# The Calling of Jujubee Forthright

# The Calling of Jujubee Forthright

a novel | **Scott Philip Stewart**

FaithWalk
PUBLISHING
Grand Haven, Michigan

©2006 Scott Philip Stewart

Published by FaithWalk Publishing
Grand Haven, Michigan 49417

All rights reserved. No part of this book may be reproduced or transmitted in any form by any means, electronic or mechanical, including photocopying and recording, or by any information storage and retrieval system, except as may be expressly permitted by the 1976 Copyright Act or by the publisher. Requests for permission should be made in writing to: FaithWalk Publishing, 333 Jackson Street, Grand Haven, Michigan, 49417.

Scripture quotations are taken from the Holy Bible, King James Version, Cambridge, 1769.

Printed in the United States of America
11 10 09 08 07 06          7 6 5 4 3 2 1

Library of Congress Cataloging-in-Publication Data

Stewart, Scott Philip.
 The calling of Jujubee Forthright : a novel / by Scott Philip Stewart.
  p. cm.
 ISBN-13: 978-1-932902-58-7 (pbk. : alk. paper)
 ISBN-10: 1-932902-58-9
 1. Auctioneers—Fiction. 2. Georgia—Fiction. 3. Revivals—Fiction. I. Title.
 PS3619.T53C35 2006
 —dc22
         2005034647

 Dedication

To the Friend of Sinners—my Friend—Jesus of Nazareth

    As always, for those I love best:
          Mom & Dad
      Lena, Scott, Chace, Aidan
          & Bennie

# Acknowledgments

Thanks to Dirk Wierenga, Louann Werksma, and Ginny McFadden of FaithWalk Publishing for believing in my friends Ryne O'Casey and Jujubee Forthright.

Thanks to my friends Pastor Tommy Morris, Greg Chatham, Shelley McKenzie, and Jeff Dockman for teaching me—in word and deed—what this wondrous thing called grace is all about.

 *Prologue*

IF YOU HAVE EVER BEEN TO THE TOWN OF MEDLYN IN THE NORTH GEORGIA MOUNTAINS and been accused of being "blasphemious" by a great big man with a head of hair thick and black as a bearcoat, chances are you made the acquaintance of James Jackson Baldwin Forthright. If you had, you might or might not cherish it, but you would certainly remember it. He was Jimmy Jack B. Forthright before the Lord called him; Jimmy Jack B. Forthright—"without the double-you," as he puts it—thereafter. (One of him, he was fond of saying, is more than enough.) Most everyone called him Jujubee, after that old movie candy that can either break or stick to your teeth.

If I told you that Jujubee was once married to a woman named Dots you probably wouldn't believe me. But it's true. Her given name was Dorothy, but, according to Jujubee, they all called her Dots (not just Dot), after that other rubbery old movie candy that also has a tendency to stick to your dental work or your teeth if you have any. They were Jujubee and Dots. And, according to Jujubee Forthright, it was on account of his sin that *they* hadn't stuck together. That is how he summed up their relationship after, he said, the Lord showed him the "error in his ways." Jujubee sometimes proclaimed that his message was sweet candy for a bitter world, all right, but that what he wanted most of all was for it to stick not to your teeth but to your heart.

That is the Jujubee Forthright I *first* met one breezy Friday evening late in the summer of a year early in the twenty-first century in the town of Medlyn, Georgia, at the Town & Country Auction House, which was on the plat of land just east of the campus of Wentworth College, where for many years I taught philosophy. I know, I know: saying "first met" is usually redundant—like saying "honest truth." Is there any such thing as a *dis*honest version of the truth? I'm sorry, I taught philosophy. I'm a doctor of it, in fact, a professor of it—emeritus. And even now, though I profess faith, I still take a little philosophy for my head's sake, from time to time. As a recovering philosopher I happen to think that there just might be a *dishonest* version of the truth, but here's the honest truth on Jimmy Jack B. Forthright:

I have met him for the *first* time many, many times over the several months I have been (as we say in the mountains of Georgia) *knowing him.* Knowing someone is contrasted with knowing *of* someone, which is reserved for those with whom we are merely acquainted. Well meaning folks from other regions of the United States might think we're all a bunch of ignoramuses because of the way we talk down here, but a classicist would see in this habit of our language (and in a great deal of our other habits as well if they would quit sniggling about our pronunciation long enough) the distinction between the *aorist* tense denoting simple past action and the *imperfect*, a richer past tense denoting continuing action in past time.

*Aha!* Now *that* captures it perfectly. I doubt that anybody who met Jujubee Forthright more than once, and was from this part of the world, would use the simple past and say I *knew* him. He was not a simple man, Jimmy Jack B. Forthright, not the kind of man you could honestly say you *simply knew.*

Or rather he really was so simple (there I go again) that he was downright complex.

I must say this before going on ... And I shall try my best to keep from getting philosophical about things as I tell you this story, because Jimmy Jack B. Forthright and the story of his calling is much more practical than philosophical, and it's a lot more interesting than my own story—trust me on that; it is a story about the heart and hands, not so much about the head. And it's about as subtle and nuanced as a pig in rut, and for me here's just how practical it was: I believe in Jesus Christ because of a five-foot-tall, three-hundred-pound auctioneer named Jujubee Forthright, who was called by God to do something really special.

It's *that* simple.

I have talked to many people who were knowing Jujubee Forthright, and I have drawn on their accounts and I believe what they told me. They are good people such as Francine Mae Fuller of Medlyn, Georgia. Everybody but Jujubee called Francine Mae Fuller "Fanny." Jujubee called her Miss Franny, he said, for three reasons. One, because he always had. Two, because he had once gotten his own "hindparts tore up but good" by his stepfather for using *that* f-word. Three, because "Fanny" didn't seem to fit right with either her maiden name or her married name: Fanny Mae Waddell and Fanny Mae Fuller, respectively. Besides, he told me, he could recall a time way back when he was a little boy when Francine Fuller was no bigger around than a stovepipe chimney and the name Fanny seemed a whole lot less likely to be *misinterpretated.*

My sources are honest people such as *Charles C. "Doughtree" Doherty, Jr.,* of Shirley Grove, a banjo picker; and a dulcimer player named *Burden Blue* from a town called Pink—Pink, Georgia. Oh—and I'm not making any of this up—there's a man named *Bennett Monroe,* who was called Merlin—Merlin Monroe—a plumber from Hollywood, Georgia, who played the fiddle like mad and who had a big role to play after we got back from the coast. Yes, they are good, honest people and do not lie. And all are still alive and living in Georgia, U.S.A.

In one of my father's few tender moments in the pulpit (he was a minister and a Presbyterian, in that order), he said (I believe off-script for once) that perhaps once in a lifetime, if we are blessed, we will encounter someone whose story is worth telling. I am blessed indeed, and so I am going to tell you the story of Jujubee Forthright's calling (or re-calling, as he put it) and his response.

* * *

Now when I told Jujubee that I wanted to tell the story, I assured him that I would have the book meticulously edited, and here's what he had to say about that. "*Mediculous* edit? Not sure I'm clear on what that means, but it sounds to me like a cross between doctoring up and being ridiculous. And that's a big part of what's wrong with Lord Jesus's church in our day. Don't edit the truth, Dewey. Tell it plain out, just the way it all happened. I'm not a man with letters—you yourself have got enough of those for the both of us—so I don't expect to find myself in your story looking like Cary Grant, dancing like Fred Astaire, and talking like Billy Graham."

So here's the story told plain out, with the truth unedited, beginning with the night I met Jujubee Forthright for that very first time ... .

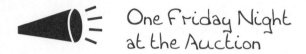# One Friday Night at the Auction

THE TOWN & COUNTRY AUCTION HOUSE was set on the 400 block of U.S. Highway 76, which is the Main Street through the town of Medlyn, northwest of Toccoa, in the mountains of north Georgia. The "Teensie" (for T & C), as it was known to locals, was a 40-foot-wide by 60-foot-deep by 22-foot-high cinderblock structure, painted gray, with two picture windows on either side of the main entrance, which faced Main Street. Inside, the brushed concrete floors were covered with well worn gray-green indoor-outdoor carpet, except for an area in the main auction room which Jujubee had covered in a great big swath of gold shag carpet he had acquired in an estate sale down in Shirley Grove, Georgia.

There was a counter in the front area of the Teensie that doubled as a ticket window and snack bar with the standard snack bar fare: hot dogs, fountain drinks, coffee, cocoa, movie candy (including Jujubes and Dots), pretzels, Goody powders, pickles, and Tums. That was also where patrons bought their admission tickets to the auction for a dollar each, which wasn't a bad deal: half of the door's take went to the lucky man or woman whose ticket was drawn in the mid-auction raffle called "The Special." (The more tickets you bought the better your chances of winning, so the auctioneer himself, Jimmy Jack B. "Jujubee" Forthright, often used to buy two but had never, to anyone's memory, won the special jackpot during the fifteen years he presided over the auction after his stepfather Allis Blackwell and his half-brother Borger passed on and by default the auction became Jujubee's.)

The Teensie Auction was held on Friday and Saturday nights. But, of the two, the Friday night event was what they called "The Big One." It drew the dealers with the best merchandise and folks from as far away as Hiawassee and Clarkesville. The population of Medlyn proper (not counting the student body and faculty of Wentworth College) has held steady at about 1,200 for the past twenty years. So when I report that the Friday night auction at the Teensie—which ran at the same time as the stock car race on the Medlyn Dirt Track—regularly drew 300 people, you'll appreciate just how *big* an event it was. The entertainment at the Friday night auction was better, too; Jujubee would often light down from his auctioneer stand (if a 300-pound man's descent from a chair set on a platform ten feet above the ground could be called *lighting* down ... and in Jujubee's case it could; he was surprisingly light on his feet for a man of such stature). He would get down on the stage, take up his vintage mother-of-pearl Hohner accordion with gold-gilded bellows, and sit in with the Teensie Weensie Band on selected numbers.

I confess I have lived the whole of my life in Medlyn, Georgia—with the exception of the years I was away at graduate school: Duke University in Durham, North Carolina—and I had managed to reach the age of sixty without ever attending the Town & Country Auction—despite (no, *because of*) the fact that the campus of Wentworth College was on the plat of land just west of it. You see, there was a great divide in Medlyn between the Wentworth College folks (Wentworth is an exclusive, monied Presbyterian institution) on the one hand, and, on the other, the non-Wentworth College folks (who were mainly Baptists, though to be fair there were a few Methodist and holiness snake-handler types in town, too). I used to think it was just out of ignorance that the townfolk of the other Medlyn referred to us as Wentworth*less*. Be that as it may, the Town & Country Auction as run first by Allis Blackwell and then by Jujubee was no Sotheby's and it was, as I'm sure you've guessed, quite a bit more country than town, and the only reason I ventured in there that Friday night, the twenty-third day of August, was because I had heard a rather incredible rumor about a lawn gnome that Fanny Fuller, my oldest and dearest friend who just happened to be credibility itself, had won at the auction the month before; and I determined to buy one for myself.

The rumor was this: God would "lay hold to" the lawn gnome and it would glow—a saffron glow, as Fanny described it—though most of this "gospel" was according to Jorge Ruiz, the young man who mowed Fanny's lawn and edged around her driveway. Once, Jorge said, it even spoke—though in English or Spanish he couldn't say.

Fanny Fuller was a Christian, of the sensible sort. I was not. In fact, I was at the eye of a great storm that was just then about to roll into Medlyn from the four winds over a book I had written called *Honest to God*. I have never been one for bookburnings because ideas are hard to get lit and tend to flame back up like trick birthday candles, but I must say I have since participated in burning a few copies of my own book. It's okay, because in this case the ideas have been burnt up, too, thanks again to Jujubee Forthright and the good news he *showed* me.

My book *Honest to God* was … anything but. I was depressed when I wrote it—and depressed when I saw the press it was receiving (much more bothered by it than I would have been when I still had dark hair). There I was, teaching philosophy and religion at Wentworth College (in fact, I was the Chief of Sinners: I was the head of the Philosophy Department) and I found myself at that stage of life having neither the wisdom of philosophy nor the faith of religion. What misery. So I wrote the book, a hymn to misery, and it was stirring up quite a bit of controversy. It seems that certain alumni, who had received advance copies to review, were alarmed at my theology.

*Did I not believe anything?* they asked in their letters. It was a fair question if not a particularly novel one. "Academic freedom is one thing," wrote one retired pastor of a prominent church in Charlotte you would know if I named him, "license to heresy is *another*." And if in fact I didn't believe in anything, they charged, how then could I "in good faith" discharge my duties as a teacher of the impressionable youth sent by parents who expected, as a return on their investment of a hundred and some thousand dollars (the cost of a Wentworth baccalaureate), a faithful education—or at the very least not a faithless or faith-destroying one.

That smarted.

My favorite philosopher was Diogenes the Cynic, and alas it seems I was too good a disciple. I was born *David* Umberton Hazelriggs III, but I changed my name to Diogenes while away at Duke, and even all those years later when I would go for a top-down spin around Medlyn of a Saturday morning in my midnight blue '62 Big Healey 3000 (a worldly treasure I have since let go) with my little Shih Tzu named Dog Maddox (as in dogmatics) riding shotgun in the passenger seat beside me, I did wear a T-shirt with a picture of a dog on it and lettering on the front that read, "Four on the Floor: A Dogmatic Transmission."

I thought it was clever, though nobody ever got it, and sometimes now I don't really get it, either. The garment now serves, believe it or not, as a dust rag to tidy up guest rooms at the home … .

But I am getting a little ahead of myself.

So, anyway, many of the young men and women enrolled at Wentworth were seminary-bound—at least before they enrolled in my classes—so let's just say it was a bit of a maelstrom on the way. I knew that word of my book had gotten to the Very Right Honorable Professor Dr. Alisdair Calvin Knox, lately of Aviemore, Scotland, President of Wentworth College. He was a cantankerous Grinch and never smiled. He had directed his secretary to summon me to his office at 10:00 on Monday morning. When I told Will Reardon, a junior colleague in the Chemistry department, about the presidential summons, he was wry and suggested that I present the "blokey old curmudgeon"—*his* words—with a bottle of Scotch—good Speyside whiskey, the very finest I could afford, preferably a single malt with a moody palate and peaty finish. And, he added, if Knox started pouring on the shepherd pie Scots accent, I was advised to drink the stuff myself.

Which was all to say: Things were bound to get dicey. President Knox's one-on-one appointments with faculty members were referred to as "come-to-Jesus meetings" at which Knox issued an invitation and you either turned or burned. If not being published often enough or in the right types of journals could get you all that, I frowned to think what publishing a book of heresy would get me.

So there was a lot on my mind that Thursday morning when Fanny Fuller called and said there was something in her backyard that I just had to see for myself. She would put on a rebel pot roast and expect me there at her place at six. I would have gone anyway, even without the added enticements of a prophetic lawn gnome and a rebel pot roast—as Fanny called her roast on account of the secret southern concoction of herbs and spices she seasoned it with. It is the best roast I have ever eaten, better by far than the best Yankee pot roast I ever had.

I have always loved it … .

And since I have digressed this far in telling about the night I met Jujubee Forthright at the Teensie auction house, let me say this: I have always loved Francine Mae Waddell Fuller. I had a crush on her that lasted from the September of our seventh grade year at Medlyn Middle School until … well, until this very day. This despite the fact that she was married to Earl Edwin Fuller, Jr.—whom we all called Early—for thirty-six years. Early Fuller died two years and eight months before, and—in the year or so since that fortuitous Thursday—I have been seeing quite a bit of Fanny.

My good fortunes with Fanny, too, I suppose, when it comes right down to it, I owe to Jujubee Forthright. Some might say Jujubee was a divider in the ministry that followed his calling—but I suppose you cannot divide without at the same time uniting.

To sum up my interest in the lawn gnome: I did have a rebel pot roast with Fanny Fuller that Thursday evening. We lingered over dessert—one of Fanny's blue-ribbon cobblers, blackberry, I think—and chatted, more and more about the gnome as day dimmed to dusk and the back porch light emitted a saffron glow all its own. Then I helped Fanny into her black silk cape (which I teased reminded me of a Medieval cloak) and put on my eight-quarters Gatsby driving cap (Fanny said, "driving cap, my foot; it's a newsboy," and we both laughed) and we went out back and strolled down the little flagstone walk that led down by Early's shed, and ended up standing two feet from the water (Fanny's house was one of six built around Lake Sorghum, a charming setting).

"Here it is," Fanny said. She gestured toward the lawn gnome, which was standing somewhere in the gray mist of dusk, which was gathering in earnest by then.

Eyes training about knee-level, I turned nonchalantly (I always tried to be nonchalant about everything when I was with Fanny) and the glasses flew off my face as though I had been struck. I shrieked. So much for nonchalance. I'm sure I said something on the order of "good heavens" or such, too, and shuddered as I stood there wondering how I could have missed it, the big thing. I must have mistaken it for a tree. It was a giant among gnomes. I had expected the blasted thing to be knee-high and so kept my eyes trained downward to spy it out and also to keep from losing my footing and pitching into the lake. And here I was face-to-face with it; the tip of the thing's hat was above my head. I rubbed my eyes beneath my spectacles and shook my head.

Fanny said, "Why good heavens, David! I am so sorry." (So sorry she was sniggering a little.) "I certainly didn't mean for it to scare the daylights out of you." I was always just David to Fanny (or David Umberton Hazelriggs when she was making a point) because she knew me long before I met and became Diogenes. Besides, she said, "Diogenes" suited me no better than a corncob pipe and overalls, which had something to do with the fact that Fanny thought I was perfectly suited for the academy. A true-blue dandy, I was. David or Diogenes: I was a Wentworth man, she said (by which she meant nothing more than that I was not a person who used contractions even when speaking).

But that misty night out back at Fanny Fuller's I muttered a few contractions—words that should never be contracted—as I gathered my breath and blasphemed at the burly six-foot-tall lawn gnome that was eyeing me down in the flickering shadows of Early's tool shed.

"See it?" she asked. "There. Look!"

I looked at the thing. Looked hard at it, I tell you. I wanted to see "it"—whatever Fanny saw when she looked at it, whatever Jorge Ruiz heard it say when it spoke to him in English or Spanish or some heavenly tongue ear hath not heard, deep unto deep, wanted to be baptized in its saffron glow, to hear the voice of God coming from its pursed wooden lips so that for just once he could issue forth the PRONOUNCEMENT of all time and convince me that Diogenes the Cynic was wrong and that there was, after all, some meaning in something. In anything.

That's where I was at the time—where, as the younger folks now say—my *head* was.

But as for that lawn gnome's head, well, I did just about everything I could think to do to behold that glow, to see "it." I looked at it with glasses on, glasses off. I screwed my eyes shut and then squinted and looked through my eyelashes. I tried looking at it through my right eye with my left closed, and vice versa. And again. And once more with feeling. But for all that I just didn't see a thing, and it didn't utter so much as a peep.

I said, "Do *you* see something that I don't?"

Fanny said, "A great many things, I should say."

"Touché," I shot back. "It's bad enough the thing nearly killed me. Have you considered that the glow might not be from above but from below, the fires of … . And now the insult to injury."

Fanny said, "Poor dear. Bless your heart."

I said, "I'll live. What I meant is, are you seeing it do anything right now, anything peculiar going on with this gnome?"

She said, "No. Not right now." She put her right hand on her hip and massaged the back of her neck with her left. "It's not something that happens all the time, like you wave a wand and 'Poof!' it does its song and dance."

"Oh," I said. "How coy of it." I wondered if *it* was something that happened when the setting sun cast its melting saffron glow on the world, wondered if *it* talked a blue streak only when Jorge was drinking beer and working the lawn tools. Typical cynic I was. But Fanny was not, and didn't like it when I was, so I just shrugged—happy for the company and the slightly tart aftertaste of blackberries on my palate.

Just then, Fanny yanked the shawl from her shoulders and, in one swooping sweep of the thing, managed to lasso the lawn gnome's head with the precision of a seasoned cowboy ringing a fat calf. I was astonished. There stood Fanny, a retired elementary school teacher who was often heard to bemoan the effects of age, roping the head of this strange thing with the skill of Annie Oakley shooting the ash off Kaiser Wilhelm's cigarette.

She said, "Get under the covers with it and you *will* see it, too. Sometimes it takes this type thing to see it."

Now, to be honest, I was given to wonder how many other twilit experiments she had conducted out here in the backyard trying to make the thing light up. And I wouldn't have done this for anybody on earth but Fanny, but I was desperate. So I hitched the fingers of each hand under the hem of Fanny's wrap, which at the moment hung down to the gnome's waist, and lifted, slowly lifted, each corner, as though I had been called to the morgue to identify a body and was left alone to pull back the sheet. Slowly, dreadfully, I ducked my head under the wrap and eased in so I was nose-to-nose with the thing, my glasses at first clicking against the point of its nose … and in the pitch black darkness, I tell you, I did see something, something in its eyes burning like tiki torches at a luau.

And I felt warm. There might have been any number of explanations for it, but at the moment I suspended disbelief and let go my inner cynic, which had kept me miserable, if resigned and well adjusted, all these years. To explain something is, alas, not to explain it away. We philosophers have an old logical truth that says "to affirm one thing is not to deny another." So, to say that I felt warmed because it was a humid late August night in the Deep South—and, after all, I had my head tucked up under a satin shawl—is not to say that the Lord was not warming my heart, strangely warming it, too, with a Wesleyan warmth. And to say that I saw what looked like twin tiki torches burning in the wooden gnome's eyes because a glint of yellow light from Fanny Fuller's back porch lamp was reflecting off my shoes is not to say that the Lord was not opening my eyes to a new way of seeing.

I didn't think all this just then—as the flickering tiki glow filled my eyes and warmed my cheeks. As I said, that's not where my head was back then. But my heart was moved.

When I emerged from the shawl a little while later (Fanny says I was under there a full twelve minutes though I noted that she wasn't wearing her watch), I felt so unsteady that I had to take a moment, recline on the dewy grass on the bank, and let it pass. Then Fanny helped me onto my feet and into the house and plied me with her sweet tea.

She said, "I just knew you would see it for yourself, David. Now don't you want to get you one?"

By the time I had finished half a glass of sweet tea and the ceiling fan in her parlor had dried the sweat on my brow, I had all but explained away my encounter with the lawn gnome. It was the heat and humidity and the concentration of carbon dioxide under Fanny's black shawl. It was exhaustion. It was *Honest to God* and the big mess I was about to get in over it. It was being in love with Francine Mae "Fanny" Fuller and wanting so badly to see what she saw, hear what she heard, believe what she believed ... .

But I kept all this to myself and simply told Fanny that I rather liked the idea of being able to visit her and the gnome at her house and, in fact, would like to have sessions with it on a more or less regular basis (the ulterior motive, of course, being that it gave me an excuse for seeing a little more of Fanny). Besides, how could we be sure the Lord was visiting more than one of the gnomes, which, like people, are each and every one unique creations. Fanny snorted as politely as anyone ever did. Nice try.

As far as I knew, there was only one burning bush, one talking donkey, one ... one ... one what else? I wondered. Drew a blank.

Fanny said, "David Umberton Hazelriggs. Diogenes. *Puh.*"

I said that another bush in the area wouldn't have been anything more than just another bush. A bush by any other name ... . Another donkey was just another beast of burden doing what a donkey does—not talking.

My tune changed, as they say, when Fanny asked me out on a date the following night. A Friday night date. Early had been dead, she said, almost two years. Her proper period of mourning was over. She wasn't getting any younger—though, she noted, she wasn't getting any older, either, and she was not wearing a watch. She was, had been, holding steady at fifty-five. That way, she said, it would sound a little better, even if she looked a little worse, every year of her life.

Suddenly I did want one—a lawn gnome—that I could call my very own. At least, we decided, we could set it up in my yard and run some extensive (and time-consuming) tests on it. Try the shawl, or capelet (as Fanny insisted her wrap was called), or one of my sport coats on it, whatever else we could think to try to get it to do its thing. We could stand it at different angles at different hours of the day and see what happened. Thus I accepted Fanny's invitation to escort her to the Teensie Auction House in hopes that the dealer from whom Fanny had acquired the giant gnome (for an undisclosed sum) the month before would return with another one and lay it on the block.

I realize I am a little long in coming to the point: I have said that—*all* that—to account for how I ended up in the Town & Country Auction House on that Friday evening, August 23, the night I *first* met Jimmy Jack B. Forthright and my life took a turn that was beyond me, beyond Diogenes the Cynic, beyond anything I might ever have imagined.

On that Friday evening, at precisely five o'clock, I again made the right-hand turn just past a mailbox lettered: Fuller, E. E., Jr. Seeing Early's initials there in the sturdy black letters was a little peculiar, but I carried on, without so much as a tap of the brakes, trying to recall if I'd ever noticed the mailbox before. I popped the shifter on the old Austin Healey down into second gear and let her engine redline it all the way down the long meandering blacktop drive that led through the wooded lot to Fanny's house—in the backyard of which was the giant gnome that was, ostensibly, the reason for our being together for the second night in a row.

It started out as not so much a date as a mission, but whatever it was, I was giddy with excitement. So off we went, and yes I did open the door for Fanny.

Fanny had wanted to cook, but I insisted that we go to the Dillard House, about a half hour from Medlyn, which I knew Fanny loved. I said: "Humor me. This is my first date in thirty years."

Fanny said, "It didn't have to be."

We had the top down. It was a balmy, overcast day—just such a day for which an English roadster was made—and Fanny pulled off her sunglasses and our eyes locked.

"Those eyes," I said. "If Gene Tierney was fair of face, Fanny Fuller is beauty itself." I was sweet-talking, sure, but truth to tell I have always thought Fanny every bit as ravishing as Gene Tierney (and no, I'm not *that* old; I saw her at picture shows in my student days in Durham—and, even at that, they weren't first runs).

"See what I mean," she said. "Thirty years, my foot. Now what woman wouldn't kill for a slice of such charm—even if it so much nonsense." She tossed her head back, said, "How's this? I haven't been on a date in *forty* years."

"Touché," I said, and on we drove, fast if not furious, to the Dillard House for dinner.

Over dinner a little later Fanny shook her head at me, with a look that said "for shame." She scolded, "David Umberton Hazelriggs. You can eat that with your hands. It's finger food."

"No it's not and no you can't in the refectory at Wentworth College," I said.

"*Refectory*," she said. "Is that what they call the mess hall? I'm surprised fried chicken's on the menu at Wentworth College." She was enjoying her cabbage casserole.

"It is," I said. "Honest to God." I thought about my book and worried more just then about what Fanny would think of it than about what President Knox, all the Wentworth alumni, and even what God, with whom I was urging all and sundry to be honest, thought of it. I continued slicing little strips of the fried chicken breast from the bone and putting them into my mouth by way of fork. Fanny seemed amused by it, but she let it go.

"I am looking forward to the auction," I said.

"You are not," she retorted, and added, "speaking of being honest to God."

I shuddered a little. If Fanny Fuller has a singular gift (and, of course, I would argue she has a great many) it was a special *charism* in the body of Christ: She was endowed with the gift of speaking humbling truth. Later, I learned from Jujubee Forthright himself what they—the good, decent, and common folks of Medlyn, Georgia—called it when Fanny "called them out"—a "Fanny-spankin'." Though, as I said before, Jujubee himself always referred to her as Miss Franny. I had just been Fanny-spanked, I suppose.

"What I mean," I said, "is that I think it will be interesting."

She said, "Oh, it probably will be—in a 'cross-cultural' kind of way for you, David, your being a man of the world and high culture and all that jazz. You'll see a specimen or two of the species known as hillbilly, but I'll bet you fifty cents to a nickel no one gets lynched from the rafters in there tonight."

"You're on," I said.

She said, "That's only on the *second* Friday of every month."

"Then we'll have to come again."

"Not on the second Friday we won't. That's my race night. You've never been to the dirt track, either, have you?"

"I drove by it once."

Between bites of acorn squash, she said, "I can't make peace with the fact that a debonair man such as yourself who sports about in a nineteen hundred and sixty-two Austin Healey MK three thousand with a 'driving' cap on isn't a race enthusiast."

The Friday night race at the Medlyn Dirt Track, which hosted such "special" events as the Monstravaganza Tractor Pull, and which was built in the swale just downwind of the Medlyn landfill, was a far cry from the European Grand Prix, but I could never say such a thing to Fanny. And not just because I'd be sure to get a Fanny-spankin', either, but because Fanny would have none of that class warfare

*The calling of Jujubee Forthright*

nonsense. She had a foot in both camps, a foot in neither, meaning just this: Fanny was one of those rare Medlynians who had never, ever, believed the tale of two cities—Wentworth and non-Wentworth; cultured vs. redneck; Baptist vs. Presbyterian (for the record, as I said, there are a few Methodists and fewer Pentecostals in Medlyn). Fanny refused to subscribe to the propaganda about our little town in the mountains of north Georgia. To Fanny Fuller there were people and there were animals and there were things.

Oh, and above them all, there was God.

Fanny proved she was right by living what she believed about Medlyn.

She said, "If you have it in your mind to believe in two Medlyns, you'll find two; if you believe there's only one, that is exactly what you will find." Fanny had it in her mind to believe in only one Medlyn—and that is *exactly* what she found. And no one I knew ever presumed to assign Fanny Fuller, born Francine Mae Waddell, to one Medlyn or to the other. It was where she came from. Her father was a Presbyterian-bred, Nagoochee-groomed Wentworth man of letters who chose to forgo a promising career in "higher learning" for the higher calling of local school administration—*public* school administration. He served as principal of three high schools in the county during his storied career. Her mother was a Baptist-bred graduate of Shelnutt County High School. She was, Fanny said, a career volunteer—plain and simple. She was the town's matron saint.

Fanny opted to attend high school at Shelnutt County High, though her father would have preferred that she attend the Hanna Mitchell All Girls' Preparatory Academy in Hayesville, North Carolina, which was a Wentworth prep school. Fanny argued that all of her friends were going to Shelnutt (all except for *me*; I went to the Milford School, which was also a Wentworth prep school). If Shelnutt was good enough for mother, it was good enough for daughter. After high school, Fanny opted out of the legacy scholarship to Wentworth and went instead to (caution for Wentworth alumni: prepare to cross yourself, rend your clothes, or skip this line) to Georgia State College in Atlanta, which had a superior teacher training program.

In high school, she fell in love with Early Fuller who after graduation went to the Oconee Vo-Technical Institute in Athens and earned his associates degree in auto mechanics. After college, the young couple settled back in Medlyn. Fanny taught first grade; Early opened a full-service gas station and raced cars—3:16 was his number—on Friday nights at the Medlyn Dirt Track.

I went to Wentworth in the *other* Medlyn then to Duke and ate my heart out.

Honest to God.

And I've been doing it for the past forty-some years.

Honest to God.

"There's that charm again," she said, with a glancing blow of those Gene Tierney eyes, after I had told her that the pastry chef at the Dillard House could stand to take a few pointers on the art of cobbling blackberries from a lovely lady I knew, a lovely lady with beautiful eyes from the town of OneMedlyn.

The drive back from the Dillard House to the Town & Country Auction House was set to be all glory. I was able to lay aside *Honest to God* and all the grief it would bring and felt so absolutely at peace there beside Fanny that I can say this: The only thing a teenage boy on a hot date had on me this night was a dram of testosterone and a size 30 waistline.

I had never married, not so much because I was pining for Fanny Fuller (though I did a little of that, too) as because I never found the "right" woman and never called any woman I found "right." I dated until I was thirty, then in a ceremony attended by only a few colleagues at Wentworth College (at which I was at that time up for tenure) I confirmed myself as a bachelor. It was little more than an excuse to drink wine, that ceremony. When you fancy yourself a philosopher, it is no trifling matter to admit being shallow, but let me just say for the record that there were no Gene Tierney lookalikes among the faculty or student body of Wentworth College. And had there been, well, I really didn't want to complicate my life with a family. I might have had a change of heart if Gene Tierney (from the era of *Laura*) had shown up batting those sad girlish eyes and said she just had to have me. I certainly would have if Fanny had come strolling down the promenade in Durham with a pageboy haircut, a red pantsuit with little sequins stitched on its front, and said *she* just had to have me.

Neither did.

So I will blame it all on a Greek philosopher who lived three and a half centuries before Christ, a philosopher whom I met in a Western Civilization course: Diogenes of Sinope, the Cynic, who lived in a bathtub and questioned both the meaning and the value of everything and consigned me, so long as I believed in him, to ruin—ruin by way of "the easy life":

>     Even bronze groweth old with time, but thy fame,
>         Diogenes, not all Eternity shall take away.
>     For thou alone didst point out to mortals
>         the lesson of self-sufficiency,
>     and the path for the best and easiest life.
>         (Diogenes *Laertius* VI, 78).

That was my quest.

>     My name is Diogenes, my nickname is dog.
>     Ferryman you bring the dead men
>         to the other side of Hades,
>     bring me also, and if I did something
>         in my whole life,
>     it is that I relieved the human life
>         from any useless pride!

He did no such thing, of course. And what *useless pride* on his part to assume he had!

I became a Cynic.

Meantime, Fanny and Early were finding themselves unable to have children of their own. I have heard rumors as to why it wasn't completely unexpected but, to tell you the truth, I just filed it away in a generic "fertility issue" file and let it be. So the Fullers became foster parents and, in the twenty or so years they served, Fanny and Early fostered nearly sixty orphans of Shelnutt County.

God love them.

To folks on both sides of the Wentworth divide in Medlyn, Fanny Fuller was a saint.

I had seventy children each semester. We went home every afternoon—they to their homes and I to mine.

It was only as we were on the way from the Dillard House to the Auction House that I learned that the auctioneer (whom I knew by name only), Jimmy Jack B. Forthright, had been one of the sixty. Fanny started to tell the story ...

She said, "You may think his place is tacky, David. The Teensie is not a country club. It is a country auction. All I ask is that you bear in mind that Jujubee—that's what everybody calls him, and you should, too—well, he had a rough start. He has not had the advantages some of us have, David. We two, for instance. His stepfather—common-law stepfather, Allis—was an alcoholic."

I said, "I think I heard that once."

"Well," she said, "then trust me when I tell you that you didn't hear the half of it—the *bad* half of it. Allis was—well, not to mince words—he was a devil. When he was sober he was a demon; when he was drunk, he was the devil himself. He used to beat Jujubee's mother, Celia, and when Jujubee was old enough to understand and would try to take up for her, he would beat poor Jujubee nearly to death."

I said, "Oh my." I heard Fanny's voice break just a little, and though I didn't cut my eyes to the left to see, I could tell that she was moved, perhaps to tears. And suddenly my heart went out to this man—whom I would call Jujubee—I knew only in name.

Fanny went on. "It was after one such beating that he came to live with Early and me. He showed up for school one day favoring his right leg, but—bless his heart—he was doing his best so nobody would notice. If you have ever tried to walk on a foot that's pins-and-needles asleep, you can imagine. He grimaced with every step. And of course I didn't want to make a scene and embarrass him. Jujubee was always bashful, some of it on account of his weight. He was always right big. Besides, I knew of Allis and Celia and their situation, so I took him aside and said, 'How'd you stub your toe, Jimmy, or is it a splinter lodged up in it?' Poor thing dropped his head, his face melted, and he started crying, without making a sound."

I toe-tapped the Big Healey's throttle the sooner to have finished with this sad tale. I don't know exactly how long it had been since I let such a dreadful story linger in my mind—years, I'm sure. In my quest for the best and easiest life, I had spent decades insulating myself against the reality that such atrocious things happen not just out there in the world but in my own community of Medlyn. It was the "evil" acts in the wide blue yonder that I cataloged as evidence against a loving God in my book. That tack, however intellectually precarious I now consider it, always worked to keep the danger at bay. What better way to avoid feeling pain than not thinking about it?

At any rate, I just preferred not to let the dark reality of life upset the perfect balance of my mind and emotions. But just then I was torn: Part of me wanted nothing more than to hear Fanny Fuller tell the story of young Jujubee Forthright.

Fanny said, "I will spare you the worst of it, David."

Out of the corner of my eye, I saw Fanny shiver, and I was inclined to say "God be thanked." But I didn't.

Fanny cinched the frog loop of her capelet together beneath her chin. "But Jujubee calmed down enough to tell me that about a week or so before, Allis had gone evil berserk and cut the blood out of his legs with a razor strop so bad that they were welted from ankle to rump. I helped carry him down to the school nurse who called both the police and the rescue squad and they carried Jujubee off in an ambulance to Clayton General."

"Oh my." My throat was tight. I reached up and gave a little yank on my bowtie. I hadn't realized till Fanny pointed it out: We were going ninety miles an hour. I eased off the throttle.

"That's not the worst of it, I'm afraid," Fanny said. "You see, one of the wounds, in particular, on Jujubee's right calf, got infected. He had blood poisoning that turned to gangrene, and the long and the short of it is that they ended up having to take his right leg off. He came to live with Early and me until Celia finally managed to get shut of Allis and get herself back on her feet—she, too, had a drinking problem to contend with. She was 'a wino,' in Early's words. Anyway, when she got herself together somewhat Jujubee went back home and lived with his mother."

I had many questions for Fanny: How long was Jujubee with them? Was he ever outfitted with a prosthesis and ambulatory, or was he confined to a wheelchair? What happened after he went back into the custody of his mother? Whatever became of Allis Blackwell? (One calamity after another, I hoped.) Was he charged with the crime of child abuse? Did he serve time? Did he die a scoundrel—but an indigent, derelict scoundrel, harmless, hardly able to draw a breath without the help of some wicked wretch bunkmate named Boris? I nearly wished it so.

But before I could ask any of them, she said, "Put your signal on now, David. We'd best go in the lower lot. The upper will be full by now."

I made a gentle right and pulled us slowly into the east parking lot, feathering the throttle to roll the Big Healey over the gritty lot of gravel-packed red clay. The last thing I wanted was to make a big scene (you might not believe it coming from a man who drove a 1962 Austin Healey roadster, but even for those given to making scenes, timing is everything, or rather *place*). With Fanny's help navigating, I backed the Big Healey in between a new green Buick four-door sedan and an old primer-gray Ford half-ton pickup. I parked a little closer to the Buick, of course, for my door's sake.

The mingled scent of popcorn, magnolias, and honeycomb was strong—reminiscent of a long-ago outing with Grandmother Hazelriggs to a parking lot carnival in Blairsville. The smell of cotton candy had mingled with the earthy smell of sweating flesh, rotten bark, and funky imitation leather work boots. The air was heavy with gear oil and axle grease, too, and I pulled the kerchief from my pocket and mopped my forehead. Whatever it was, it was invisible. (I had half expected to see black grit on the kerchief.) There was the awful grinding trill of a machine out behind an outbuilding, spraying goldenrod sparks out through the dusk with pops and hisses, and hillbilly music blaring loud through cheap speakers, music I couldn't have identified by artist or title for all the money in the world.

Tearing myself from my reverie, I turned to Fanny and asked, "Do you mind if I take your hand in mine, Madam?"

Fanny just said "No" even as she proffered her arm. "What kind of gentleman has to ask such a question as that?"

"The kind who had rather not find himself dragged before a student-faculty tribunal for making unwanted advances."

"Oh brother," she said. "Has it come to that?"

"Yes, well, I'm afraid it has," I told her. Wentworth College had recently adopted a graduated consent policy and all such consent had to be stipulated in writing, ratified by signature, and bear the great seal of Wentworth College. "If

I had a pen," I told Fanny, "we could put this in writing and save ourselves a trip to court."

Fanny clucked her tongue. "That is the most unromantic thing I have ever heard of. And this from the very people who won't eat fried chicken with their hands in their *refectory*."

"The very ones," I said.

Fanny said, "I doubt all that's really necessary for the fifty-something set."

"Speak for yourself," I told her. I was more conscious than usual of the simple act of walking, and I wondered how Jujubee Forthright got around. I tried hard to place him. I would have sworn an oath that I had seen him about town before—and there might have been two Medlyns or only one, but either way it was a small town. I would have told you straight-faced that I could pick Jimmy Jack B. Forthright out of a lineup. But Fanny's description of him—or the image formed in my mind from his story as she told it—just didn't square with any composite I could have created with the help of a forensic artist.

She said, "This auction might be just the thing we need to ground you, David Umberton Hazelriggs, the *third*."

I said, "To ground me, you say?" I was enjoying the softness of her forearm brushing so lightly against my own, making the hair stand on end, enjoying, too, the possible meaning behind her saying that the auction might be just the thing that *we*—which I hoped meant, Fanny Mae Fuller and David Umberton Hazelriggs, together, as a team, a dynamic duo—need to ground ... me. If I had been a man of faith at that moment I would have whispered a prayer: Please, Lord, let it be so; nevertheless, not my will but thine be done.

But I wasn't, so I just tried to be on my best behavior, charm her as best I could. And the best I could at that moment was to let her take the lead. The auction was, after all, her turf and I was content to play the daytripper to her tour guide. There were a lot of sights to see, a lot to take in. The place was a shrine to redneck Americana. Now I am aware that some people think the moniker "redneck" is equivalent to a racial slur, but those I have met during these past several months who refer to themselves as such do so proudly. It's a loaded word, and those who use it to describe themselves can, I assure you, bear that load. At first glance, the plight of the redneck auctiongoers struck me as the plight of the migrant Okies must have struck Steinbeck, it was so exaggerated: a parody because it was a cause, a curiosity and not something I in my case or he in his had any intimate knowledge of: outsiders looking in and not seeing what was really there. That's the way it struck me. I had lived all of my life here in the same small town as these people (*same* to hear Fanny's "One Medlyn Under God" speech, anyway), and here I stood like a wide-eyed kibitzer at a freak show. Shame on me.

But it *was* a spectacle for me. The NASCAR memorabilia, Lord. I have since learned the special significance of the numeral 3 in Christian sacred literature (for starters: the triune Godhead). I could tell it was special to the auctiongoers, too—a certain form of it, the top tilted to the right, always either red or black, was all over the place. Now of course I knew who Dale Earnhardt was, though I admit I was amazed at the spectacular press that followed his death inasmuch as I was not, to Fanny's wonderment, a motorsports enthusiast. But I was amazed, too, at how many representations of the Intimidator and his famed number 3 decked the walls of the Teensie auction house.

To be fair, there were memorabilia as well for Bill Elliott, "Awesome Bill from Dawsonville," who hailed from a neighboring county and was a champion in his own right. And there were busts aplenty of Ugga V, Ugga VI, or whatever incarnation was the current University of Georgia canine mascot, but the runnerup to Dale Earnhardt was old number 3:16—local hero Early Fuller, my date's late husband, my late friend. There were autographed glossies of Early standing atop his Ford pumping fists into the sky in the Medlyn Dirt Track's victory circle; relishing a congratulatory kiss from his wife, Fanny, standing beside a trophy as tall as she, the spray of some drink misting them like stardust ... .

I learned that night that a simple "How do?" or "How you?" went a long way—much longer, in fact, than an awkward attempt at striking up a conversation about things one (let's be honest, if not to God to ourselves: I) knew nothing about. Fanny knew everybody. She had taught most of the folks at the auction their times-tables, how to read, where Georgia is on the map. I knew only Fanny. So I shook a lot of hands and tipped the brim of my eight-quarters cap in response to a tap of a ten-gallon hat or a poplin trucker cap.

"Ma'am, I'm pleased," I said when Fanny introduced me to one or another of her friends, aware that my accent was rather more Medlyn southern than Raleigh-Durham southern that night.

I was glad that Fanny introduced me as "Mr. David" to children and simply as David to everyone else. Doctor or Professor would have done branded me "Other Medlyn." The name Diogenes would have shown me for the dandy I was. And the mere mention of Wentworth College would have (or so I imagined then) gotten me tossed out on my ear.

It was a date, so at Fanny's urging, I shelled out three dollars for a large bucket of buttered popcorn and two fountain Cokes and caught up with Fanny as she made her way into the auction hall. Oh, a close third in number behind Early Fuller memorabilia were cigarettes—a pack of Lucky Strikes on the counter; a pack of Chesterfield Kings on a barstool, and cigarette smoke everywhere thick and pungent as tear gas. Squinting through the silvery ghost-like clouds of smoke, Fanny found us a place about midway down the row of seats on the right side of the hall. The house band—the Teensie Weensie Bluegrass Band—was still on the stand, over to our left, playing a bluegrass number (of the "plum pitiful" genre) whose tune I knew, then didn't know.

"What song is that, Fanny?"

"'I'm Blue and I'm Lonesome Too,'" she said.

I said, "It's nice."

"Just sit down," she told me.

I really wasn't making fun; the song had a nice melody. The seating in the hall was a pastiche of chairs and benches of every style and period, not to mention color. We were sitting on a pair of vintage movie theatre seats covered in threadbare red velour. There were rips and soils and cigarette burns I couldn't seem to keep from stretching with my fingertips as the night wore on. I just sat down.

A moment later, everyone started clapping and whistling and otherwise carrying on, and I said, "What's this about?"

She said, "Things are about to get underway. Why there's my big old Jujubee now."

"What—?" I could say no more when my eyes first fell on Jujubee Forthright, and I knew right away that I had never seen him before ... I could make a positive nonidentification. Though given his size I could not image that it was possible that the two us had lived in O little town of Medlyn all our lives and that somehow I could have missed seeing him.

He was humungous. It was the first word I thought when I saw him, and to this day I can find no better word for it.

Buttery popcorn was overflowing from the bucket where I had it wedged between my knees and, when Fanny noticed it, she remarked, "David, what in the world is going on with you? You look like you've seen a ghost, and I don't imagine those nice gray gabardines will ever be the same."

I shrugged. I had no idea Jujubee Forthright would be such an imposing figure, so much bigger than life.

Fanny said, "David Umberton Hazelriggs, you mean to tell me that you have never before seen Jujubee Forthright?"

"I'm quite sure I haven't," I said. A little boy standing just behind my chair starting laughing—real belly-laughing filled with joy—and when I looked up I saw that Jujubee, who had just made his way up to the auctioneer seat on a riser a good eight feet above us, was waving at the full house of auctiongoers.

Then I was laughing, and Fanny called me down, saying, "Now David Umberton Hazelriggs it's not polite to laugh at fat people."

"No, Fanny," I said. "I'm not laughing *at* him; I'm just very happy, for some reason, all of the sudden. They don't spike their Coca-cola, do they?"

Then she got it, seeing, I think, that the whole time I was talking my eyes were fixed on Jujubee Forthright way up there above us. She said, "Jujubee has a way about him that makes people smile—and not just because he's big. I'm sorry, David, for assuming the worst."

I said, "Yeah, well, I'm hurt."

"Hush," she told me.

To this day I can't say for sure why I did what I did next: I waved back at Jujubee Forthright, waved with my fingers nodding slowly up and down the way grownups wave at babies, and for a good long time. And when I glanced about, self-consciously, I discovered that nearly everyone else was also waving up at his giant form in pressed denim bib overalls and a short-sleeve checked shirt hovering there above us.

The band broke into a double-time bluegrass rendition of the Moody Blues' song "The Voice," and the crowd, as one, stood up. I confess I didn't know "The Voice" as anything but a catchy tune prior to that night, but a few days later I called around and ended up driving all the way out to the record store in Blairsville to buy the album, as if to capture that magic and keep it for all time.

"The Voice" became the theme song of the movement. It was our anthem, a hymn to the ministry to which God was about to call Jujubee Forthright.

But on seeing him that first time, I was smitten. He waved and blew kisses for a couple of minutes; then, from his station above us, Jujubee Forthright reached out and grabbed a little pinch of air and we all sat down.

He said, "Evening, y'all." And I tell you this: his voice was every bit as robust as the man himself and was ... African-American. Southern African-American. I scanned the room and found that Jujubee's voice was not the only African-American thing in the building: There were black people at the auction, and a few Mexicans or otherwise Hispanic, a man who looked like the Indian chief on the TV commercial back in the 1960s, the one who used to get all choked up over littering—all, mind you, at a "redneck" auction. They weren't supposed to be, I thought; that didn't fit the stereotype of this *other* Medlyn. How ironic that the country auction was more "culturally diverse" than the country club, certainly more colorful than the sanitized, whitewashed student body of Wentworth College.

The dregs all settle at the bottom, they might say. And apparently the cream was always white. I shook my head.

Jujubee Forthright was a mini-giant—if that is possible—and I couldn't help but think that it was by grace alone that Allis Blackwell died of liver cirrhosis instead of a bear hug—that much of the rest of the story I had gotten out of Fanny as we were making our way across the parking lot to the auction house.

I eased down into the lumpy seat of the chair with the coil of the springs playing the devil on my skinny rump, and my left foot went cold. I looked down to see why and found that I had kicked over my paper cup of Coca-cola. It was seeping down through the canvas shoe and pooling up on the concrete floor.

Fanny looked down, said, "Don't worry about it; worse things have been spilt on this floor," and then she squeezed my hand. I clenched my toes to wring out the sticky Coke, and we waited for Jujubee Forthright to call the auction to order.

Here's how the auction worked: Down front to our right (that would be stage left) there was a partition running parallel to the back wall of the auction house (and offset from it by about twelve feet) that extended from the wall to our right about a third of the way across the room. The partition rose to about four feet of the 15-foot ceiling. The Auctioneer's Table was set so the top of it was flush with the top of the partition and there were three chairs behind the table (set on what must have been a mightily reinforced flooring of some sort), at the center of which sat Jujubee Forthright.

Whoever on earth might have thought it a good idea to design the set such that a five-foot-four, 300-pound man who wore a prosthesis was required to mount the auctioneer stand by way of a ladder or staircase I still don't know. (Jujubee would not give up the set designer when I asked him about it.) Though for dramatic effect it simply couldn't have been any better—for high and lifted up, there he sat, at the center of the table, the larger-than-life personage of Jujubee Forthright.

Down to our left (stage right) there was a little cinderblock wall, about four feet high, that extended about twelve feet from the left wall of the building. A platform perhaps six feet deep on top of it served as a bandstand for the Teensie Weensie house band. Behind the bandstand, at the front left corner of the building, there was a big double door, which served as a staging area. The dealer who was "on the dock" would back his vehicle up to the door and one or two assistants would help him unload his merchandise and haul it out onto the auction block—which was a folding school table.

The calling of Jujubee Forthright

The call to order commenced. "Welcome to the Town Countr'Auction, oh," Jujubee Forthright bellowed, in a voice that ranged from baritone to bass and back again. "How 'bout say we get this here show on the road? We got dealers all up in there roarin' to go, vans a-rollin' in like forty goin' north, and I'm a setting here roarin' to go, too. *Come* on!"

I had never heard (nor have since) anything like that voice. When Jujubee Forthright spoke it was more like song than speech—the inflection, the stresses falling on all the wrong—or at least unexpected—syllables. He said, "I'm just a roAHrinnnnnnnn to go-oh."

Was I the only one in the whole smoky place who thought that maybe Timothy Leary had been tending the punch bowl at our strange little masquerade party? It really was almost a hallucinogenic experience. I was transfixed—smitten, if not stricken—with the man, I admit. Maybe, I thought, it was a trick of the light; maybe it was the fact that Fanny had transported me across the great divide that yawned so wide between Wentworth College and the Teensie Auction; maybe it was the man himself—the improbability of him.

Maybe, just maybe, it was the inbreak of grace in the life of a sinner who hadn't the wherewithal to realize it.

When I finally stole my eyes away from him, I was surprised to find that everybody else was carrying on as though nothing was happening. A man in a blue mechanic's coverall yawned; a woman in a mumu and pink horn-rimmed glasses swatted a child's bottom; Fanny studied the high-gloss fingernails on her left hand with those Gene Tierney eyes.

I said, "Is it always like this?"

Fanny said, "Give it a minute. It's just getting started. It'll pick up and get going here in a little bit."

I said, "No, that's not what I mean. It's not dragging. There's something almost electric in the air."

The look on her face told me that she had no earthly idea what I was talking about. Either that, or at first she took it as sarcasm. She said, "Electric?"

"Well, yes," I said.

Then she smiled, as if she got it, elbowed me in the arm. "You're quite taken by him, aren't you? By Jujubee?"

"*Quite*," I said, trying to shrug it off.

She bit her lip, said, "Now you just behave yourself, David Umberton Hazelriggs."

I was not sure what she meant by that, but I said, "Of course. He is something else."

Fanny said, "He sure is. My little nephew Worthy Waddell always says, 'I love me some Jujubee.' There's nobody quite like him."

I said, "I should say there isn't." I laughed. Little Worthy Waddell must have been *quite* as taken by him as I.

The first dealer on the dock was a skinny fellow in hunting camos and snakeskin boots. A blond fair-skinned boy I took to be his son helped him haul his merchandise out onto the stage. The first item up was a metal appliance of some sort. I thought it might be a mini-dishwasher.

Jujubee started auction-rambling in earnest, with his opening line: "Who'll-give-a-start?—let's-go-tell-me-what-you-want-to-gib on this nice little one of kind copper-color't—exactly what is that thing anyways, Ray-mond?"

Raymond turned to his left and looked up at Jujubee and said something I couldn't hear. Then Jujubee nodded, spoke into the microphone, "It's a trash compaction thing. You don't see too many like that anymore. No sir, they don't make 'em the likes of that nowadays."

Fanny said, "They sure don't. They haven't made them like that since about nineteen seventy-three. You'll have to just bear with some of this stuff, David. *Les pieces de junque.* Though somebody could probably put a trash compactor to good use."

I said, "Is he, Raymond, the dealer in gnomes?"

Fanny said, "No. That was the only time I saw that gentleman. Somebody said he was a flea marketer out of Franklin, North Carolina. Even Jujubee said he wasn't sure exactly who he was. Whoever he was, he said he was coming back."

Jujubee Forthright cradled his chins (he later told me that it took more than one chin to hold up a head as big as his) in his left hand and used his right to hold the black microphone in front of his face. And in that voice that went from Al Jarreau to Louis Armstrong and back in the span of a sentence, he sang the auction call in a scat. "Five dollah here, five dollah now six. Five dollah: now six … . Five now six-six, five now six. And uh five-five-five gimme six, got five, gimme half, got five, and a half, got a half, and a quarter and a half, gimme six … . Now a half, need six, got a half gimme six, now a half-half-half, gimme six, gimme six, now a half, now a half, got a six. [Pause for a little wind. Then:] Got a six, gimme half, need a half, got a six, got a six, now a half, give a half, need a half. I got a half. Now s'en … . Come on with it y'all. Don't let this nice little dee-luxe gen-u-ine Maytag trash-a-majig get away from y'all all up in here. Y'all be sorry if you do 'cause it may *not* come again. Says he's only got one of these here. Says it's better'n stuff, ain't half as rusty."

I said, "I thought the saying was, 'It's better than snuff, ain't half as dusty.'"

Fanny said, "Does it make any difference, David?"

Jujubee intoned, "Got sev' now a half, and a half … . "

And on it went in that same manner for a few minutes more until Jujubee, bobbing his big head in utter disbelief that none of us was willing to pledge another fifty cents for the coppertone trash compactor, smacked his heavy palm (he didn't need a gavel) on the table and said, "Sold for eight dollars and a half to lucky Number Seven, the pretty little lady in the blue dress all up in here on row number four and seat number," he squinted, "whatever it is. Eight dollars and a half. A trash machine gone. Gone sold."

The clerk who sat at Jujubee's left hand recorded the transaction in a ledger while an auction hand in striped engineer overalls jogged across the stage and tagged the trash compactor and helped the dealer's son set it off to the side. Then the plain dealer and his son brought out a gas-powered weedeater and a bow rake and square point shovel—both with wooden handles and both about shot.

Jujubee looked down and looked them over, then said: "Folk, you can't find 'em like these here at the Wal-Mark."

Fanny muttered, "I should say you can't. That stuff was made before Sam Walton's time."

Jujubee held the microphone against his chest while he exchanged a few words with the dealer. Then he spoke into the microphone and told us: "He says all this is for one money. One money takes it all; all this merchandise, such as it is. You're bidding on the orange weedeater and the garden rake the wife can use to tend all those pretty little flowers all up in there in the flowerbed out yonder in your backyard and the square mortar shovel she can use to whomp you in the lower forty as oft as you get out of line." Then he sucked in a lot of wind and off he went with that raspy singsong run-on opening line he used (I was to learn) to start the bidding for each and every item: "Who'll give a start? Let's go. Tell me what you wanna give."

"That's almost mesmerizing," I said to myself in a whisper, but somehow Fanny heard it.

She said "David Umberton Hazelriggs, you're enjoying this quite a bit, aren't you? Now come on: Aren't you sorry you haven't come before?"

"I am," I said, thinking: mesmerizing and poetic, as I listened to Jujubee ramble his way through the musically hypnotic deal as the bids rose in half dollar increments all the way to "twelve dollars and a half." Jujubee's speech pattern had more verbal tics and filler-phrases than anyone else's I've ever known. His language, drawn in that rich mocha-American tone, was chock full of phrases such as "or what have you here" and "such as it is" and "if you will." I had a friend who specialized in psycholinguistics, and I wondered that night what he would make of a transcript of Jujubee's speech—a tape and a transcript. It had to be heard to be appreciated. I myself had no idea what to make of it. But I loved it. It was, like the man himself, so full-bodied—and no more or less nonsense, I decided, than my own book *Honest to God*, which was full of self-conscious safe little phrases that cloaked a danger dark and dirty.

Two hours and seven dealers later, there was still no sign of the unknown dealer from whom Fanny had acquired her lawn gnome. I was, however, a hand-knitted dog sweater to the good. Dog Maddox, my Shih Tzu, needed a light winter garment. He was none too fond of the dog coat I ordered from a mail order vendor the previous year. It made the poor creature (who is disposed to a mild manner) itch so bad that he would morph into a rampant beast and play the devil all through the house. Fanny helped me carry out the transaction. I had to request a "number" to open an account with the auction house then just stay seated: The attendant would deliver my merchandise, which I would pay for by cash or check, at the checkout counter when we got ready to leave.

Anyway, it was only after I had driven the price of that homespun blue knit dog sweater up to $8.50 that I discovered that it was not, as I had assumed, a one-of-a-kind garment. The dealer, a grandmatronly-looking woman a few years older than I, promptly snapped her fingers and her granddaughterly-looking assistant brought out a box full of the sweaters and Jujubee said, "Who wants to get in on this deal, or what have you here? She says she's got more and she'll sell each and every one for that price of eight dollars and a half. They must be stole' if she can let them go for that. Come on up and take a good look at 'em, feel of them with your own hands. This one has got all the frills and a lacy taffy collar and all like that."

To be honest, by the time I reached the $7.50 mark I had decided to hold and let the only other bidder (a heavyset woman with no teeth) have it for eight dollars because the lacy collar—turns out it was *taffeta*—was a little too effeminate even for a rather girlish Shih Tzu. But I made the mistake of raising a bite of popcorn to my mouth, and Jujubee thought I was raising the ante, and it was too late to turn back. All I could do then was hope the woman wanted it badly enough to pay a dollar more for it than her last bid. She didn't. So, with Jujubee up there going on about how it was a good thing they weren't in the business to make money, what with such priceless dog shirts practically being given away, and with the eyes of every red-blooded real man in the place on me, I looked up at the attendant who delivered the dog sweater to me and I promptly transferred it to Fanny who, gracefully, took it and said thank you. She held it up by the sleeves to inspect it.

A woman behind us leaned over and said, as loud as she could, "Did you get you a dog, Miss Fanny?"

Fanny said, "No, but maybe Corky can get some use out of it." Corky was Fanny's 20-year-old gray tomcat, and you couldn't have gotten that dog sweater on him without first killing him. I knew that much.

The transaction wasn't lost on Jujubee, either. He said: "I reckon that'll look mighty nice on you, Miss Franny, though it might require a little alternation." Then he looked on me and winked: "You're a gentleman, sir."

I winked back at him.

A little later, when the auction ended and the crowd was breaking up, Fanny sought out the heavy-set woman with no teeth who had bid $7.50 for the dog sweater and said, "Barker'll look cute as a button in this, Miss Melba." She handed Miss Melba the sweater, discreetly, and hugged her neck.

As we were walking away, she said, "It's not Dog Maddox's color."

"It certainly is not," I said. "You've always been a saint."

"Hardly," she said. "But let's go marching in and visit with Jujubee for a little bit."

As we made our way down front through the slowly dispersing crowd, a strange sensation came over me. The only thing I can think that does it justice is ... I was overcome with a case of the vapors, as a Victorian maiden might have put it. I was pleasantly warm yet painfully cold—with a coffin-cold chill of death; I was right there in my own skin and, strangely, as detached from myself as I had ever been. Of a sudden I had a sense of place—of, that is, being *out* of place: Why the devil was I here? For three hours I had suspended disbelief, but really, I was a stranger in a strange land. I had come to see a man about a gnome .... A gnome that, according to Fanny and Jorge, was the Oracle of Medlyn. Their delusion had become my own out there by Early's tool shed with a gut full of blackberry cobbler and not much else to live for.

So I had come. It is true I would have accompanied Saint Fanny to Dante's ninth level if she had only asked, but there was more to it than all that. I was, I told myself, way beyond immune to puppy love—a 60-year-old bachelor, confirmed thirty years over, who hadn't entertained an amorous (much less lusty) thought in decades. I can tell you this: If philosophy gives you a lot to live by—enough wisdom and folly to keep a person occupied for, what, sixty years in my case—it doesn't give you anything to die by.

And that's why I was there at the auction, I guess.

When my father died in the pulpit one Sunday morning back in 1974 at age sixty-one, he was the longest-living Hazelriggs male on record. When I reflect on his death I think first that my father would have been less troubled by the indignity of dropping dead during the Sunday service than by the fact that he was only on point two of his three-point sermon. He was a man who liked to finish things. I do think he would have found something satisfying in the grand object lesson that was his death, though: the shepherd dying while tending his flock—laying his life down if not *for* them then *before* them. There was an echo, if faint, of the Passion in that.

My mother had passed last summer, in her eighty-fifth year, and she was, quite literally, my last link to the human race. If Jujubee Forthright was an amputee, I was but an amputated limb, which was worse by far any which way you cut it, so to speak. With neither ancestor nor descendant among the living, who was I? There was not another person on the whole *bloody* earth with whom I shared … blood. So I had only recently become aware of my own mortality, and the only thing more depressing than that was becoming aware of my own *triviality*.

I didn't have the faith of my mother. I didn't have the nerve of my father, didn't have his Calvinist sense of Providence to comfort me. I was not predestined to do anything, or be anything. Or so I was thinking at the time.

So I got angry and wrote a book called *Honest to God* because it was easier to be honest with him than with myself because being honest with myself entailed facing head-on the plain fact that I had done so very little with my life and nothing—not a single solitary thing—that would outlive me. All that talk about *mid-life crisis* and *marking time* and *pondering one's legacy* is not all mere rhetoric—especially for those, such as myself at the time, who believed only in this life, neither finding nor taking consolation in the Christian afterlife or in Eastern reincarnation. There was no big mission I had accomplished. I was going to die and pass on into obscurity. So *Honest to God* was supposed to be my last (my *only*) great work, my *magnum opus*. I could live on, if not as a great philosopher whose name was spoken in the same breath as Socrates and John Stuart Mill, at least as an iconoclastic wig who, like Socrates, corrupted the youth of Wentworth … who shined the light of cynicism in the dark places of Calvinism.

And now here I was at the Teensie Auction on my way to meet Jujubee Forthright, and Lord knows it had the feel of an altar call as Fanny led me by the hand across the stage.

"Hey there, honey," Fanny said, as she approached Jujubee.

He closed his short arms around her and said, "Miss Franny, how you?" His voice was all Louis Armstrong now.

"I'm fine," she said. "I have somebody I'd like you to meet. Jujubee Forthright, this is my friend, David Hazelriggs."

At five-feet-four he hadn't needed to bend over to hug Fanny, so he didn't need to straighten up to shake my hand. He just rocked back a little at the waist and pivoted to his right and looked up at me for a moment before he reached out and took hold of my hand.

He said, "Hey, there, sir. I'm pleased to meet you and thank you for coming out the auction tonight with Miss Franny."

It was then I noticed for the first time his signature manner of looking at something. Even when he was not up in the box seat auctioning off merchandise, Jujubee Forthright had this habit (though for all I knew it was as involuntary as a blink of the eye) of all the time bobbing his head from side to side, making figures eight lying on their side, with a little dip in the middle. Each cycle——say from right to [dip] to left and back——took about three seconds, and it was all the more notable because of this: When his head was moving right to left, his right eye was closed; when it was moving left to right, his left eye was closed. And I can honestly say that, in all the time I've been knowing Jujubee, I have never once seen him awake with both eyes either open or shut at the time.

I cleared my throat, said, "I'm pleased to meet you," and shook his heavy hand.

He said, "Well all right then. And I'm pretty-pleased to meet you, too ... or what have you here."

I was not convinced that he was pretty-pleased, but I took no offense at the last phrase, having heard it close fully half the sentences he had uttered over the preceding three hours. His head was bobbing and weaving like a buoy at low tide. That, like his singsong cadence, was somewhat mesmerizing.

Fanny said, "Jujubee, we thought we might find a gnome like the one I got last month."

In response he asked, "Talkin' bout that dwarf thing with a beard stood about—" he raised his hand slowly to eye-level "—about yea high, right?"

Fanny said, "That's the very one."

He said, "That old dealer didn't come up in here tonight, now did he-*ah*-uh?" He ended the sentence with such a rise-and-fall you would have thought he was bringing the national anthem to a close. Fanny didn't seem to notice, and I couldn't do anything but stand there fixated on his head bobbing to and fro and his eyes blinking on and off like an old-fashioned switchboard.

Jujubee said, "But now, let's see, I do have another one of them dwarf-a-mabobs like you like back in the back up in there somewhere. For some reason that dealer-man left it behind him when he left off out of here that night. I had Peanut Butterbean and them set it aside, or what have you here."

We followed Jujubee through a hanging bead door with a multicolored Elvis image and back into a shadowy storage room behind the stage. The Coke was sticky between my toes as I walked.

Jujubee said, "I'd have Peanut Butterbean fetch it even now, if need be. But I picture he's out back gettin' him a little sip a something strong and pepp'ry about now with Dark Vader and them, or what have you here. Anywho, I seen that big old dwarf all back up in here somewhere just this afternoon."

"Don't trouble yourself, Jujubee," Fanny told him. "We'll come again some other time. You need to take you some rest. You look like you're still a little peaked from that bug that got a hold of you."

I said, "Of course. Don't trouble your—

Jujubee said, "Ooooh, there it sits, such as it is, down in the hole there yonder."

For the first time since shaking his hand, I took my eyes off of Jujubee Forthright. There, in a dark corner of the room—made darker because I was blocking the light from the auction hall—was a little hollow about six feet square recessed about four feet into the floor with five stairs leading down into it. And, sure enough, there it sat, the giant gnome, obviously cast from the very same mold as the one in Fanny's backyard.

"I would recognize that face anywhere," I said, recalling the face-to-face encounter I'd had with its kin out by the lake.

Jujubee shifted his weight onto his left (real) leg and swung his right (prosthetic) leg out in front of him. He was not so much walking as bounding or stilting, it seemed, and when he went to step down onto the first step something gave way and with a loud cry he went down face first but managed, somehow, to roll over in midair before falling into the gnome, the back of his head coming down hard on the gnome's own hard head, and crashing onto the floor. And I attest that I saw the gnome glow saffron in the tar black corner of the Town & Country Auction House on the 400 block of Main Street in Medlyn, Georgia, just an instant before Jujubee's head collided with it ... .

"Mercy!" Fanny shouted. "Jujubee?" In an instant, she was down the stairs and on the floor of the hollow with him, tending to him.

"Good heavens," I said, going down the stairs on my behind, in part because I wasn't at all sure there were any stairs left to trust a foot to. "Are you all right?"

A moment passed, with Fanny down on her knees beside him with his head resting in the crook of her arm, literally flat on the floor, before his guttural response to my question came, and when it did, I was astonished: "Yes, Jesus," he said.

I said, "He thinks I'm Jesus."

Fanny said, "Shhh. Hush minute."

"Yes, Jesus—or what have you here ... . Yes. Here am I. Send me. *Right?*"

I suspected at first that he had suffered a rather severe head injury and made for the door. "I'll summon a doctor, an ambulance."

"Great Phoenician," he said, the delirium playing the devil on his pronunciation. I wondered if he was referring to the Great Physician, which even a devout cynic such as I then was knew was a name for Jesus. "Great Siren Phoenician Woman," he said, and just then a siren screamed through the Medlyn night and a great clap of thunder shook the whole building.

I had crawled to the top of the steps and by the time the rolling thunderclap moved on, Fanny said, "Wait a minute, David."

*Wait?* I thought. It's clear the man has knocked himself silly, lying there muttering gibberish.

"Okay, Lord Jesus, yes," Jujubee said. "'The wind bloweth where it listeth, and thou hearest the sound thereof, but canst not tell whence it cometh and whither it goeth: so is every one that is born of the Spirit.' John three and verse number eight. Or what have you here."

"Well I'll be," I said. "What in the world is going on here?"

"Jujubee knows a lot of Scripture," she said.

A moment later, Jujubee was sobbing, dealing with the Lord and, from the sound of it, the Lord was dealing with him. I was quite ill equipped to do anything but stand there and listen as the poor man confessed thirty years or so of sins to the Lord. For her part, Fanny was there as a midwife delivering him of the great outpouring of transgression. "There now," she said. "Lay it to rest in the arms of the Savior, honey."

After a little while of this—being a man of the mind, not of the heart—I thought it might be best to leave the two of them in that Madonna and Child pose and perhaps see if I couldn't track down Peanut Butterbean and Dark Vader and get me a little sip of something strong out behind the Teensie Auction House.

But Fanny read my thoughts. She said, "You need to hear this as much as he needs to speak it," and I wondered if perhaps the same held true for every priest who ever climbed into the confessional booth. Though for the life of me I confess I had no idea what Fanny was talking about, specifically. I who was no priest had no business eavesdropping on another man's confession—especially that of a man who had just fallen down the stairs and knocked the sense out of him and was lying on the floor weeping like a baby. Why I was not even a confessing Christian; I was a professing cynic—long ago a Cynic with a capital C, that night just a cynic with a small c.

Now, for the record, Fanny denies any memory of having ordered me to stay put there in the shadows and hear out Jujubee's protracted confession. She neither denies nor admits telling me to sit down and shut up when I questioned her order. But so many astonishing things were happening in that moment that, well, who knows for sure what he said or did.

Jujubee Forthright went on. "'For while they be folded together as thorns, and while they are drunken as drunkards, they shall be devoured as stubble fully dry. There is one come out of thee, that imagineth evil against the Lord, a wicked counselor' or what have you here. *Right?* 'Thus saith the Lord. Though they be quiet, and likewise many, yet thus shall they be cut down, when he shall pass through.

Though I have afflicted thee, I will afflict thee no more.' Nahum chapter one and verse ten through twelve."

I said, "We need to get him to a hospital." Of all the passages of Scripture one might memorize—the Twenty-Third Psalm, the Beatitudes—Why this, I wondered, this obscure, rather dark passage from Nahum?

Fanny shook her head no, and Jujubee went on quoting Scripture and weeping and confessing still more deep dark sins as he lay there on the floor between Fanny on his right side and the giant gnome on his left.

"Here am I; send me," he said, over and over and over again.

It was well past midnight by the time Jujubee revived and we managed to help him back to his house, which was 300 feet back of the Auction House. We tucked him into bed, and Fanny kissed his cheek. "We'll see you tomorrow, Jujubee. Take your rest. You're going to need it, angel."

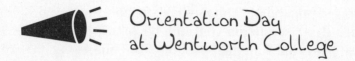# Orientation Day at Wentworth College

THE FOLLOWING MONDAY MORNING FOUND ME IN MY OFFICE—ROOM NUMBER 602—on the top floor of Wentworth College's Guilford Hall. Having served the college longer than anyone else except Mrs. Lucille Eckridge, Dean Mobley's secretary—who arrived on August 1, 1971, two weeks before I—I had earned perhaps the most coveted office on campus. It was a large Belgian-oak-paneled suite subdivided into an office proper and a reading area warmly lit with sconce lamps and fitted out with finely scrolled antique bookcases, an oversized club chair for reading, and a writing table and straight-back chair in which I had sat, none too comfortably, as I prepared all three drafts of *Honest to God*.

I certainly had the finest view of all, thanks to the great picture window that swept over the quadrangle below and the gentle slopes of the Blue Ridge Mountains that made a soft zigzag of the horizon. A stand of tall pines to the east was a saving grace that concealed the unsightly tract of land on which was set the Town & Country Auction and Jujubee Forthright's old two-story farmhouse, which was, to speak the truth, ramshackle. This morning, though, I stood with my nose practically touching the glass and lifted up onto my tiptoes to try to catch a glimpse of something—perhaps saving grace itself—on Jujubee Forthright's property.

But alas, the landscapers had carried out their orders too well.

I hadn't seen Jujubee Forthright or Fanny Fuller since early Saturday morning when we tucked him into bed and I drove Fanny home, neither of us saying much of anything, until I walked her to the door and saw her safely in. Before

I left, she said she would like me to join her that evening at the dirt track for the Saturday night races. She plied me with the gracious offer of a home-cooked meal. We could check in on Jujubee, she said, on our way to the Medlyn Dirt Track.

Of course, I accepted, though I wondered if I might not be pressing my luck. Early Fuller was the racer and the Medlyn Dirt Track was where he raced Car 3:16 until, by Fanny's own account, he accepted the fact that, if racing was not necessarily a young man's sport, it was necessarily not an old man's sport. So he hung up his racing helmet and put his master mechanic skills to work as an engine builder, car owner, and crew chief. His number, 3:16, which he had chosen for two good reasons—the obvious was the reference to John 3:16 and the less obvious was that Fanny was born on March 16—was retired on the Saturday night after his passing. He had left his mark on motorsports in Medlyn, and there was a flag bearing his name and number flying at the entrance to the Medlyn Dirt Track.

As it turned out, I had apparently caught whatever "bug" had Jujubee looking peaked even before he and the giant gnome nearly plunged down the stairs to their death in the backroom of the auction house Friday night. I was too weak to get out of bed on Saturday and, though I implored her not to, Fanny insisted and came over with a big pot of chicken soup—homemade of course—ginger ale, and a generations-old honey-lemon (hard) tea brew for just such ailments as I had. I didn't ask her whether by chance she had treated Jujubee with it … that would have helped to explain a lot.

I had intended to spend a good portion of the weekend polishing the address I was to deliver to the incoming freshman class Monday morning: Orientation Monday. In my weakened condition I couldn't manage to do anything but glance at my unfinished speech, which, I beg your pardon, was on the order of:

"Always answer a question, even a direct one, with a question. Always question an answer—even a straight one—with a question. Remember that seeing has very little to do with believing and that *believing* has everything to do with seeing. Remember that forty is a critical age. Therefore: Never trust anyone under forty. Never trust anyone over forty. Remember that you have no such thing as free will. Remember that you are no such thing as determined. Figure out, then, just what you are."

For the most part it was the same speech I had given more than twenty times before. It was certainly not going to get me a golden gavel from the Toastmasters, but it always seemed to go over reasonably well with the students—so easily impressed are the children. I did discover a subtle trend in looking back at years of speech notes: Each one was a little more cynical than the last.

I thought quite a bit about Jujubee's confession as I spent the weekend in bed, for the most part, reading the book of Nahum over and over. I pictured him lying there on the floor of the shadowy storage room between Fanny and the gnome, sobbing. I heard the various inflections in the way he said "Here am I, send me," with the stress, in turn, on each of the words, none of the words, then finally on all of them. Something in the way he said it screamed: *I've said all this before, but this time, this time ... I mean it.*

But what I thought about mostly was how he had managed to confess his sins, more or less nonstop (the stops were when he was punctuating confession with Scripture passages more or less related, as far as I could tell, to his sin), for over an hour. I reckoned then that I couldn't have confessed my sin for one full minute. Perhaps, I thought, it was better for one to be honest to oneself before presuming to be honest to God. Or to anyone else.

What a sin that was.

And it meant just these two things: One, I had learned too well from my master, Digoenes the Cynic, how to cloak my pride in a fussy, self-righteous air of humility. How much pride does it take to question everything?

Quite a bit, I tell you.

Two, I had not one minute's worth of confession not so much because I was righteous (though I would have told you with a straight face that I was a "good" person—"good" when measured against other mortals, which was my only point of reference—because I had never raped or killed anyone or kicked the walker out from under an old person) as because I was a coward. I'd never had the moxie to sin boldly. All my sins were of the "mild" variety, which I am sure gall the Lord precisely because they are so smug, so room temperature lukewarm. And there's no sense in compounding moral error with cowardice.

If Socrates was the wisest man of all because he knew that he was a fool, as the Delphic Oracle proclaimed, then maybe the most righteous man of all is the one who knows best that he, in the words of Saint Paul, has no righteousness of his own.

I did not know that then. I discovered it when I heard Jujubee Forthright deliver a message on the Pharisee and the sinner and decided that I myself wanted to go home justified that day. I now know that I could easily have spent three hours on my mild, socially acceptable sin—PRIDE.

Strange, I thought, as I stood at the window of my Wentworth office straining to catch a glimpse of the auction house and sipping my honey-lemon tea, how the confession of Jujubee Forthright seemed to include every sin but pride.

I peered absently out the window at the bustle of youthful students rushing up the hickory-lined cobblestone promenade as cocksure as Xenophon's mercenaries on their up-country march to Persia … . The Wentworth College Class of whatever had arrived, those dear children, either very smart or very rich but very seldom very both. They were on their way to the Rymer Auditorium for Dean Mobley's orientation address, which was scheduled for 10:00 A.M., and their colorful new clothes were a brilliant foreground against the slate-gray day with the clouds hung low in the late summer sky. Lightning flashed in the west and I knew that the tempest that had arrived with an arresting bolt of thunder during the Confession of Jujubee Forthright was not through with us yet.

Though as the time drew nigh for my appointment with President Knox I couldn't help but think of another tempest, the tempest within, a tempest of my own making, honest to God. In Shakespeare's words, "The tempest in my mind / Doth from my senses take all feeling." I drew in a deep breath and gripped the back of the chair to steady myself. I was hardly well enough to be out of bed, much less traipsing around campus, but I was loath to cancel the appointment with President Knox because I needed to know what he intended to do about me and *Honest to God*.

With tenure comes license to say just about any fool thing one wants with impunity. As a cynic, though, I hardly had the fortitude that comes with true conviction. Notoriety is a pathetic substitute for renown; but it is better by far than being but a semicolon in the great book of History. This is what I was thinking at the time.

Just as I was about to turn from the cold window and gather my things for the meeting with President Knox, my eyes fixed on something very improbable. There in that rich smart multitude padding toward Guilford Hall, bringing up the rear, if you will, was the largest student I had ever seen at Wentworth College. I removed my glasses and strained my eyes to see. Money, I thought, *a great deal of money*, was the only explanation for his matriculation at Wentworth. We had no football team and, as everyone knows, Presbyterians, whatever else they may or may not be, are not fat people.

As the students drew closer, he got larger, of course, and his size relative to the other students and his peculiar bounding gait became ever more remarkable. He was wearing blue overalls over a red flannel shirt. And as everyone knows, Presbyterians, whatever else they may or may not wear, do *not* wear overalls and flannel shirts.

"Jujubee Forthright," I whispered, my breath fogging the window pane. *Whatever on earth?* If I had never stepped into his world before the Friday night auction, he had never to my knowledge stepped into mine. And here he was bounding down the main promenade in the Wentworth quadrangle.

He disappeared did Jujubee Forthright after lumbering up the steps leading to the colonnade at the entrance to Guilford Hall. I could not explain it then, but I felt a joy unspeakable as I stood there before the window watching the place he had just been, and even in my influenza-weakened condition, and even though I was facing the unpleasant prospect of a humiliating visit with President Knox, I stood there joyful and clapped my hands and laughed a laugh that bellowed up from my gut—not *at* Jujubee Forthright but *because of* him and, if anything, *at* myself.

A few minutes later I was seated in the waiting area outside the President's chamber thumbing my way through *Fortune* magazine, wondering what on earth had brought Jujubee Forthright to campus, and eavesdropping on a conversation between President Knox's secretary, the comely prim and proper Martha Kitchens, and a sophomore whom I knew only by face. Young Martha, whose husband was a junior faculty member in the English department, was positively giddy about the exceptional quality of the incoming class. On paper, she said, they were the most distinguished ever. Their admission test scores and grade point averages, she said, surpassed any class in the 150-year history of Wentworth. Including my own class, I noted, the class of 1964.

She lowered her voice to a whisper and bit her lip as she said, "Dean Mobley has high hopes. He said this is the class that's going to do something really big."

And at that very moment, I kid you not, Jujubee Forthright rounded the corner and came bounding into President Knox's reception area with a family-size black Bible in his right hand. Martha Kitchens drew back in her chair and crossed her hands over her bosom. "Excuse me," she said.

He said, "I'm awful sorry, ma'am." He sounded a little like Barry White, but he had the whitest skin I have ever seen; the whitest skin and the blackest voice. "I didn't mean to startle you, or what have you here. *Right?*"

I was on my feet. "Jujubee Forthright, how are you?"

"Good morning, Mr. Hazelriggs," he said, with those eyes blinking on again off again and his head sweet-papa-dipping all around.

"Jujubee Forthright," I said. "Good morning to you." I was surprised he remembered my name, though if he were the least bit surprised to happen upon me sitting there leafing through *Fortune* magazine outside President Knox's office, he gave no hint of it. I had as yet to learn that Jujubee Forthright never forgot anything.

"Peanut Butterbean and them helped me get your dwarf put back together."

Who knows what poor Martha Kitchens must have been thinking, but she was all eyes, darting, as she stood up and sidestepped her way a few steps out toward the far corner of her desk, for all the world as if she might run screaming down the hall.

The young student bowed out and left us to it, and I said, "Ms. Martha Kitchens, I would like you to meet my friend, Mr. Jujubee Forthright, a businessman in our community."

Martha Kitchens looked me in the eye—as if I might give her some supercilious indication that the jig was up, by Jove, and she should run, run, as fast as she could, and summon campus security at once while, for my part, I would stay behind and try to fend off this obese ogre in farmer's overalls with hair like a black bear while trying to sound the nearest fire alarm I could get to. I tilted my head toward Jujubee, said, "Jujubee Forthright, this is Martha Kitchens, President Knox's executive assistant."

"How do, ma'am," he said, without looking her in the eye. "I didn't mean to startle you there."

"Mr. Forthright," Martha said, as she exhaled a long breath. She made it back behind her desk and sat down. "Is there something I can do for you?" I could tell she was almost afraid to ask that question. What vile thing might such a man as this request?

"I've been called of the Lord, or what have you," he said. "I'm inter'sted in rolling in some Bible classes here. *Right?*"

Poor Martha Kitchens.

Poor Jujubee Forthright.

That's all I could think just then. What a dreadfully awkward situation for both of them. "I've been called of the Lord," he said. I remembered how many times during his auction house confession Jujubee had said, "Here am I. Send me."

I lowered my head, feeling so sorry for him that I almost fainted with the vapors, and thought again of Xenophon's mercenaries in the *Anabasis*, recalled how boldly they had marched to the aid of old Cyrus and how valiantly they had retreated after his death in battle. In what spirit would Jujubee Forthright retreat from this place? I wondered. In what spirit would I retreat from my "come-to-Jesus meeting" with President Knox? Was I cast in the role of Cyrus?

"Perhaps," I said, with a wink and nod, "I could talk to Mr. Forthright about Wentworth—orient him a bit, answer any questions he has."

Martha's head was bobbing in time with Jujubee's. He gently picked up an eight-by-ten photograph of Althea Knox, President Knox's adolescent daughter, his only daughter, the daughter to end all daughters, the seraphic belle of the angel ball and, of course, the fairest of them all … and all this was mocking, of course, for the man's sickening devotion to his daughter was a favorite topic of my young colleagues (those, at any rate, who were young enough to really despise a man). Alisdair Knox's daughter was not so much pride and joy as she was his *only* joy, and to tell the truth she was, the dear Althea, a wondrous work wrought by a Master—though she was hardly the wholesome being her name suggested (the name Althea comes from a Greek word meaning "wholesome") and her adoring father presumed her to be, according to those young colleagues whose children attended prep school with her.

I thought for a moment that poor Martha Kitchens was going to faint. She crossed her hands over her heart and her eyes were impossibly bigger than usual behind her thick lenses. She pleaded, "Oh, oh, please do be careful with that," as if Jujubee were holding in his unwashed hands the holy grail.

Jujubee said, "What a beautiful young woman."

"An angel," Martha Kitchens said. Then, as if to a child, "Now let's put that back down in its place and not touch it again."

Jujubee set the picture back in its appointed place, and Martha Kitchens was just about to say something else when the door opened wide and President Knox stood in the threshold of his office. "Get yersel in, Hazelriggs," he said. "Martha: the tea." Then he noticed Jujubee Forthright. "And who are ye, my man, if a body might ask: Whit are ye daein here?"

Jujubee stood up and answered, "I have been called of the Lord, or what have you. And I'm inter'sted in rolling in some Bible classes, or what have you here."

I said, "President Knox, this gentleman is Jujubee Forth—"

"Ye are acquaint wi this lad, Hazelriggs?"

I nodded.

"So, then," he said, turning to Jujubee: "Well, say away then."

"Say away," Jujubee said, those eyes doing their lazy blink. "Sir, I am James Jackson Baldwin Forthright, of Medlyn, Georgia, if you will. Many people calls me Jujubee, and you can if you'd like." He was glib, Jujubee was, and I found myself feeling only a little less sorry for him. He bounded right up and extended his short arm. "Lord Jesus called me to the gospel ministry Friday past—*re-called* me really. *Right?*"

President Knox echoed, "Right?" But I am quite sure that Alisdair Knox had never in his life heard "tell o such as that." He did not know what to say.

"Yes sir," Jujubee said, "he most certainly did. I fell down them steps, but he called my name and you know what he said, if you will, he said: Get up and go on. That's what he said, sir. And I reckon from his tone he meant it this time."

If at that very moment Jujubee had broken into Louis Armstrong's "What a Wonderful World," he wouldn't have had to modulate his voice or tone one bit. For some reason I know not, I spoke up and said: "I was there when it happened."

President Knox looked at me, then back at Jujubee and said, "The Laird Jesus said git ye'rsel up and gae … *where?*"

"To go unto the ends of the earth, if need be," Jujubee said. "Go and carry out a mission, which was: 'The Spirit of the Lord is upon me, because he hath anointed me to preach the Gospel to the poor; he hath sent me to heal the brokenhearted, to preach deliverance to the captives, and recovering of sight to the blind, to set at liberty them that are bruised. To preach the acceptable year of the Lord.' Luke four and verse eighteen and nineteen."

"Aye. I see," Knox said. "And that brung ye *here* to me?"

Jujubee said, "Yessir, it did."

Knox to Jujubee: "Ye're a Reformed, are ye?"

"I'm trying to," Jujubee said, and it was clear that he had no idea what Knox was asking—which was whether Jujubee was a Presbyterian (or at least *not* something else). "Or what have you here. I've swore off it and haven't done it in a good long while."

I had no idea what Jujubee was talking about but it seemed a prime time to intervene. "He's actually in the Wesleyan tradition."

"Dear Lord," Knox said. He rubbed his eyes beneath the spectacles.

On our way home from tucking in Jujubee early Saturday morning Fanny had told me all about Jujubee's church affiliation. So I said, "He attends the Good Shepherd A.M.E. church in Medlyn."

"Ach," Knox said, his voice catching. "Well, then, are ye well prepared academically?"

Jujubee looked over at me as is if I myself were a glowing lawn gnome. He said, "No sir, I'm not. I finished the tenth grade." His straight white teeth were sparkling. "But I was young then, or what have you here, and there was a great and terrible many things going on in my life … ."

Knox scratched his head and bared his teeth. "Do ye not know, my lad, that we've a process to wit: admissions? Ye cannot very well come roarin doon onto the campus and get on, like that." He snapped his fingers.

Jujubee said, "My stepfather Allis had a devil of strong drink, or what have you here, and he would lay hold to me—"

"President Knox," I said, interrupting. I simply could not stand by idle and let Jujubee Forthright lay bare his soul, his tortured past, the better to spring the trap Alisdair Knox was setting for him. I could not let him cast his pearls before swine so that Knox could in turn cast his swine before pearls. Jujubee Forthright was not Wentworth material; he would not be a Wentworth man. It was that simple. "Mr. Forthright—"

Knox turned to me. "What did ye say?"

I said, "I was going to say, sir, that this gentleman was not in any way suggesting that he intended to simply 'come roarin doon onto the campus and get on, like that.'" I snapped my fingers.

Knox looked me off. "I meant, what name did ye call him?" He turned to Jujubee. "What is ye'r name, lad?"

He said, again: "James Jackson Baldwin Forthright."

"Well, that's a fine name," Knox said. "I myself am Alisdair Knox." He cocked his head and looked down, over the rims of his half-lens spectacles, at Jujubee's sextuple-E feet shod in a pair of black high-top Chuck Taylor sneakers. The change in President Knox's demeanor was so abrupt that I suspected, at once, that the name meant something to him. Maybe it was what a psychiatrist would call transference; perhaps his favorite schoolmarm in the Scottish Highlands of Aviemore was a Forthright. It was something, the change that came over the man.

President Knox, never accused of being a diplomat, curtsied. He shook Jujubee's hand. And there was something in his eyes that struck me. The only thing I can liken it to is caution. It was said of Alisdair Knox that he was not a man who suffered fools—period—and I am in no wise suggesting that Jujubee Forthright was a fool (he had more wisdom in his eyetooth than Knox and I together had in our heads), but to a "blokey old curmudgeon" such as Knox you can see how Jujubee could seem like a fool. Nevertheless, to my astonishment, Knox all of a sudden was no longer dismissive.

"Mr. Forthright," he said, motioning towards the sofa. "Please take ye a seat here for but a moment, while I tend to Hazeriggs here." He showed Jujubee into the oversized club chair in the corner. I hoped it would hold up. Then he said, "Martha Kitchens will accommodate ye."

Then he placed his hand at the back of my elbow and steered me into his office. At the door, he turned to Martha: "See that ye give the lad some tea."

I stood there with a copy of *Honest to God* under my arm and no bottle of single malt with a moody palate and peaty finish. Maybe, I thought, it wouldn't be called for after all.

I drew out my pocket watch: It was 10:50 A.M. "The time, sir," I said. I was tempted to call him "Alisdair," which is how he had introduced himself to Jujubee Forthright. He insisted that all students, staff, and faculty address him with the term of respect appropriate to their status relative to his: President was preferable to Professor or Doctor for a faculty member such as I.

He said, "What is that to you, dear Hazelriggs?"

I said, "My orientation address is scheduled to commence in a few moments' time, sir, and you know that Dean Mobley never takes his whole hour."

"About that," he said, "faer not. Ye will not be gaein' tae that this day." He gestured toward the loveseat, a Victorian affair that might have been comfortable in that era of discomfort.

I sat down. "Fear not?"

He sat down behind his desk and raised a copy of *Honest to God* toward me. "I read the buik through many times owre, *Honest to Gawd*," he said. "This bulks lairge in ma mind. They, the Board and the alumni, have cried on me tae put ye *oot*."

I said, "But I am tenured and have committed no moral turpitude. Whatever happened to academic freedom?"

He shook his head. "I myself have nae objections. However, it is all academic if'n the Board gaes all amok and eliminates the department of Philosophy ootright. They've long spoken of daeing just that."

"That's unthinkable," I said. "At a liberal arts college?"

"Arts and sciences now, man. Ye're well to oblige that every school is in the first place a *financial* institution," he said. "The alumni are at your back, at my back. They're aye quarellin wi ane anither aboot it."

"I see," I said. In a way, I confess, it was a relief.

"Myself, I do no' care what you write. I myself am a man of the Economics. And withoot the five pun note I've no ax to grind. Philosophy is ah so much blether tae me. But I am no' gaun tae hang for it either. The meetin'll be on Tuesday the tenth. Ye'll have tae behave yersel meantime. And ye're classes, well, Saunders will relieve ye till all is square."

Relieved of my classes? Caught by surprise by this turn of events, I nevertheless rallied immediately and said, "I will do my best, mean time."

The whole time he was talking to me, he was riffling through a manila file folder he had pulled from a drawer of his desk, shuffling papers as only a man of economics could. Then his eye fixed on some item on a sheet of stationery. When he lifted his eyes from the paper and trained his gaze back on me, I saw something there I could only identify as suspicion … or malice. "Ah," he said, exhaling. "That's why ye brung him then—the big lad there what's fond of his meat—why, he's your collateral."

"What?"

"James Forthright," he said. "He owns the auction due east, no? The Toon an' Coontry."

"He does."

He lowered his head and stared at me hard with those steely Scottish eyes, and his gray brow was furrowed. "And," he said. "Is there anything else? If so, say away, my man."

I looked at him there in his argyle sweater with his whistle-white hair slicked back, and I said, "What else should there be, *Alisdair*? What else?"

"Nothing" was his answer, but I was all questions—questions I sensed would be imprudent to ask. He said, "How long are ye knowin' him?"

I started to lie, but didn't, for two reasons: First, I am in the habit of telling the truth. I learned that from both my Calvinist father and my Cynical namesake, Diogenes. Second, I was not sure what was passing between us, even though I was quite certain that the question was anything but innocent or idly curious. "I met him this past Friday night."

"For the very first time?"

I nodded, thinking: *You wouldn't hang* with *me or* for *me, but you'll tie the noose; you'll hang me.*

Knox rose, once again smug then, and said, "Well, ye'll see him out then, I trust, your new frein. Now, it's aboot time for ma meetin' with the Board. We are set to sail to the sea on the morrow for the Pew-n-Pulp meetin'—I trust ye'll not be coming. Now, carry on then as well as ye can, do explain tae the lad that we hae certain standards for admission—the S-A-T, the G-P-A, and the like. Wit is it? *The Presbyterians value an educated clergy and informed laity.* Well, the Foondament'lists doont, and they have a Bible school in the laigh cellar a wee bit doon the pike. He's more suited tae that, the laddie, and that tae him. Godspeed to ye and haste ye back. Now good day, Hazelriggs."

Liar.

\* \* \*

In my office, Jujubee said, "I reckon that's what they call 'the school of hard Knox.'"

I said, "I'm sorry."

"I'm not a real good fit here, am I?" Jujubee asked. "My body's too big and my brain's too small and nothing else about me is just right either. *Right?*" He was sitting in the club chair in the reading room half of my office where I led him after President Knox dismissed us. "They really don't want some big old fat man wears overalls and talks like a colored, if you will, that's dropped out in the tenth grade shamblin' about all up in there. And if you must know I was the first in a long line to make it that far up. But anywho you learn quick in the auction business that there's no harm in asking. The worst they can say is 'No,' and sometimes they say 'Yes.' Well, no is not the *worst* they can say—they can say a lot worse—but you know what I mean."

"President Knox is a stickler for details," I said.

"He's stuck, all right. Stuck smack dab in the mist of the details of his past. We all of us are, if you will. Some of us more than others. *Right?*" He sat there, his head doing its undulating bob, eyes blinking on and off like a lighthouse beacon, though in slower cycles now. "My heart breaks for him," he said. He crossed his right hand over his heart.

"What do you mean?" I confess I took no pity on Alisdair Knox. "You know Alisdair Knox—before today?"

"No, not in a how-do sort of way, I don't. I've never seen him before. But in another way, I know him well. I know pain and I know fear," he said. "I know how they look and how they sound, how they smell and how they feel. *Right?*"

I resisted the impulse to agree with his rhetorical "right?" It was still new to me. But this time I was stunned. I eased back against the edge of the writing table. "Yes," I said, wanting him to go on, not about Alisdair Knox's pain. Truth to tell, at that very moment I couldn't have cared less about Alisdair Knox and whether his kilt chafed or not. I took him at face value: for a snake. It was Jujubee Forthright whom I could not seem to take at face value. It was Jujubee Forthright I cared about just then, whose story I wanted to hear in his *own* words.

There was a glaze in his eye and a hair in his throat when he said: "No one on earth has ever loved that man—really loved *him*, or what have you here. And he himself has never loved a soul on God's green earth—not loved in truth, for the worse along with the better, when all the facts are out and the stink of the world is reeking all around. Anywho, see: Even that that dimple-cheek daughter of his smiling so sweet in that picture up in there with Miss Martha Kitchens, the one the flesh would trade eternity in heaven for fifteen minutes flat with, he loves himself in her more than he loves her as she really is, with all the facts out, truth be known. That's the way of a man to love. Lord Jesus said, 'But I know you, that ye have not the love of God in you.' Gospel of John, chapter five and verse forty-two."

The pronouncement rang so true that it was in that moment I, a cynic, first admitted the possibility that Jujubee Forthright had been called by God that Friday night in the shadowy back room at the Town & Country Auction House. I was tempted to ask him what he saw and heard and smelled and felt with regard to myself, but I resisted. I was not ready to hear it—whatever it was.

"This is your book," he said. "*Honest to God*, or what have you."

"Perhaps more 'what have you' than *honest* to God," I said.

He said, "*Right?* Die-oh-genius, is that how you say it?"

"It's Die-*AH*-juh-knees," I corrected. "Not that it really matters."

"Ah," he said. "Of course it is. It's a name I've never heard."

"Few have," I said.

He cleared his throat. "Die-o-genes?"

"Much better," I said. "It's not everyday one runs across a Tom, Dick, and Diogenes. My mother and father named me David. I named myself Diogenes, after a Greek philosopher who lived in a bathtub." Then I gave him a Golden Book version of the story of Diogenes of Sinope, the Cynic, the way a father might explain to a small child who George Washington was, by way of the legend of the cherry tree.

"He lived in a bathtub?" he said. "Why did he take to a tub?"

"Maybe he was crazy," I said. It occurred to me in that moment that perhaps crazy was, after all, what Diogenes really was.

Jujubee said, "Hmm. Wonder did he feel dirty, or what have you? Is that what it was? Maybe nobody ever told him that the blood of Jesus washes away all the grime of the past?"

"Perhaps," I said. "When he was a young man he and his father, Icesias, who was a banker, were brought up on charges of debasing the public coin and exiled from their hometown. Diogenes moved to Athens—Athens, *Greece*, that is—and joined the cynic school under Antisthenes—"

"Them Greeks had some names on 'em."

"Right," I said.

"So, that might have been what it was that was eating old Die-oh-genes bad enough to make him want to get all up in there in his tub, then, or what have you here. Ask me, people'll do just about any fool thing to get shut of the past. The answer's real simple, if you will. Anyhoo, I reckon there's worse places to live than a bathtub. Thing of it is, I've lived in worse places myself. I'd have to take up in a hot tub though, probably, one of them big old Jacuzzi pools.

"Well, your initials suits you, I reckon: Die-oh-genes Umbert'n Hazelriggs? D-U-H: DUH. That's the boilt-down version of what"—he glanced back at my first name on the book cover—"Die-oh-genes there had to say."

Then it was I who said, "Right," and began to wonder, just in that moment, who was condescending to whom. If I talked down to Jujubee; he talked up to me—and there's nothing like being talked up to to make you feel humble—even if you are, as I was, a master of condescension. The students, even at such an exclusive private college as Wentworth, are not what they used to be. He was right, Jujubee: Diogenes the Cynic would have liked our English slang word *duh* perhaps better than all the rest.

Then Jujubee said, "I'm not having a easy time with the pronouncement of your name. How about if I just call you Dewey?"

"Dewey?" I said. I clucked my tongue just then, I am sure of it. Why wouldn't I have? From Diogenes to Dewey: Just. Like. That.

"Be a doer of the word and not a hearer only."

"Amen," I said to Jujubee Forthright.

I thought about Allis Blackwell, his stepfather, and in what horrific ways Fanny had said he mistreated Jujubee, and just then I might have felt some measure of the pity for Jujubee that Jujubee himself felt for Alisdair Knox. Maybe if I had been a father I would have had the vocabulary to describe the wave of sentiment that flowed over me just then. It was two parts protective to three parts heartbreak. I said, "I think President Knox was right about one thing: You and Wentworth are not a match made in heaven. I think it's quite possible that you have too much sense for this place."

"That's not the truth," he said.

I said, "Besides, ministry preparation is not one of Wentworth's strengths. Trust me on that." I thought of the angry letters I had received from pastor-alumni of Wentworth; if some small part of me was exacting revenge, a larger part was merely speaking the truth. I had on several occasions had the misfortune of having to sit through their oratories at convocation ceremonies in the Trenton Chapel on the Wentworth campus.

Jujubee was getting up onto his feet. "You are a kind man," he told me.

That was the first time anyone had used the word "kind" to describe me. The very first in my nearly sixty years of life. "Now *that*," I said, "is not the truth."

"Oh, my dear friend Dewey, but it is." He stood there nodding, and it struck me then for the first time that for all the expressions I had seen him make, I had never seen him smile.

"I have to run, or what have you here. I'm going to see Miss Bagwell over't the clinic. Her folks has done gone on— every last one of them but Nickel—and he's bad to drink, if you will. We do what we can, but the bottle's good for undoing it."

"Miss Bagwell," I said. "She's the one you took up the offering for at the auction the other night."

"Yessir, that's her. But it's not so much an offering as repaying a loan, right? It's all of us's way of doing for her what she's always done for us, or what have you here." He shifted onto his left—his real—leg, I think. "She took a hard spill some few months back and busted her left hip, so she's been laid up in there at the clinic for a spell. Every Monday

I take her a plate from Cindy's for lunch and a quart Mason jar or two of their sweet tea. She likes their meatloaf and greens."

"That's very kind of you, Jujubee," I said. And I meant it. I must confess two things at this point: One: Not only had I never dined at Cindy's, a country cooking restaurant just outside of Medlyn with rockers on the porch and sweat tea served in Mason jars, but I would have been hard-pressed to find the place on a dare. Two: I was playing a bit of the fool because Fanny, during one of her chicken soup drops at the house on Saturday, had told me that Jujubee applied the proceeds from the offering and raffle to pay Miss Bagwell's house note and bills. He made up the difference from his own wallet.

Jujubee said, "Anybody'd do that for somebody they love."

"Hmm," I said, wanting to say *wrong again*. "Alisdair mentioned a Bible school in town that you might want to look into."

Jujubee said, "Fundamental First?"

"That has a familiar ring to it." I recalled Knox's shepherd's pie Scottish brogue: *The Foondament'lists have a Bible school in the laigh cellar a wee bit doon the pike.*

He said, "They're right hard-shell, or what have you, I've heard. They don't mix much, and Tammy Tillis told me one time she heard they said auctioning was of the devil and they'd better not catch any of their members over't the Teensie of a Friday night with them moneychangers. She said it might have something to do with the colored people being there and the Spanics."

I said, "Good heavens. It's hardly a den of iniquity."

"Don't judge it by your first trip. It might not be a den of antiquity, but it's not exactly holy ground, either, or what have you here. Peanut Butterbean cranks up Lynyrd Skynyrd on his car stereo and they start imbibing the liquor and dancing barefoot out in the back lot if the moon is full or if it's not. One time they had to carry Willie Stedman away for prancing across the side lot in his birthday suit. Buck naked if he was a white fellow with four teeth. He told me he never took his underpants off, but others said make no mistake about it but he did too and they're not apt to lie giving a description such as they give, and anywho the po-lice got called. They've been called out more times than one to turn the music down and break up a fistfight, if need be. The things you can find out there of a Sunday morning when you're heading out to church makes you wonder some, if you will."

I said, "I see." I could picture it. After Fanny and I had managed to get Jujubee up on his feet when the confession petered out, a few people helped us carry him up the front stairs of his house and work him into his bed. If I couldn't have picked any one of them out of a police line-up, I wouldn't have been surprised in the least measure to find any of them in one.

"Well, the thing of it is, it couldn't hurt much to go and see," he said, "or what have you here. They're right next to me to the east. I feel like I got to get me some training to do all that the Lord Jesus called me to do. He means it this time, if you will. And I got this funny feeling this time, too, that I'm either going to do it or die."

"By all means, then, do it."

"I need some training, right?"

I started to say: *To the contrary, nothing will ruin the ministry of a young man quicker!* I merely shrugged.

Jujubee said, "All I've ever done is run a auction, or what have you here. Well, that's not the truth. It's all I've ever done *half* decent. And I'm not all that good at that, *right?* I drove a truck for a few months, too, and did various odd jobs in the season of my sin. Some were right odd; some were *real* odd."

I said, "I'll be happy to go with you to the Bible school, if you think it might help."

"It couldn't hurt. *Right?*"

Again, I merely shrugged.

"We might could go first thing in the morning?"

"Certainly we could. Why don't I pick you up at the auction house at nine o'clock, and we'll go together."

"Nine-ish is good. You can pick up your dwarf then, too, or what have you here. *Right?*"

\* \* \*

After I saw Jujubee out at half past eleven, I sat awhile at the writing table in my office drinking a pint of Fanny's honey-lemon brew and feeling my gall rise to a frothy boil. The very idea that the Wentworth College Board of Trustees, charged with keeping that sacred trust, was ready to do away with the philosophy department on account of my book vexed me. That struck me as being as eminently sensible as burning down the house to kill the rat in the laigh cellar. If *Honest to God* was the problem, have done with *me,* by God—me, Diogenes Umberton Hazelriggs, author of heresy—but spare the discipline of ideas and its noble quest for truth, for beauty, for virtue.

Though, of course, I had to acknowledge, after Fanny's honey-lemon brew began to do its work, that the number of Wentworth students who elected to major in philosophy had been declining since, well, since sometime during Clinton's second term, and enrollment in pure philosophy classes excluding the Western Civilization sequence I taught was hardly enough on its own to justify keeping the department. *But still.* For all I knew, though, the whole caper was nothing more than Alisdair Knox's blather and bluff.

I sat there with my eyes closed, midway between wake and sleep, and the image of Alisdair Knox with that slick white hair and those beady eyes when they scanned from the stationery to me and he said: "Ah. That's why ye brung him then—the big lad there what's fond of his meat—why he's your collat'ral."

*Collateral?*

Collateral *what?* Collateral evidence. Collateral damage. Collateral relative. Collateral loan. I went over to the bookshelf opposite the window and pulled Volume II of my 20-volume set of the *Oxford English Dictionary* from the stack. I shuffled back to the entry for collateral and read the entire piece, to be sure Knox had not meant by collateral some obscure Scottish perversion of the term. I decided he hadn't. I was almost as confused as I was annoyed just then. What had the man seen on that leaf of dark brown stationery that made him suspect that I had "brung" Jujubee Forthright to serve as my collateral.

"James Forthright," he had said. "He owns the auction due east, no? The Toon an' Coontry." Then he stared at me, hard, searching for something. "And … is there anything else? If so, say away, my man."

Then by irresistible force of habit I had said No, instead of misleading him with an outright lie: Yes, or with a coy: Maybe I do and maybe I don't. I have many times since then wondered how things might have turned out differently if I had looked into that varicolored argyle tartan and defied both my father and Diogenes of Sinope and lied my fanny off. I cannot say for sure how things would have been different, but I know they would have been. Or maybe they would have turned out exactly as they did, because what I did next is this:

I got up off my duff, feeling some little relief from the honey-lemon tea, and crept down the hall, close to the wall with palms flat, all of which was hardly necessary because the orientation processional would stop next at the campus refectory in Dinwiddie Hall across the quadrangle. I approached Martha Kitchens' workstation, which was vacant, of course. Martha would have recovered by now from her initial encounter with Jujubee Forthright and would be there dining with the quality incoming class *in loco obKnoxious* for the President who was meeting in the holy of holies in Windsor Hall with the Board of Trustees for all I knew plotting just then to lay the ax to the root of the philosophy department and seal my fate.

I walked directly into President Knox's office and was sliding papers in that manila folder this way and that like a con man in a pea and shell game before it dawned on me that, of course, campus security would be monitoring the office. I shuffled down through the sheets of stationery until I saw the name "James Forthright" then quickly slid it off the desk. Then I dropped to my knees and crawled around on the floor in front of that Victorian loveseat under the guise of—I would say during the interrogation—searching for the, uh, the Wentworth class ring that had slipped off my finger perhaps during my earlier meeting with President Knox.

I folded the sheet of stationery in half and slipped it into the interior pocket of my Harris Tweed sportcoat and, back on my feet, made a show of slipping my class ring onto the ring finger of my left hand. I brushed my hands together as though they were cymbals, breathed a huge sigh of relief, smiled for the camera, then left.

 # A Visit to Fundamental First

THE NEXT MORNING I WOKE UP FEELING MUCH BETTER—I mean, not just much better than I had the day before, but much better than I had in a very, very long time. I recall sitting out on my back porch in my striped pajamas and matching nightcap sipping coffee and seeing the first dazzling rays of the morning sun form a halo above the dome of Bannister Mountain. And as I sat there in the cool of the day with the morning breeze loosening the last leaves of summer from the hardwoods, I entered into some sort of contemplative state not unlike prayer. I was awed by the surpassing beauty of the sunrise, the majesty of the moment, and I thought of the Tertullian's saying *Rosam tibi si obtulero, non fastidies creatorem.*

"If I give you a rose you will not disdain its creator."

My father would have been proud, I think. He preached from the early church fathers nearly as oft as he preached from the Bible, it seemed, during certain phases of my childhood. And it was my boyhood reading of the anthologies of the church fathers, in the textbooks from my father's seminary classes in Patristics that I smuggled out of his library—*smuggled* lest he mistake my interest for "seeing things his way"—that sparked my love affair with philosophy, ironically, and not theology.

I drained my coffee, stood up and moved in close to the rail of the deck and, fixing my eyes on the numinous halo over Bannister Mountain, said aloud: "O God, bless Jujubee Forthright."

If it was a simple prayer, it was a significant act. You see, I had not addressed God, in prayer or in any other wise, in Lord knows how long. That five-word petition on behalf of

Jujubee Forthright was the shortest and sincerest prayer, I am sure, I have ever prayed.

When I passed along Alisdair Knox's suggestion about the *Foond'mentalist Bible school* to Jujubee Forthright, I did so with the best of intentions. Lord knows, I did. I confess I didn't know much about Fundamentalists, in general, nor about Fundamental First Church of Medlyn, Georgia, in particular.

I might say at this point: Beloved, if I had but only known ... .

I did know this, however: Jujubee's academic options were limited because he had dropped out of high school in the tenth grade. (And it was only later that I would learn that he had worked with a tutor he met in a twelve-step group and passed a test to receive a high school equivalency diploma, which he needed to get the job driving a truck.) But he wanted training, as much as anything else I guessed, to provide him with some measure of confidence in discharging the duties of his calling. So the Bible school in the "laigh cellar" of the church might fit the bill. It was hard to imagine it would be given to academic rigor, whatever else it might be given to.

As I stood in the shower that morning, I decided that the skills of the auctioneer are not so different from those of the pulpiteer. In both cases, job one is presiding over a negotiation between interested parties—between one bidder one and another, in the case of the auctioneer—and between God and the devil, in the case of the pulpiteer. And Jujubee Forthright certainly had presence; he captivated me who, in Fanny's words, was "quite taken" with the young man as he held court from his seat high above the floor of the Town & Country Auction House.

It wasn't until I got behind the wheel of the Big Healey that it dawned on me that there was little chance that we could fit Jujubee Forthright into the passenger seat of my car, which was built long and narrow, and Jujubee was, well, built short and wide. The Big Healey might be big, but it wasn't that big. I thought it might be awkward, and I fretted some about it on the way down the mountain.

When I pulled into the front lot of the auction house a few minutes before 9:00 A.M. Jujubee was already standing out front flat-footed in the long shadows of morning in a two-piece double-breasted suit, navy with wide white chalkstripes, set a good two inches apart, and a shimmering gray pocket square point up in his breast pocket. He had on a blue clip-on tie, not quite the navy blue of his suit, with bold canary yellow stripes running down at 45-degree angles toward his right shoulder. He had on brown dress shoes with a gold buckle across the instep; they were shiny but not new, as I could see by the heavy wear showing light gray on the outer edges of the soles. He was holding the family-size black leather Bible crossed over his heart with his right hand and he waved at me with his left.

It was the first time I had seen him in anything but his overalls, and I couldn't help but wonder why he had worn the blue denim overalls and plaid shirtsleeves to Wentworth and saved the suit for Fundamental First. Maybe he attributed his experience at Wentworth (the school of hard Knox, as he put it) to his dress and thought a suit might improve his chances at Fundamental First.

Beside him, a good foot taller than he and not a third as wide, stood the lawn gnome back in one piece and looking none the worse for his run-in with Jujubee in the shadowy room behind the Elvis Presley bead curtain at the auction house. It was the first time I had gotten a good look at the thing in the unforgiving light of day, with his onyx-black eyes, fire-engine-red pointy hat, white bearded face, and green bib-front overalls with short pants. It was a grotesque-looking thing, seen in any light, and likely to scare small children.

I stepped out of the car, said, "Good morning, Jujubee. You look very nice. I feel underdressed." I had on a pair of khaki slacks, a navy blue brushed cotton golf shirt, and navy canvas shoes.

He said, "You look neat as a pin, Dewey Hazelriggs. I'd be in Osh Gosh myself and wouldn't have gone and got myself all gussied out to the nines in my Sunday suit and all like that if I didn't have to make a court appearance this morning."

I said, "A court appearance, you say." Now to be honest I was curious, though I didn't want to be forward. Who knew what shenanigans the likes of Dark Vader and Willie Stedman might have gotten into this time when Peanut Butterbean cranked up Lynyrd Skynyrd out behind the auction house? I tried to picture Jujubee in the dock at the Medlyn City Court gussied out to the nines in his Sunday suit, testifying under oath as a plaintiff, a defendant, an *amicus curia* expert witness on standard auctioneering practice ... .

I said, "Are you sure you won't be late on account of the Bible college interview?"

Jujubee said, "Nah. I don't reckon we'll be there too awful long, such as it is." He looked at my car, as if sizing it up. "I don't think we need to drive over there to the Fu-Fi. We could take the truck, if need be ... . "

Need would most certainly be, I thought, if we were going to drive. The passenger seat was at least a foot too narrow to accommodate Jujubee.

He said, "But it's a cool morning and it's not that far, so what say we just hoof it up there? If it's all right with you."

I looked over at his old GMC box truck parked at the right side of the road, sideways so that passing traffic could read the message painted on the box in big red letters:

T & C Auction, Inc.<br>
425 Main Street (U.S. Highway 76)<br>
Medlyn, Ga.<br>
874-9801<br>
J.J.B. Forth right, Dealer<br>
We Buy Estates, Liquidations, Close-Outs

I said, "What happened to the *W* in your name on your truck?" I asked.

"Lord Jesus told me to let it go," he said, "or what have you here. I was all up in there at the church house on Sunday and Bishop Lester Watts said, he said, 'Lord Jesus has called somebody in the sound of my voice to do something. Tell me, Lord Jayzus!' or what have you here, right? So Maurice and a couple of us got up flat on our feet—we do that when the Holy Ghost starts listething about—with the holy hands lifted way up in the air, and I said, 'Tell it, brother Lester.' He looked me dead in the eye and said, 'You get yourself up here right now. Come *on* with it.' He put his hands on his hips and rocked back on his heels and puffed his chest out. He's not as big as a minute. He said, 'You best put a move on, or what have you here, and get your big business up here. Tellin' me to "tell it." Boy: STOP! Boy, tell you what. I bet I'll come on over there and smack me some big old face. Smack hail out a you—right clean out a you, boy.' He was grittin' his teeth and his eyes was all bugged out. Now this wad'n the first time I've been called out up in there at the meeting, if need be. I don't know if you've ever seen Bishop Lester. He stands about up to my shoulders, and I'm five-foot-four high in my dress shoes and I make about six or seven of him, if you will, when it comes to the width. He's ninety-seven years old and ornery as a hog-tied cat that's been dipped down in some water, if need be, and he'll call you out in the aisles and pull your pants down and spank your hindparts but good right there in view of the whole congregation."

"Oh my," I said, or what have you. I said something innocuous, as I pictured Jujubee bent over old Bishop Lester's knee down front in the Good Shepherd A.M.E. church. It was almost too much to think about.

"Well not literary," he said. "I'm just saying is all."

For a long moment, neither of us said a thing. But we did take off walking out toward the sidewalk that would lead us up to Fundamental First. Jujubee smelt strong of spearmint bath soap and corn meal.

I said, "Pardon me for interrupting you in mid-story, Jujubee."

He said, "Anywho, Bishop Lester laid hands on me and screwed his eyes shut and said, 'I gots me da word of knowledge, yes, yes I do. And something's going on. Lord Jesus says, "There's too much of you. T-W-O: two much." If you got da ears to hear, you bet' hear it, boy.' Then he slapped me in the face, the way he does when he's slaying folk in the Spirit or threatening to slay 'em in the flesh, and I went down. And as I was layin' there in the floor at his feet with folk all up in there around me prayin' and carryin' on: I heard Jesus say, 'Henceforth, ye shall be forth right. No more double-you—that's been your problem all right along, or what have you here. Ye shall go forth and be right, and be Forthright.' So after I'd woken up and they got me back down at the house, I took me a paintbrush and a can of white paint out and crossed out that double-you from my name on the both sides of the truck, such as it is."

"Go forth and be right," I said. I played Jesus's command regarding the double-you over and over in my mind and, for even as convinced a big C cynic as I then was, it did sound like something Jesus might say, it had the ring of truth about it, as I'd heard my father once describe how he could tell canonical books of the Bible from the books of the Apocrypha (though I think he used the word veracity, the ring of veracity). "That's astonishing."

He said, "That Jesus, Lord, he has a way of astonishing you, if need be."

A passing car honked twice and Jujubee's arm went up like a toll gate and waved. The auction house was set in a swale between two cities set on a hill—Wentworth College on the east and Fundamental First on the west—so the trip from the auction house to Fundamental First required a steep uphill climb. Jujubee slowed up a bit, not on account of him and his prosthesis. He was fine; I, on the other hand, was panting and had a case of shin splints—symptomology I attributed to my recent illness.

As we made our way, slower now, up the sidewalk to the Fundamental First Church, Jujubee told me what business he had in court that day—that is, after I had baited him into telling me with such transparent lures as, "I hope you didn't get a traffic ticket speeding in your GMC truck," to which he responded: "That's not why I'm summoned to court. I don't mind telling you, if need be. Seems like you're wanting to know pretty bad."

I said, "It was that obvious, eh?"

He said, "Anything you ever want to know about, Dewey, just come out with it and ask, if you will. Miss Franny's trying to get her land rezoned. You know—well, I don't know if you do know—but anywho even if you don't I don't reckon it's like it's top-secret anywho. Miss Franny's nephew Worthington, which we all call him Worthy—that's her brother Marion Waddell's son—or what have you here, and well he's afflicted something terrible—Worthy is, not Marion—well. Marion's wife Pauline passed on last year and left Marion to care for Worthy all alone—not that it was her fault, so to speak: She had cancer. And Marion, God love him, he's got the sugar for one thing and more problems than a math book, for another, and Miss Franny's made up her mind that both of em's gonna come live with her, if you will, and anywho, she says now's the time to take and turn that red brick house up in there next to their place that she and Early was letting out to them old folks that's gone to live on some island somewhere into a group home, if she can get it rezoned, or what have you here, now that the tenements has moved out. She's going all out, she is *that*. She's had this idea for the longest time of giving people that's got various and assorted problems, if you will, some nice place to live. She took me in way back—she and Early did."

"I'm not surprised in the least," I said. "That woman is a saint, if ever there lived one."

He said, "Believe me, if you will, she is. Anywho, as my property backs up to her and Early's property, they summoned me into the court to see if I had any objections, or what have you here, to the rezoning. Last week, the City Council bound it over because there was some parties, if you will, opposed to it, and I guess the judge will have to decide the matter, such as it is."

"That's too bad," I said. "I hope she prevails." I had never thought ill of those who opposed such good Samaritan causes as Fanny's group home. They always struck me, when I would see them on the evening news, as upstanding pillar-of-the-community types who had worked hard for their little slice of the American dream and opposed this or that project only on the reasonable commonwealth grounds that it would disturb the peace or adversely affect the value of their property. But I, who had no right to do so, judged them harshly just then. They were mean-spirited and selfish and had no right to frustrate Fanny's plan to do God's bidding! Was it easy for me to say? You bet it was—I, who lived on a secluded 10-acre wooded plot on the side of a mountain. I guess the group home put a human, Fanny face on the issue for me.

"We'll see about all that, if need be," Jujubee said. "'And the King shall answer and say unto them, Verily I say unto you, Inasmuch as ye have done it unto one of the least of these my brethren, ye have done it unto me.' Matthew twenty-five and verse forty."

We followed the signs pointing the way around to the side of the church and down a walkway that led to a gray metal door with a black-on-white sign:

Mount Sinai Fundamental
Bible College & Institute of Theology
Separated * Independent * King James

"Holy Moses," I said, leaning back against the retaining wall in the cool shade, toes pointed down to relieve my shin splints. And behold Jujubee stood at the door and knocked then stepped back and stood flat-footed in front of the door, waiting, still but for his head doing its slow motion Ray Charles bob. I wondered how on earth he managed to get around so well considering not only his size but the fact that he had a prosthesis. I was tempted to ask him about it. He had, after all, given me carte blanche to ask him about anything. But since Fanny was the one who had told me about Allis Blackwell's razor strop and the infection that became an amputation, I let it be for the time being.

He said, "That was a good one, or what have you here." His voice bellowed the low register of a tuba. "Holy Moses and Mount Sinai Bible College."

"Forgive me," I said. "That was a poor attempt at humor."

The door opened about halfway before it caught on the sloping concrete walk, and a gray-haired woman in a charcoal Mother Hubbard dress looked up at Jujubee and started to say something before her voice, like the door, caught on something—most likely the expanse of Jujubee Forthright. Her left hand, quite involuntarily I'm sure, rose up to her mouth and she seemed to lean harder into the open door.

Jujubee said, "Good morning, ma'am. I am James Jackson Baldwin Forthright—with no double-you—of Medlyn, Georgia, if you will. Most folk calls me Jujubee, and you can too if you'd like. Lord Jesus has called me to the Gospel ministry Friday past—*re-called* me really. *Right?* And so I've come to get my path prepared, or what have you here."

"I see," she said. "You're a preacher boy. Pardon me. I was thinking something else there for a minute. Now help me get this door open a little more or you'll never fit in here."

Jujubee said, "Yes, ma'am."

It was only when Jujubee pivoted a little to open the door that she saw me. She said, "Have you been called, too, or are you his father?"

I pushed off from the retaining wall and was about to say something benign—probably on the order of *I'm here for moral support*—when Jujubee said, "Yes, he is, if you will. Only he doesn't know it yet."

With a single simple motion, Jujubee had managed to get the door open all the way, albeit with the grating scrape of metal on concrete. The woman in the frock stepped aside and showed us into the eight-by-ten receiving area of the Mount Sinai Fundamental Bible College & School of Theology. It was no Wentworth College. Worn brown indoor-outdoor carpet covered the floor, cheap yellow-tone sheet paneling the walls; two mismatched file cabinets stood against the wall just to the right of the gray metal desk, its top not cluttered in the least, and on it was a faux wood nameplate engraved: *Sister Brenda Cheeley, Receptionist.* There was a card table with several stacks of mimeographed brochures and fliers on top, all bearing the official gold-stickered seal of the Mount Sinai Fundamental Bible College & Institute of Theology. And presenting all this in the harshest possible light was a bank of fluorescent lights in the low drop ceiling that I could have stood flat-footed and reached up and knuckled with my clenched fist.

The guest seating consisted of a 1970s settee that looked as if it might have been purchased at the Town & Country Auction for a winning bid of five dollars, and we all knew that there was simply no way in the world that it would support Jujubee Forthright—even with a single-you. So out of respect, I guess, I stood rather in the middle of the room next to Jujubee in the direction of the narrow dim-lit hall and Sister Brenda, standing now behind her desk.

She said, "Dr. Wiley's out in the print shop tending to an issue. He will be back any minute. I'm Brender Cheeley. Would you gentleman care for some coffee?"

Jujubee said, "No, Sister Brender Cheeley, but thank you very much all the same, if you will, ma'am," and I shook my head and winked. Then we all held our places and I wondered what, if anything, Jujubee meant when he said that I was called of the Lord, too, or his father, too, only I didn't know it yet.

From somewhere down the hall, I heard one door open and another close. Sister Brenda asked for our names and wrote them down on a small notepad and then excused herself and went off down the hall with a sideways gait not unlike Dog Maddox's with her hips rotated to about two o'clock. Near the end of the hall she took a hard right into an office and I could hear her talking, in a lowered tone of voice, with a man I assumed was Dr. Wiley.

Back in the office a minute later, she said, "Dr. Wiley will see you now."

Jujubee tipped his head toward her. "Thank you, Sister Brender."

She pursed her lips and nodded. "Dr. Wiley's office is at the end of the hall. Just head straight on back."

There was no way we were going to make the narrow pass two abreast, so, after giving Sister Brenda a wink and a nod, I followed Jujubee down the hall. Sister Brenda, for reasons known only perhaps to God, had pulled the door closed before coming back down the hall, so Jujubee knuckled the door lightly.

"'m' on in," Dr. Wiley said in a yawning southern accent.

We entered and beheld the man, who was about my gray age with a head too big for his size 34 body and a good bit more square than round. He stood up behind his desk, laid both palms flat on his desktop, looked us over with those faraway eyes that put me in mind of Dr. euGene Scott and said: "Well, glory."

"Praise the Lord," Jujubee said. He was standing a foot in front of Dr. Wiley's desk. He smoothed his slacks with his right hand. The big black family Bible was still clutched over his heart in his left hand.

"Praise his name," Dr. Wiley said, squinting at Jujubee.

I nodded my head, I think, and kept quiet, I'm sure. I had no earthly idea what to say.

Jujubee said, "Hallelujah."
"Blessed be the name of the Lord," Dr. Wiley responded.
Jujubee said, "Glory be."
The man said, "Hosanna."
Jujubee said, "Thank you Jesus."
The man said, "I'm Dr. J.C.Wiley. You can call me Reverend, Doctor, Professor, President—any of those that suit you."

"Amen, Reverend," Jujubee said. He ran his hand through his thick black hair. "Whew, I'm glad that's over. There for a minute I thought you was going to bust out with another of them holy sayings, and to tell you the truth, I was just about holy-sayinged out."

Dr. Wiley said, "I see," though he didn't seem at all amused, and one look at Jujubee convinced me that he was merely stating a fact, not trying to be clever. They just looked at each other for a long moment. Then Dr. Wiley shook Jujubee's hand and Jujubee said, "Good morning, sir. I am James Jackson Baldwin Forthright—with no double-you—of Medlyn, Georgia, if you will. Many folk calls me Jujubee, and you can too if you'd like. Lord Jesus has called me to the Gospel ministry Friday past—*re-called* me really. *Right?* And so I've come to get my path prepared, or what have you here."

It was a signature, I thought, word-for-word what he had told Sister Brenda Cheeley a few minutes before and Martha Kitchens yesterday outside President Knox's office at Wentworth.

Dr. Wiley shook Jujubee's hand, then he turned to me and took my hand, said. "And you would be—?"

"I am—" I cleared my throat, thinking of who I would be, come to think of it. "I'm David Hazelriggs. I am a friend of Mr. Forthright." Not doctor, not professor, not Diogenes: I was, in Fanny's words, just David, plain and simple. How liberating that was.

"I see," he said. "James and David. They're two good names, they are, good Bible names."

Good thing I had gone with David, plain and simple, instead of Diogenes, which for all it might or might not have meant to Dr. Wiley, was decidedly *not* a Bible name, good or otherwise.

Jujubee said, "Mind if I set my big old business down?"

Dr. J.C. Wiley shrugged his shoulders. "By all means."

I took the smaller of the two chairs in the office, a hardwood affair like a porch rocker without the rockers, leaving the loveseat to Jujubee, who settled very carefully down onto it, though when anchor hit bottom we all heard the splintery cry of wood stress. I timed another throat clearing to cover as much of it as I could.

Then we sat in silence for a full minute, the most awkward silence I have ever sat. Jujubee spent the better part of it trying to get situated more or less comfortably without ending up on the floor with the loveseat in pieces around him. He had his prosthetic leg out straight in front of him and looked as big as I'd ever seen him—enormous even. For my part, I sat there stiff with my head back against the sill of the frosted glass window and peered through the swarm of dust in the golden shaft of morning at Dr. Wiley's "ego wall" strung with diplomas hanging askew and advertising unlikely degrees from unlikelier schools: a B.M. from Mount Carmel Theological Seminary; an M.E.S. from Holy Trinity Divinity; an S.T.D. from Fundamental Baptist; a B.S. from F.I.T.—Fundamental Institute of Theology.

*Feng shui* is one thing, and karma is another, I thought, but this office was, perhaps by design, the most uninviting, uncomfortable place on earth—had to be, or so I thought, and it was about to get even more so.

The saving grace in the room—if there was one—was the portrait of a cherub-faced boy with full flushed cheeks like moist dough and curly blond forelocks and eyes the sea blue-green of turquoise. He might have been five, might have been fifteen—I guess angels don't show their age. The longer I looked at that face, though, the more I saw the resemblance to Dr. J.C.Wiley before the earning of all those degrees had taken their toll.

Dr. Wiley broke the silence. "Let's bathe it in prayer, boys," he said, and I lowered my head and closed my eyes and waited for the prayer to begin. I heard some shifting around but didn't dare open my eyes; my father had taught me better when from his vantage point in the pulpit he had seen me looking around to see who was offering up the unspoken prayer requests in the sanctuary of the Providence Presbyterian Church. "David, what say you take us to the Lord in prayer and get the joy bells of heaven all a-ringing within the halls of our heart."

*For Pete's sake*, I thought. My breath caught in my throat. Now, I have no bitter memories of childhood; my parents were of Calvinist extraction and (some would say *but*) not punitive. But I do have a sour memory or two—and all involved being called upon, always by my father, to pray in a public assembly of one type or another. My dread was not that everyone was listening but that only *one*—my father—was. And now it was because Dr. Wiley was listening and because I had not prayed—aloud or alone or at the top of my lungs—in years and had no earthly idea what kind of prayer to pray in Fundamental First.

I cleared my throat and opened my mouth and what came out was about what you would expect from a lapsed Calvinist cum big-c Cynic: "'I believe in God the Father Almighty, maker of heaven and earth, and in Jesus Christ, his only Son, our Lord—'"

"Praise the Lord," Jujubee said. "Yes, Jesus."

"... who was ... uh, was born of the Holy Spirit, conceived of the Holy Mother ..."

"Bless him, Lord," Jujubee said.

"... and was crucified under Pontius Pilate." I knew at this point that things had gone badly awry. I said, "Or what have you here, and was there then and is here now, and by whose hand we all are fed, and we thank him for our food. Amen."

Jujubee said, "Bless your heart, Dewey. Amen, amen, and amen, if you will. That was a beautiful prayer."

Dr. Wiley said, "Part of that was the Apostolic Creed, I think." I felt his eyes boring through me and couldn't bring myself to look at him—not so much because I was ashamed as because I wanted to wrap the joybells of heaven around his neck. He said, "Well, now, we're not what you'd call a creedal people here at Fundamental First."

"The *Apostles'* Creed," I corrected. If a moment before I regretted not simply reciting the Lord's Prayer, I didn't regret it all just then, knowing that they, whoever they the flock of Fundamental First might be, were *not* a creedal people.

He said, "No sir, we're a people of the book. No creed but the Bible ... that's our creed."

Jujubee, God love him, said: "I don't know if we're a credible people or not at the A.M.E., but I'm gonna tell you this one time: I liked it, all right. We say it all in union every once and a while over't the Good Shepherd when Bishop remembers it and sometimes he gets tongue-tied on it, too."

Dr. Wiley said, "Speaking of tongue-tied, just so you know, we don't talk in tongues here. You don't talk in tongues, do you?" Before Jujubee could conjure up a response, Wiley said, "Hey now. Good Shepherd A.M.E.? Is that that colored church up in the hills where Pop Lester Watts preaches?"

Jujubee said, "Yessir, it is. We call him Bishop Lester."

Dr. Wiley nodded. "He was a good friend of my granddaddy's. He's a good man. Now, don't get me wrong. I can't cotton on to all of what he stands for. But he's a good man anyway, a hard preachin' man."

"He is that," Jujubee said, and to calm myself I conjured the image of Jujubee getting called out by old Bishop Lester and charged with a mission.

"Well, I'll need a testimony for starters," Dr. Wiley said. "That's the most important part of the admission process here at the Mount Sinai Fundamental Bible College and Institute of Theology. Who will get us started?"

Jujubee looked at me with those on-again-off-again eyes and his head was bobbing around like a buoy. Jujubee said, "Well, let me see if I can't testify, or what have you here," and Dr. Wiley got a funny look on his face as if he was trying to reconcile the voice of Satchmo with the powder white face of Jujubee Forthright with that stick-straight hair that shot up a good two inches from his head like blackbear fur. Then Jujubee continued, "I was called into the ministry the first time—"

Dr. Wiley said, "Who called you to preach the first time, son?"

Jujubee said, "The Lord Jesus of Nazareth, the risen Christ, if you will. *Right?* I wasn't but thirteen years old at the time."

Dr. Wiley: "All right. Yes. A boy on the threshold of manhood."

"Such as it is," Jujubee said.

"Like my own boy, Daniel," Dr. Wiley said. He craned his neck around at the portrait of that cherub-faced boy hung beside the window. "There he is: my dearly beloved son." And the sunrays of morning cast a heavenly halo glow over Daniel's soft blond head.

Jujubee said, "He's a angel."

Dr. Wiley said, "He's a fine young man with a call on his life. He's on the strait and narrow." He swept his hands, palm over palm, and came back into himself. He said, "So, go on then with your own story."

Jujubee said, "Anywho, after two years of conviction, right heavy-duty conviction if you will, conviction borne of the Holy Ghost I gave my heart to Jesus on the first Sunday in September of nineteen hundred and seventy-sits up in there at a tent meeting over't Clarkesville, Georgia. Or what have you here."

Dr. Wiley: "Now I like it when a man can cite the day and the hour of his salvation—makes me believe he's not making believe. Good book says watch ye therefore, you know not the day."

For some reason, I did not think that was the verse he wanted to summon forth at that moment, but Jujubee said, "Or what have you here. Anywho, I got baptized wearing a big old white Bible-type bathrobe that same day all up in there in the cold and chilly waters of the little creek out back of the tent."

Dr. Wiley: "Ooh yes. Amen."

Jujubee: "Hallelujuah, too, or what have you here. And I surrendered to the call about a year later. That was when I was fourteen year old."

Dr. Wiley: "Boy, that'll preach. You've got the voice for it, too. I can picture it now, thundering forth shouting glory down. But, do tell how come he had to 're-call' you, as you put it?"

"Oh, sir, I fell away." Jujubee shook his head. On a scale of one to ten for easy to talk to, with one being easy and ten being hard, Dr. J.C.Wiley was about an eight-and-a-half, but it still felt good, Jujubee told me later, to just say those words: *I fell away*. It was confession and it felt clean, clean down to the soul.

Dr. Wiley: "Having put your hand to the plough, you fell away, did you?"

Jujubee: "Yessir, I did. Big time, too. Boy, did I fall away, way away, such as it is, I fell away. Mmmmmm. Sinful times, if you will. I've got more degrees in backsliding than you got on your wall back there."

Dr. Wiley: "You sowed you some wild oats, did you?"

I noted the way Dr. Wiley was baiting the hook for Jujubee. He sat there with his elbows on the armrests of his chair, and the points of his fingertips pressed together made a little steeple under his chin and he synchronized the slow-motion nodding of his head more or less with Jujubee's head-bobbing. I just had the dreadful feeling, as I sat there listening to Jujubee recount his misspent youth after that day of glory when he had invited Jesus into his heart back in September of 1976, that things were apt as not to take a bad turn any minute. There was something about the momentum he was gaining—sin after sin and grace abounding more and more—something about the way Dr. J.C.Wiley's eyes were narrowing to slits by the confession.

I had heard it all during the Auction House confession, of course, Jujubee's catalog of sin and vice. But it all seemed different, as the giant gnome had seemed different, in the golden light of morning. The most sensational sin was that time during his employment as an over-the-road truck driver of moon pies when he was first hospitalized then incarcerated following an incident involving six cans of beer, an eighteen-wheel Kenworth hauling fifty tons of dry bulk with a jake brake that didn't work, five state troopers (two from Georgia, three from Tennessee), a man named Heyweird, and blonde-haired doll named Edna Mae Shilgroth, a doll with the face of Barbie and the body of Kewpie (though for all he knew it could have been vice-versa—"more vice than versa, if memory serves," he said) that went down outside Lenoir City, Tennessee. There was Dots and the whole sad relationship they had because, in Jujubee's words, it was hard not to mistake relations for love, such as it is, when you'd had things done to you like he had. There was the hate pent up inside him like molten magma that never—God be thanked, if need be—spewed forth in a fury of vengeance and saw through the plan he had hatched to kill Allis Blackwell and his son, Jujubee's stepbrother, Borger, after first torturing them a good long time. On this last he said, and I believed it and I'm sure Dr. J.C.Wiley did, too, that he hadn't a murderous bone in his body, much less a torturous one, though he did have a vengeful one and a murderous lust in his heart. And vengeance was his, saith the Lord, and a murderous thought was as bad for the one thinking it as the deed itself—though, of course, not for the one about whom it was thought.

*And who wouldn't have been vengeful—justifiably so?* was all I could think as I sat there listening to the balance of his confession for sins the most of which were hardly more heinous than the mess I had made of the Apostles' Creed when I was opening us in prayer.

Jujubee said, "That just about wraps up the sins of co-mission, for the most part, or what have you here, right? Now the sins of o-mission, that's where but for the grace of Lord Jesus I'd be slow-roasting on a spit over a bonfire that burneth with brimstone flames a hell fire and run through with a skewer with Eve's apple stuck in my mouth. The thing of it is I wasted more'n twenty years of my life, such as it is, in a backslidden state, not letting the Jesus who was in me from that day and hour I said, 'Come on in,' live through me. A double-you life, see. I just wonder if Jesus is grieved more by all the good things we don't do than by all the bad things we do."

That was a profound concept, and I was trying, as one of my students at the time would have put it, to get my mind around it—to really get it—when it became apparent that Dr. J.C. Wiley didn't. He said, "And Dots?"

I had a feeling I knew where this was going.

Jujubee said, "Well Dots she up and left me one Friday evening about ten-fifteen, in the spring of a year I don't know by number, or what have you here, and well now anywho I can't say as I blame her anymore than she would have blamed me for loading up the LTD and motoring out from here to yonder with a Mason jar of eighty-six-proof Kool-Aid in the glovebox and a tear in my eye."

All Dr. Wiley said, after all that, was: "But you're going to tell me that y'all were able to get it all patched up then?"

Jujubee said: "You ever seen you a heap of ashes in the fireplace the morning after the big blaze? Can you imagine trying to get all up in there and resemble those ashes back into a seasoned pine log, such as it is?"

"Ashes to ashes and dust to dust," Dr. Wiley said. "That's just about what the good Lord's fixing to do for all his true children when we get our new body, amen? The dead in

Christ shall rise first—and it won't be a freak show when all the dead who are in no better shape than that heap in your fireplace rise up to meet the Savior in the air."

"Amen," Jujubee said.

Dr. Wiley: "So where's Dots now, your wife Dots?"

Jujubee: "Last I heard she was living all up in a trailer house in the Tallulee Trailer Court, so to speak, over Blue Ridge way with a fellow name Bo Cecil Morton and a yellow dog name Big'n, or what have you here."

"Well now, see, boys, we got us a problem here, then, bigger than I thought." Dr. Wiley cleared his throat. "When a man desireth to preach the Gospel he's got to meet certain requirements. First Timothy three and one: 'This is a true saying, If a man desire the office of a bishop, he desireth a good work. A bishop then must be blameless—"

"'the husband of one wife,'" Jujubee said.

"First Timothy three two," Dr. Wiley said, and when he said it he laid his hands palm down on his desktop, and with a simple cock of his head and a simple tap of his fingertips he settled the whole matter with the subtle finality of a conductor bringing the concert to a close with a final sad stroke of his baton.

Jujubee said, "I could go on to verse three, or what have you here, about a bishop not being given to wine, no striker, not greedy of filthy lucre, and all such as that, but I think you're about to wrap it all up for me."

Dr. Wiley: "There's sins and mistakes, and we all make them, and then there's *sins* and *mistakes*."

"And that's one that's worse than all the others, if need be." Jujubee hugged that big black cracked leather Bible to his chest and doubled over—as certainly as ever a man of his size could be said to double over. He looked down at the gold buckles on his shoes. "If this is a checklist of the past, I'm done for with a capital F. I flunk. I fail. You see, I think I know where all this is going to. And, no offense," he said, looking down at his watch, "but I'm due at the courthouse in a half hour on a official matter, so I think I can save us all a couple minutes and a lot of breath, or what have you here. I'm hearing 'fatty fatty two by four' all over again. And believe me, I've heard it all before. Why I've stared the Grim Reefer gray in the face, and here it is: I know I'm not smart, such as it is. Nobody has to tell me that anymore."

Jujubee, eyes still trained, one after the other, on his shoes, big black Bible still close to his heart, paused. And neither I nor Dr. J.C. Wiley said a word or made a move, I because I was heartbroken, he because … well, God only knows why. Again, if I had been a father, or a friend, or a lover, if I had ever had a child or a close friend or a lover, if I had ever been anything, anything more substantial than a damned professor of, well, of anything or of nothing at all, I suppose I would have had the vocabulary for what was happening inside me as I listened to Jujubee after he said "And here it is." I understood for the first time the value of the tears I drew from my father's eyes one Easter Sunday when I told him, who had just finished delivering an eloquent sunrise sermon on the empty tomb, that I, his son, a lad of some sixteen years, was dismayed if not disgusted by the fact that a man of his intelligence could be so naïve as to believe that Jesus woke back up. It was one of the three times I saw him cry, and the memory was the more vivid for my having caused it.

I felt something like tears welling in my own eyes just then—for my father and for myself, my pitiful prideful puerile self, and for Jujubee Forthright, who said:

"I knew I wasn't 'Wentworth material,' or what have you here, when I let out down Main Street about this time yes'day morning and marched my big old behind, such as it is, right up to floor number six of that building where they told me I could find the man. I'm twice as old, three times as big, and not half as smart as them kids with their nice soft faces and their matching clothes and their polite manners and all like that. And come to find out I'm not Mount Sinai material either. I could've told you all that. I'm just saying is all. Ask me, I've broke every last one of them rules and regulations the Apostle Paul set out when he was holding forth to Timothy. I've been given to wine and had it given to me, and been filthy with lucre, too, whatever that is, and I've been married and divorced and dallied a time or two, for all I know. I'm guilty as sin. Plain and simple."

He said, "And all of that, all of that and a whole lot more, up in there in the pitch darkness of my prayer closet is just what I've been trying to tell Lord Jesus for lo these past couple of five years. I've been saying, 'But now, dear Jesus, I'm not worthy. True dat!' And he keeps on saying—not softly and tenderly now—'Who says it's about you, Jimmy Jack B. Forthright? What if it's about *me*? And here you've give me the slip for twenty-some-odd years.' He, Jesus, says: 'Okie-dokie, so you're a sinner.' I say, 'Who you tellin?' He says, 'Let's move on then. Can't we get past all this?' He lowers his voice, such as it is, and says, 'What if the whole problem, the real problem, maybe even at rockbottom the only real problem is that it's always been all about you? What if you're doing it all over again?' Jesus, he says: 'Am I, Lord Jesus, worthy? Tell me now, Jimmy Jack: Well, am I? Is it not my decision to call whoever I want to do whatever such work as I want him to do? Shall not the judge of all the earth do right, or what have you here? Shall not I, Jesus, do right?'"

If Jesus had been there in the flesh in Dr. Wiley's office at the back of the Mt. Sinai Fundamental Bible College to say in his very own voice what Jujubee said he had said in the pitch dark of his prayer closet I doubt if it would have rung any more true.

Jujbee said, "Ask me, all I am is a auctioneer and accordion player. That's all I can do, half-decent anywho, for all I know, but dear Lord Jesus he keeps saying: "Whom I call I equip." Go and do the work which I am trying to call you to do. Know'm sayin?"

"An auctioneer?" Dr. J.C.Wiley, who had all this time been leaning over his desk for all the world as if he might collapse into a coma on account of the frankness of Jujubee's confession, sat bolt upright and clapped his hands into a steeple again. "I'm sorry, you said your name was Jimmy Jack ... . "

"B. Forthright," I said. I was annoyed. Had the man not heard, really heard, anything that Jujubee had been saying? The honest confession that had broken my heart had apparently not done any such thing to Dr. Wiley.

"Of course," Dr. Wiley said. And for the second time in as many days I saw an otherwise disinterested man suddenly develop a very keen, if not patronizing, interest in Jujubee Forthright, though I suspected it was for all the wrong reasons. The day before Alisdair Knox asked if Jujubee were my collateral. Now, Dr. J.C.Wiley was perhaps wondering the same thing. He drummed his fingers on his desktop and squinted not just his eyes but his whole face as a weary man might do in a winter wood at nightfall the better to make his way out—though he wouldn't be able to find one, I thought. *What was it?* I recalled that mad scene during which I had sneaked back into President Knox's office and, under pain of facing campus security or even criminal prosecution for all I knew, riffled through the file for that leaf of stationery on which his eye had fixed on some line of text. *What had I missed?*

The only reference to Jujubee was his name, typed "James Jackson Baldwin Forthwright," and a handwritten notation, in cursive script that looked to be the work of Alisdair Knox: "expiry land-lease 9/30, W4200 thru W4400/Drice Weaver." Drice Weaver was a Wentworth alumnus—"a class behind me" I liked to say. He was a year behind me in school and half a lap ahead of me in the pool. He was the star on the Wentworth swim team; I was old *Also Swam*. More recently Drice was the Weaver in Blair Polson Weaver, the Atlanta law firm of record for Wentworth College. I assumed that the cipher meant that Wentworth College intended to purchase Jujubee Forthright's land just east of the campus. This theory would explain why Alisdair Knox had downshifted his tango to a waltz when he had learned who that big lad in bib overalls *what likes his meat* was. Perhaps he thought by feigning kindheartedness, or at least a wee bit of courtesy, he could drive down the asking price for the property; he was, after all, a man of economics.

*So what was the story with the preacher?* Dr. J.C.Wiley looked like a man suffering a terrible case of constipation. His face was crimson, his lips pursed. He said, "Brother Forthright, are you sure you was saved before all that with Dots happened? I mean, see here, we usually don't hold against a man things that's happened before the Lord saves his soul."

Jujubee said, "But you hold things that's happened since—even if he's confessed. I'm of a like mind with you, Dr. J.C.Wiley. I am a wretch, a vile wretch, but Jesus, well, he is not. I am most certainly not fit to speak out in the name of the Lord, but I don't think that means that, if he takes a notion, he can't speak through me. He spoke out of Balaam's ass. Well," he said, the color pouring into his cheeks like tomato soup in a white bowl, "not lit'rally, or what have you here. *Right?* So if he can do that, such as it is, I imagine he can speak through such an one as I."

*And the forgiveness of sins,* I thought, finding one of the lost articles of the Apostles' Creed that hadn't made it into my compulsory opening prayer.

Dr. Wiley said, "Well, I keep going back to there's sins and then there's sins."

"That's a good one," Jujubee said. "I don't know that I've heard of it before this morning."

Dr. J.C.Wiley winked. "Now, are you sure you weren't just caught up in the moment back when you was fourteen and just *thought* you was saved when in point of fact you wasn't? 'Many are called; few are chosen.'"

Jujubee said, "Is that what that passage means? That statement of beliefs I read out yonder hanging on the wall in Miss Brender Cheeley's room, it said y'all believed in 'once saved always saved,' if need be, and now sounds like I'm hearing that you're not sure my salvation took the first time."

Jujubee Forthright—it struck me again—for all the tics and tacks his face made, and he was a man of a thousand expressions, with those on-again-off-again eyes doing their lazy blink like a lighthouse beacon, and that big head bobbing like a buoy in the bay: That face never smiled. If he had intended his statement as a gotcha, as a "Well-isn't-that-ironic?" commentary on Dr. J.C.Wiley's questioning whether once saved he had always been saved—even during the Dots years—it couldn't be proved by his face. That face could do a lot of things, but it did not give Jujubee Forthright away.

"Oh brother now," Dr. J.C.Wiley said. "I'm a fundamental through and through. I was an alternate pall-bearer at the funeral of that great saint of God Oliver B. Greene. Bless God, I do believe with a whole heart in the perseverance of the saints. Lord said: 'No man will snatch ye out of my hands.' All that and more. But you've got to be saved–I mean *really* saved, not just baptized and confirmed, but washed in the wonderworking power of the blood of the lamb, as the old hymnist put it."

"Amen," Jujubee said, with a long A. "Ayman." He spoke a verse of the old hymn: "'Would you be free from the burden of sin? There's power in the blood, power in the blood.'"

Dr. Wiley sang the next line, in his raspy baritone: "'Would you o'er evil a victory win? There's wonderful power in the blood.'"

Then they were singing the chorus of spirited old camp-meeting hymn together, and I was tapping my foot:

"There is power, power,
wonder working power
In the blood of the Lamb;
There is power, power,
wonder working power
In the precious blood of the Lamb.'

When they finished the chorus, Jujubee said, "Praise be. You know what my favorite verse of that hymn is, the verse that drives me to my knees at the altar every time? It's that part goes:" (He was solo now.)

"Would you be whiter,
much whiter than snow?
There's power in the blood,
power in the blood;
Sin stains are lost in its life giving flow.
There's wonderful power in the blood."

Jujubee said, "Sin stains are lost in its life giving flow. Thank you, Lord Jesus."

Dr. J.C. Wiley seemed a little touched, too. He shifted in his seat. "Now look here, boys, if you was saved—once saved and always saved—and washed in the precious blood of the lamb, then we've got us another option." He leaned forward and swiped his tongue over his thin top lip, cleared his throat. "You can go lay ahold of your wife Dots. Bring back that sister that's gone awhorin' over't Blue Ridge with Bocephus Morton—"

"Bo Cecil," Jujubee said. "Bo. Cecil. Morton."

Dr. Wiley: "He could be Little Bo Peep for all I care. Whatever his name is is not the issue here. Preserving your marriage is."

"Thing of it is," Jujubee told him, setting the record straight in a voice that was a little bit Louis Armstrong, a little bit Al Jolson and my dear old mammy, a little bit of everything in between. He said, "Ask me, she's married to Bo Cecil—or was last I heard of her. So, now, that would be one weird situation if I was to take and go over to Blue Ridge and light into the Tallulee trailer park and all and get all up in there in folk business."

Dr. Wiley: "But then, boys," he said, lowering his head and voice in a casket-side manner, "see, why then it would be kosher—well, not kosher exactly, maybe Jesus kosher. There's a scarce man among us who hasn't from time to time hit a patch of marital turbulence but come out of it without going down in flames. You see where I'm coming from?"

I saw it clearly enough and, from any angle and in any lighting, it was the most ridiculous scene imaginable.

Jujubee said, "I'm not as sure where you're coming from, such as it is, as I am of where you're going to. You just hit it square in the head with that last thing you said, so to speak."

Dr. Wiley: "Good, good, then once you round up Dots and get it all put back together you come on back and let's sit down and talk about you coming to study here at Mount Sinai ... ."

Jujubee: "Well, that's not exactly what I was talking about. You said, 'You see where I'm coming from?' And that's the problem, Dr. J.C.Wiley. That's been my problem. It's not about where we're *coming from*; it's about where we're *going*. And anywho that's what Jesus has been telling me when he comes in of a night whenas I'm laid all up in there on my pallet in the pitch dark of the night. He says, 'I don't care where you been or what you done. Read what my friends want to tell you about me, my friends Matthew and Mark and Luke and John. And tell me what's important?' So I took Jesus up on his bet, or what have you here: It wasn't really a bet. Jesus doesn't gamble. I read it backwards and forwards. I hid that word in my heart that I might not sin against him. You know what I learned?"

He continued, "Here it is. Here's what's important: Jesus didn't never give one hoot about where anyone he ever met was coming from. If it was the rich young ruler—he didn't care about the *riches*, didn't care about the *young*, didn't care about the *ruling*. If it was Matthew the tax agent, ripping people off for all they was worth, such as it was, Jesus didn't care about that checkered past. If it was the Pharisees or if it was the Sad duckies that came to him for one reason or the other, well, he didn't care if they'd graduated at the top of their class at the Wentworth College or the Mount Sinai Fundamental Bible institution and could quote Scripture like the burning bush. If it was the Samaritan woman, he didn't bat one lash about whether she was colored or not. It didn't make one bit of difference to him. Look it up for yourself and you'll see. The blind and the crippled, the harlots of the night and the cheaters of the day in their birthday suit out in the graveyard. Where they'd come from and who they'd been and what they'd done didn't bother Jesus one teeny weeny little bit."

I was mesmerized again, though this time it had as much to do, or more, with the message he was delivering as with the way he was delivering it. I hadn't cracked open the Gospels in Lord knew how long—but that theme of Jesus that Jujubee was preaching as the BIG THEME was, I thought, the best kept secret of the Good News, the *euangelos*, the glad tidings of great joy of Jesus of Nazareth. It was the pearl of great price. The kingdom of God.

Dr. Wiley: "But the Apostle Paul said—"

Jujubee cut him off: "Oh, I know, but see, it wasn't the Apostle Paul that's been coming to me in the pitch dark of my room of a night and dealing with me. Not that I'm saying Jesus and Paul are at odds, right? I believe the Bible, every letter of it, to be the inherent word of God, but see Jesus put the comma, so to speak, in a different place for me. I got thinking about it. And the devil of the past is: You can't do anything about it. *Right?* Now, let's say I was to let out of here and go lay aholt to Dots and restore her to a sound mind, that wouldn't make one whit of difference about the past—about all the things I did and said back then when I was lapping up sin like it was mother's milk warm from the teat. I heard somebody say one time that you can never go back home again, if need be, and I got thinking about it and all like that and see that's the only place we got to go. Home's not your mama. Lord knows it wasn't mine. It's in the bosom of the Lord and we'll either go home—not *again*—or we'll never have a home. Home is all about the future, and nothing about the past, and when you feel homesick it's not for anyplace back there, it's for someplace you've never been before—because nobody who was back there is back there anymore, right? They're all in front of us now. And anywho even if you could go back, you wouldn't fit in because you're not who you was back then either anymore."

The sun went suddenly behind a cloud outside, I guess, because the room became a darker shade of gray. Jujubee's countenance, if anything, was brighter for it. He said:

"Ask me, if I was the devil here's what I'd take and do. I would call together my whole force of demons and present them each and every one with a electric screwdriver."

I broke in, "Why is that, Jujubee?" I was enjoying his oratory as much, or more, than any I had ever heard, and nonetheless, I assure you, precisely because Dr. Wiley seemed to be enjoying it so little—perhaps as little, or less, than any oratory he had ever heard. I still didn't know where he and Mount Sinai fit into my grand theory of the Town & Country Auction on the block for the highest bidder, be it Drice Weaver on behalf of Wentworth or Dr. J.C. Wiley on behalf of Fundamental First. The only thing I could think at that moment was that Wiley, too, had designs on the site of the Town & Country Auction, which was just west of Mount Sinai. But it was Jujubee I had on my mind and whatever he, as the devil, intended to do with all those electric screwdrivers.

Jujubee said, "Blessed art thou, Dewey Hazelriggs. Here's what I'd do: I'd charge them to work like the devil to screw people's heads on backwards. Remember that scene in *The Exorcist* where that poor little old girl's head started spinning around like a top? Truth to tell, now, I never seen of it myself, such as it was. But I heard about it. Anywho, see, if their head was screwed on backwards they'd have no choice but to keep looking back at where they'd been instead of ahead at where they're going, or could be going, or should be going. And speaking of Apostle Paul, I want to do what he did and press on, not push back. And if I really wanted to do it up, I'd get them to walk backward instead of forward. Ever stop and wonder why the good Lord put our eyes in the front of our head instead of in the back? Which way are we supposed to be looking? The devil wants to keep us from going home. He wants to keep me from going to court, such as it is."

With that, he looked down at his silver wristwatch, the stretch band of which was taut on his arm, and said, "Lord have mercy, I got to go."

## Fanny's Day in Court

WE TOOK THE SCENIC ROUTE BACK DOWN FROM MOUNT SINAI to the Town & Country Auction House. We walked north along the fenceline that separated Jujubee's property from (I assumed at the time) a plat owned by the Fundamental First Church of Medlyn, Georgia. We took the grassy strip past the rear parking lot of the church and a few whitewashed cinderblock outbuildings and, when we were alongside the graveyard, I said, "If I didn't know better, I'd say Mount Sinai is an apt name for Dr. Wiley's school. He seems to be a bit of a legalist."

"We all of us are," Jujubee said, "when it comes and gets right down to it. I know I am. Let's go over here right quick, Dewey, or what have you here. There's something I want you to see."

What a glorious late summer morning had broken. With the smell of fresh-cut grass, dark green and clumpy at the base of the headstones, and with the morning sun warm on my cheeks and the sweet chorus of birdsong and peckerwood in my ears, I followed Jujubee Forthright at just a little distance as we crossed the graveyard lined with dogwoods toward the larger of the outbuildings. The long shadows of morning invited me to lie down and find my peace in the cool of the grass, black as death in the shade of the headstones, and I wondered what was the something that Jujubee wanted me to see.

Jujubee said, "Look up in there," and raised his arm toward the window on the side of the building.

I had to cup my hands over my squinted eyes to see through the dirty windowpane into the dark building, a warehouse with fifteen-foot ceilings and only two four-foot windows across from us on the eastern side. There was a forklift in there, and the back half of the building, which must have measured a hundred feet long, was stacked floor-to-ceiling with boxes on skids and pallets and all shrink-wrapped.

Jujubee said, "Every last one of them cartons you see up in there is full as a tick with Bibles and partials—mainly the book of John and Romans, if they still do it like they did when I was a boy and used to come over to play with Lee Jay who was Reverend Graybill's son. Reverend Graybill was the old preacher at Fundamental First, long before Dr. J.C. Wiley showed up and got here."

Jujubee weaved his head right, toward one of the smaller outbuildings. "That building over yonder is where they print pamphlets on a ink press and salvation tracts and them flyers like was up in Miss Brender Cheeley's station up in there in Mount Sinai. From here they fork them all up in a eighteen-wheel Fruehauf transfer truck with a fifty-three-foot trailer on back, and carry them down to the airport in Atlanta, such as it is. From there they wing them over to Africa and France and such for missionaries to use in winning savage souls to Christ, or what have you here."

"That's quite an operation," I said, thinking—I think now to my shame—that like the Pharisees of old, whom my father had referenced in many a sermon, they were, in Jesus's own King James words, "'composting the sea and land to make one proselyte, and when he is made, ye make him twofold more the child of hell than yourselves." Jujubee, though, had another favorite episode of Jesus versus the Pharisees in mind.

He said, "Dewey, remember that story of the publican and the Pharisee? Luke chapter eighteen and verse nine and following. It says, 'And he spake this parable unto certain which trusted in themselves that they were righteous, and despised others: Two men went up into the temple to pray; the one a Pharisee, and the other a publican. The Pharisee stood and prayed thus with himself, God, I thank thee, that I am not as other men are, extortioners, unjust, adulterers, or even as this publican. I fast twice in the week, I give tithes of all that I possess. And the publican, standing afar off, would not lift up so much as his eyes unto heaven, but smote upon his breast, saying, God be merciful to me a sinner. I tell you, this man went down to his house justified rather than the other: for every one that exalteth himself shall be abased; and he that humbleth himself shall be exalted.'"

"I love that story," I said, speaking honestly. I had a hard time finding fault—even in my most prideful Cynical agnostic ravings—with a man who would frame the whole issue of morality in such a homely story.

"I do, too," he said. "But the thing of it is: The Pharisee looked down on the publican, and we, we look down on the Pharisee, or what have you. Thing of it is I knew I wasn't going to waltz up in there and be the belle of the ball at the Fundamental First. Knew they wasn't going to roll out a scarlet carpet, or what have you here, but even if he is a little hardshell for me, he has a soft core. He has a heart for Jesus, and like that Alisdair Knox he has his cross to bear. Believe me."

I shrugged. Just what manner of man was this Jujubee Forthright? And how had his miserable life taught him how to love so much more than I could? As Dr. J.C.Wiley was seeing us out, Jujubee had looked him straight in the eye and hugged him the way you might hug John Wayne if you really wanted to break him. He said, "I love you, Brother Wiley, and I thank you for meeting with me this day. I appreciate your ministry." When they shook hands, Jujubee slipped a bill into his hand and said, "Put it toward the Bibles for kids."

Jujubee said, "So even though I might not go in for all that the Dr. J.C.Wiley stands for—like King James as the only word of God—and I might go in for a few things he stands against—maybe a little dancing once't in a while—he's no devil. Don't get me wrong. I love the King James Bible of sixteen hundred and eleven. I believe it's the inherent word of God and all like that. It's the only Bible I ever have committed anything in to rememory. It's easier to remember than all the rest but harder to understand. King James, I reckon, was more than a whit smarter than me, which ain't saying much, since I'm sure he finished at least the tenth grade in high school. Which I didn't. And dancing? It's all I can do to walk much less cut the rug and dance a jig. But I like to see people cut it up a little when I'm hammering out something jamboree-peppy on the squeezebox, or what have you here. And, too, I think Jesus is every bit as ready and willing to forgive believers—his own sheep—that's fallen into sin as he is those who sin before they got saved. Psalm one o' three and verse twelve says, 'As far as the east is from the west, so far hath he removed our transgressions from us.' I claim that verse, which is why I'm going to pack up my sins and find me the nearest ocean I can find. I'm leaving out day after tomorrow and I'd like you to join me."

"You would?" I said.

Jujubee said, "I would. I have never once been to the sea. I've heard it's deep and blue and a man can get a sense of the majesty of the Lord God Almighty if he stands there and listens to its roar. Micah chapter seven and verse eighteen and nineteen: 'Who is a God like unto thee, that pardoneth iniquity, and passeth by the transgression of the remnant of his heritage? He retaineth not his anger forever, because he delighteth in mercy. He will turn again, he will have compassion upon us; he will subdue our iniquities; and thou wilt cast all their sins *into the depths of the sea.*'"

Jujubee turned to me with his face shining, "And now the time draweth nigh, or what have you. It is time to go there to the shallow of the sea, if not to the depths. Everything is pointing to the ocean. This little circular here," he said, pulling a yellow half-sheet of paper with black print on it from between the pages of his big black preaching Bible,

"I picked it up with the Statement of Fundamental Beliefs and the schedule of two-eety-on and fees from that card table up in there in Mount Sinai."

I read it aloud: "'A Bulwark Never Failing: A Century of Standing Firm. The Centennial Meeting of the Southeastern Conference of Fundamentals. Authorized 1611 KJV Only. Separated. Fundamental. Periwinkle-by-the-Sea Resort & Conference Center. Little Chancel Island, Altar Isles, Georgia.' It starts this Wednesday."

Jujubee said, "It does, on Wednesday. Anywho, and then there was that big old poster so slick I ran my finger over it to make sure it wasn't as wet as it looked hanging up in there on the bulletin board by the elevator at Wentworth College said they was having some sort of meeting down on the Altar Isles this very week, too."

"They are indeed," I said. I pictured the fundamentalists clad in 1920s one-piece (big piece: neck to ankles) bathing suits with sewn-in modesty shorts standing across the net from half a dozen Presbyterian church ladies with their blue-rinse hair tucked up under rubber-petal bath caps in a winner-take-all beach volleyball match. "I had forgotten all about that"—*that* being the annual convention by the sea at which representatives of our denomination's educational institutions came together with denominational authorities and delegates from the churches to share—to hear the conference brochure tell it—*a time of fellowship and community*. My father had moderated the meeting once, and I can tell you that it was in fact a time of accountability at which the lectern attempted to convince the pulpit and pew that their money was being well spent. It was the Pew-n-Pulp meetin' Alisdair Knox and his band of merry men were setting sail for, the meeting he trusted, he said, I would not be attending—the subtext being: The last thing we need, Hazelriggs, is for a heretic such as ye tae storm the stage and do a reading from your book *Honest to God*. He was, after all, a man of economics, and I stood to cost well endowed Wentworth a fortune in lost tuition and, worse, lowered alumni giving.

Jujubee said, "No sir, now Dewey, I've never once been to the sea. If you was to take and spin a globe of the world on its asses around to the United States of America and stop it cold, why you could cover the places I've been in all my life with the nail of your pinky finger. I have been as far west as Lexington, Kentucky; as far north as Winston Salem, North Carolina; as far east as Greenville, South Carolina; and as far south as Valdosta, Georgia. That was my route. That's the extent of it," he said, "such as it is. We'll have us a big time, a holyacious time, in the name of Jesus. Amen? Now won't you come go with us?"

Perhaps if I'd had anything to do—better or otherwise—I would have said *thank you all the same* and declined the offer as politely as I could. No, that's not the whole truth, so strike that. The truth is that if it had been anyone other than Jujubee Forthright asking, I would have declined. But, of course, it was Jujubee asking *and* I had nothing better to do, having been relieved of my teaching duties until September tenth, two weeks hence, so I said, "Of course." And I said it again, for roughly the same reasons, when a moment later he asked me if I "wouldn't come go with him" to the City Court of Medlyn, Georgia, where he was to testify at a hearing on the matter of rezoning Fanny Fuller's rental property in the Pine Bluff subdivision.

* * *

In the Introduction to Philosophy class I taught at Wentworth, the most oft-chosen theme for the first position paper was the part of the Allegory of the Cave in Book VII of Plato's *Republic* wherein Plato has Socrates set forth for his shill Glaucon:

"Whereas if they go to the administration of public affairs, poor and hungering after their own private advantage, thinking that hence they are to snatch the chief good, order there can never be; for they will be fighting about office, and the civil and domestic broils which thus arise will be the ruin of the rulers themselves and of the whole

State ... . And the only life which looks down upon the life of political ambition is that of true philosophy. Do you know of any other?"

The appeal of the passage promoting philosophy over politics (and by extension, authority) for those fresh young eighteen-year-olds is the most natural thing in the world—all the more so for Wentworth eighteen-year-olds cradled in the ever conservative bosom of money and privilege. Identifying with Socrates' radical approach to the civil and political authorities was, my fresh silk-faced Wentworth material thought, as disinhibited as a fortnight's binge at a stark raving orgy. It was nothing of the sort. The culture in which they were cradled was, by and by and alas, as strict a chaperone tending the keys to classtity (or class chastity) as any on earth. Their non-Wentworth agemates got tattoos of gremlins and mermaids drawn on their rumps with permanent dermagraphic ink, and gold and silver rings and ball-bearings pierced on every other body part. The tattoo of Socrates' nonconformist pie-in-the-sky blather about the civil authorities was about as permanent as a peel-and-stick tattoo from a box of Cracker Jacks. At any rate, it washed off by the end of the sophomore year.

The most radical Wentworth alumnus would turn out to be, in the end, only a type of watered-down philosopher-king in the grand republic of privilege—perhaps, heaven forbid, a Democrat. And maybe if he was not royal and had no thoughts original enough to qualify him as a real *philosopher*, he would become a mere teacher of philosophy—a professor of it even—and maybe in the warm bosom of the nourishing mother Wentworth College herself. And if that alumnus had brass hoodangs, big brass hoodangs, at that—this is dangerous—he might just trade his Christian name in for a Cynical name, say of a big *p* Philosopher.

The less radical alumnus would become a big city trial lawyer in the image and likeness of Drice Weaver and—both literally and symbolically—represent Wentworth and all she stands both for and against.

I was thinking all this as I waited on a deacon's bench in a little foyer off the rotunda in the Maxey County Courthouse, looking at a fresco of the muse Justice, blind as a bat—and supposedly that was a good thing, though injustice (with its triple disability of deaf, dumb, and blind) always seemed to get the best of Justice. A moment before, the judge's clerk had ushered Fanny Fuller and Jujubee Forthright into Judge Nunnelly Sparks's chamber, along with, of all people, Drice Weaver, Esquire, Dean Mobley, Chancellor Whitmore, and a few other high-hum-yonkas from Wentworth, every last one of whom could have passed for a brother of that most Presbyterian of American Presidents, Woodrow Wilson, with their pointy-nose high holy gentleman faces and mouths slightly puckered at the center, downturned at the corners like single quotes. They, like Wilson, looked scholarly in one light with their rimless *intellectacle* eyeglasses (that tentacle-like vision trying to get a wrap on everything) and, in another, like something out of a vintage comic book—a troubled mayor of Gotham here, a troublemaking evildoer there.

I wondered why on earth Wentworth College would be interested enough in Fanny Fuller's rezoning petition to bring along all those big men on campus and that weasely wizened barrister Drice Weaver who would not tip his hat for less than 300 dollars an hour. True, Fanny's property was directly behind the college, due north, but—even at that—it just didn't add up.

Mainly what I was trying to do as I sat there looking at Justice with the stale smell of bureaucracy in my nose whilst thinking about Socrates' disdain for politics-as-usual there in the bowels of the City Court of Medlyn—the neoclassical revival design of which would have been as familiar to Socrates as the ruinous "civil and domestic broils" settled therein—was this: I was trying to avoid looking at Fanny's brother Marion Waddell's ten-year-old son, Worthy, who in Jujubee's words was "afflicted something terrible."

I looked down at the polished wood floor beneath my new blue top-siders. How easy it was—I remember realizing with an ice-cold chill at that moment—to be compassionate from a distance, from the safe out-of-touch, out-of-reach distance of theory, philosophical musing, and emotional insulation which, let's face it, is the chief business of academe. It is another matter altogether to look into the eyes of one whose pain is beyond your healing and catch yourself looking away, knowing that if you let it touch you it will only make the moment when you realize that *you* cannot touch *it* all the more chilling.

Strange things were afoot. I was *acquainted* with suffering, of course, if not on a first-name basis with it. It was suffering more than anything else that had inspired me to write *Honest to God*. "Theodicy" is the technical name for what theologians do when they set out to defend God against the charge that if he is almighty he must somehow be less than all-loving. Children starve in Addis Ababa, Ethiopia, and in Atlanta, Georgia. Earthquakes rock San Francisco, California, and Tehran, Iran, and tornadoes wipe out little white church houses in Alabama pew-packed with sweet old ladies in their pretty white dresses taking communion on Easter Sunday.

We call these outrageous tragedies "Acts of God." My book was meant not so much as an apology for God as an indictment of him. Heresy, indeed, but—I reckoned at the time of writing—justifiable heresy. I have had a lifelong aversion to suffering—my own and others'—and truth to tell I have arranged my life around avoiding it; but insulation is a perilous refuge, for I find loneliness, with all its silence and separation, a type of hell. Even as a young boy I dared not look upon suffering not so much because I didn't have the heart as because I didn't have the guts. My father, God love him, took me to the V.A. hospital in Atlanta one Saturday—I'm almost certain it was the very Saturday after the Easter Sunday on which I had told him how disappointed

I was that he believed that Jesus woke back up. If he had hoped that forcing me to look upon those heroic men wasted to quadriplegia would endear me to the God of grace, he couldn't have been more mistaken. But if I, who had not the guts so much as to look upon their wounds, hoped that I could know anything about the God of grace without looking upon them, *I* couldn't have been more mistaken.

It took nearly fifty years for me to learn that.

There sat Worthy Waddell propped up in an old Everest & Jennings Starliner wheelchair that could easily have accommodated three of him. He was wedged into the seat with two bed pillows on either side and a corner of a blanket with various faded dinosaurs battened down under each. "So then, Mr. Dewey," he said, in a still small voice as smooth as a warm breeze, "are you a friend to Mr. Jujubee Fluoride?"

"Yes, yes I am," I said, turning my head toward him but doing my dead-level best to avoid his eyes, just as I had done that sunny Saturday at the V.A. Hospital when, marching me ten-hut into one shade-drawn room after another, my father would introduce me to one or another of his friends—a crippled sergeant here, a badly-burnt captain there—with the reek of urine and witch hazel making me dizzy, my eyes water.

Worthy Waddell said, "He's not so big and fat because he eats so much, is he? He's got him a gland problem, my daddy said, so even if he was only to eat the ration of a mouse with a nip a cheese he'd still stay just as big and all as the King Kong just like he is. He don't eat much. I like Mr. Jujubee all great big and fat just like he is. He says he was a bobble-head before bobble-heads was cool. He's funny, Mr. Jujubee is." He started cackling then. "Know what Jujubee said one time? He said 'Ter'ble.' Yeahd, one time back when Daddy was stinkin' drunk he told Mr. Jujubee that one time when he was in the service they put him in a clinic where they was made to pipe hot epsom water up into his you-know-what, and Jujubee Fluoride says, 'That's ter'ble, Mr. Marion. Ter'ble.' And his face went all red and funny and them eyes got goin' haywire like wheel cap spinners. I thought I was gone fall out and roll off yonder. Uncle Winker said well even if he was to go on the Weight Watchers and trim it off Jujubee would have a bolt of skin hanging down from him all over the place like the train of a well-to-do bride and you'd need a mule and a pull-cart to trolley it all around. He picks up and carries me to McDonald's in his big old white GMC truck on Thursdays usual. And he gets us two Happy Meals. The chicken nuggets is for me, and the hamburg plain is for him. He eats the bread off it and gives me the meat and the toy. He usually has the French fries and his drink. He don't eat much, Jujubee Fluoride."

"He certainly doesn't," I said, taking his word for it, because I had never seen him so much as pop a lifesaver into his mouth, and Worthy said, "No, he certainly doesn't."

He said, "So then, Mr. Dewey, are you Aunt Fanny's new boyfriend? Uncle Early wouldn't mind none; he's dead. He's with God now, in heaven, so he won't care if you and Aunt Fanny start going together. Daddy said Aunt Fanny's taken a shine to you. So then, you might be Uncle Dewey. I liked Uncle Early a lot. He'd take and carry me to the racetrack and let me watch him work on cars. One time I even got to work the jack with the pit crew changing tires, and Uncle Early said I was as good as Cooter Brown at it. Mr. Jujubee Fluoride, he's got me a brand spanking new motor chair ordered called a Pride Jazzy eleven oh three. He says it's loaded with a Holley four-barrel carburetor with glass packs in the exhaust will make it sound like one of Uncle Early's old hot rod cars and a three-speed transmission and electric windows and air, for the girls I might like to take on a spin."

He said, "I like your nice blue shoes, Mr. Dewey. Maybe some Thursday you could come to McDonald's with us and get a hamburg meal."

I said, "Thank you, Worthy, that would be very nice." Of all the things he had asked me in his innocent stream of consciousness, bless his little heart, he had ended with the easiest question of them all to answer: Would I go to McDonald's with him and Jujubee for lunch one Thursday? It was then I made the mistake of looking not above him and not beside him but directly at him and saw there the face of a cherub, with big blue eyes and curly blond hair.

The door to the Honorable Judge Nunnelly Sparks's chambers opened and out came the Wentworth contingent. Of them, only Drice Weaver seemed to recognize me, and he gave me a 300-dollar-an-hour tilt of the head and a starter's-guns-at-dawn-smirk that said he could still take me in the fifty-meter freestyle, any pool any day. No doubt he knew about *Honest to God*. I merely looked beyond him without giving away so much as a hint of recognition. They walked on by, those learned gentlemen, and then Jujubee Forthright emerged from the chambers with a hand on Fanny Fuller's elbow for all the world as if he were John the Beloved seeing Mary home from Golgotha.

Poor Fanny was taking whatever had passed in Judge Sparks's chambers to heart, and I had not seen her countenance so dark since that rainy spring day when Early was laid to rest at the Eternal Garden cemetery. She had that forlorn Gene Tierney look then, and now all she said when I moved in close and asked if she was all right was something mumbled, something to the sad effect that maybe there were, after all, two Medlyns. Then she patted Jujubee's arm and told him she would be fine, then she went on down the hall toward Courtroom B.

Jujubee looked after her. He leaned in close and, in a raspy Satchmo whisper, said, "Thing of it is Miss Franny's not fixing to settle nothing in that fashion. We're going into court session, or what have you here, and let her rip if need be."

Jujubee and Marion Waddell walked over and Jujubee mussed Worthy's hair, said: "You up for a Happy Meal for supper this afternoon, Mr. Worthy Waddell? I could eat me a good hamburg bun about now and a pack of french fried potatoes too. How bout it?" Then he put his big arm around Worthy's father and said, "Mr. Marion, you just get you some water and check your sugar and rest your laurel and hardies, such as they are, and we'll see you in the Courtroom B over yonder in about ten minutes."

Marion mumbled "that sunnybeach" with a nod in the direction of Drice Weaver, then scuffled off toward the men's room, and Jujubee got behind Worthy's Everest & Jennings' Starliner and said, "It's come in, or what have you here, Mr. Worthy. Burden Blue's bringing your new motor chair up 's afternoon so as we can get you suited up to tool around town in a souped-up ride, or what have you here. Right?"

"Jujubee Fluoride, there's no one like you," Worthy said. "Cool out."

Then we made our way down the hall to Courtroom B for the hearing.

*　*　*

The case might well have been called *Francine Mae Fuller v. the Two Medlyns*, I thought, as I sat there listening to Drice Weaver present the case of the Two Medlyns against her. I trust you'll thank me for making a long story short here. It was indeed like something out of the plodding start of *A Tale of Two Cities*. The facts of the case were that Fanny Fuller had petitioned the Medlyn Planning and Zoning Commission to rezone her property at 3712 Sugar Maple Lane for a residential group home for disabled individuals. The five-member commission granted her request and issued a special-use permit by unanimous consent pending public notice of a hearing. Not one homeowner in the Pine Bluff Subdivision, or anyplace else for that matter, opposed the rezoning. That left three interested parties, whose property was adjacent to 3712 Sugar Maple Lane: Wentworth

College on the southeast; Jujubee Forthright and the Town & Country Auction due south; and the Fundamental First Church of Medlyn, Georgia, on the southwest. The appeal was referred to the Superior Court of Maxey County, the Honorable Judge Nunnelly Sparks presiding.

Drice Weaver was representing both appellants—Wentworth College and Fundamental First Church—on, of course, the dime of the former. Drice Weaver argued that a group home in such proximity to the college and church would expose the students of the former and the parishioners of the latter to undue risk. When Nunnelly Sparks, that grizzled old jurist, yawned and asked him to name a few, Drice Weaver said, "Well, that's precisely the problem, your honor. We simply do not know. It is the unknown that troubles us so. Mrs. Fuller's refusal to specify the exact nature of the group home's residents is, in a word, unacceptable. The term 'disabled individuals' is subject to such broad construal as to be, well, overbroad."

All this, I thought, for 300 dollars an hour. My guess was that Drice Weaver practiced law best from behind a desk dictating briefs, that sort of thing. I wondered how long it had been since he himself had stood in open court and tried a case. He cut an impressive behold-the-man figure there against the drab backdrop of Courtroom B in his sand-and-sable summer suit of perfectly cut pure silk he might have worn to a *soiree en yacht* on the French Riviera.

"Overboard or overbroad?" Judge Sparks said, perhaps thinking the same thing.

"Overbroad," Drice Weaver told him. He stood there, with his arms crossed, bouncing up and down on the balls of his Italian-loafer-shod feet.

"Aye aye then." The judge gave a sleepy nod, as if he were either not much impressed by Drice Weaver's argument, or not much impressed at this point in his career by much of anything. He looked at Fanny, said, "Mrs. Fuller, what say you?"

Fanny stood up and removed her cateye glasses with the copper-colored browline and a little sprig of ivy etched in white on each temple. She said, "We needn't make this difficult, Judge Sparks."

Fanny Fuller had no attorney to present her case, and for a moment I considered that a liability—a retired first-grade schoolteacher squaring off against a seasoned trial lawyer—but only for a moment, for she hardly needed the added force of right to be the equal of Drice Weaver. "I am not, as a matter of principle," she said, "willing to forestall my options by limiting who the least of these my brethren might be who come knocking on the door at 3712 Sugar Maple Lane. I intend for the house to be a home, a place where everyone who needs it can come and find love and acceptance. And as I am no one to judge, please don't misunderstand me."

She looked across the aisle at Drice Weaver and the Big Men on Campus seated behind the Plaintiffs' table, said, "I am saddened if not surprised that a Christian college, on one hand, and a Christian church and Bible institute, on the other, are the only people in all of Medlyn, Georgia, who have come out against this."

"Your honor," Drice Weaver said, addressing Judge Sparks up high on the bench without so much as looking over at Fanny Fuller, the coward, "I am sure that Mrs. Fuller can appreciate the fiduciary interest which both Wentworth College and the Fundamental First Church have in safeguarding their people from the r-ri—"

"Riff-raff," Fanny Fuller said. "Speak your mind. Isn't that really the word you're looking for, Mr. Weaver?"

Drice Weaver said, "Risk." His brow buckled. "From the risk posed by, well, who knows whom. I'll thank you not to finish my sentences, madam."

Fanny said, "I will thank you for not presuming to know what I will and will not appreciate, sir."

She was in rare form, she was, and a smile broke like the first shocks of an earthquake across Judge Sparks's crusty face. "Touché." He looked over at Jujubee, said, "Mr. Forthright, are you of like mind with either party?"

Jujubee stood up from the defense table, if that's what it was in a hearing like this, and stood flat-foot. "Well, now I know my piece of Teensie property is the slimmest track of land of the whole lot on Main Street, so to speak, and all such as that, but anywho—"

There it was. A quick supercilious glance passed between Drice Weaver and Dean Mobley at the very moment when Jujubee said *slimmest track*. I leaned over and cupped my hand over Worthy's ear and whispered, "I will be back in a few minutes, Worthy," then made my way up out of my seat and around his chair, which was parked at the end of the second bench on the left side of the courtroom behind the defense table at which Fanny Fuller and Marion Waddell were sitting and Jujubee was standing and addressing the court. The last thing I heard as the door swung closed behind me was: "Anywho, I'm all for it, giving Jesus's down-and-out friends a helping hand … . "

Directly across the rotunda from Courtroom B in the Maxey County Courthouse was the county records office. I had been there only once before, when settling my mother's estate, but I felt compelled to go there this morning when the fate of 3712 Sugar Maple Lane was hanging in the balance and Jujubee's slim track of land was causing so many dignified men to make silly faces. Behind the counter sat an old woman with stringy red hair and a paisley stole draped over her shoulders who introduced herself as Wanda Lafferty and said she'd be right pleased to assist me. I thought it was a come-on and I leaned in close with an elbow on the counter and said, "Young lady, just the very sight of you has assisted me some already."

She batted her lashes and I pulled the slip of paper on which I had scribbled the information from that fine leaf of stationery in Alisdair Knox's file folder out of my pocket and told Wanda Lafferty that I was looking for information on a plat of land: W4200 thru W4400.

"Plat Book six, page twenty-two" came a whistling voice from a little carrel in the corner of the office. A man emerged wearing an orange-and-green checked suit and a green felt porkpie hat with an orange feather protruding from under the orange hatband. "I do beg your pardon, my friend, but I could not help but overhear your query." He extended his hand, said, "Mitchell Bramlett's the name. I'm the village idiot."

"Nonsense," Wanda Lafferty told me with a wink as I shook Mitchell Bramlett's hand. "This here's the most celebrated real estate lawyer in the county—the state, for all I know. He's quite the town historian, too."

"I'm pleased," I said.

Mitchell Bramlett said, "Now, famous or not, I must level with my public. I wouldn't be able to cite just any old such plat number off the top of this once-gold head gone hoary, but W forty-two hundred through W forty-four hundred is not just any plat of property in Medlyn."

"It is," I said, "the site of the Town & Country Auction."

"There is that," he said. "That would be the W forty-three hundred. The forty-two and the forty-four are Wentworth College and the Fu-Fi church and graveyard, respectively."

Wanda laid the big plat book, number 6, on the counter and thumbed back to page 22. Then she spun the book around and said, "Here it is. He was right."

"Forth*wright*," he said, relishing the pun. "It is the old Isaiah Forthwright settlement."

I said, "So does it say here who owns the land?"

"Well, God does, of course," Mitchell Bramlett said. "To whom has he deeded it? That's your question, I think."

I said, "I think it is."

"Right here," he said, running the smooth fingers of his hand down o'er the legalese as he read: "'All that tract or parcel of land lying and being in Land Lot 268 of the 5th Land District of Maxey County, Georgia, and being more particularly described as follows: Beginning at an iron pin located at the intersection of the southerly right of way of Grim-Nibble Road (52 foot right of way) and the westerly right of U.S. Highway 76 (80 foot right of way); thence running along the said right of way of U.S. Highway 76,' and so on and so forth."

Bramlett turned to Wanda Lafferty and said, "Deed Book twenty-two, number 107987 dash 3."

A moment later Wanda Lafferty had Deed Book 22 from a shelf and open to the page with the numbered property. "At your service, gentlemen."

Mitchell Bramlett removed his porkpie hat and laid it on the counter, said, "By jove will you just look at this? That land—the whole of it—is owned, rather *deeded* by God to the rightful heir of Isaiah Longfellow Forthwright. Quite the town historian or not, I never knew that Wentworth College merely let the land in plat W forty-two hundred. Same with the Fu-Fi Fo Fum church."

I said, "So Jujubee Forthright owns that land from his father's line?"

"Only if he's the rightful heir. Isaiah Longfellow Forthwright died during the Hoover administration, I seem to recall, and he's the one whose name is listed in the book. Many generations have lived and died since, so who knows? What is certain are two things: One is that no part of that land is owned by Wentworth College nor by the Fundamental First Church. The other is that if Jujubee Forthright is the rightful owner it wouldn't be through his father's line. His mother, of the two, was the Forthwright."

I said, "I see. So just how would one go about finding out who the rightful owner is?"

Mitchell Bramlett said, "For starters, one would retain the services of a brilliant real estate barrister with a sharp dress and a sharper mind who would thoroughly research the matter or," he said, "one would simply leave one's number with 'quite the town historian' who, once he had satisfied his historical curiosity, would call and share the information out of the goodness of his warm, kind heart."

I left my numbers—home and office—with Mitchell Bramlett, who gave me his business card, and, after thanking him ever so kindly and kissing Wanda Lafferty's wrist, I went back across the rotunda to the hearing in Courtroom B, which by now was in recess for lunch. I caught up with Jujubee and Marion and Worthy Waddell in the big, sunny atrium on the south end of the courthouse.

Jujubee said, "Dewey Hazelriggs, I say unto you, I'm about to bust out with the fire of Jesus. Miss Franny's fit to be tied, or what have you here. I've seen her mad before, but never nothing like this."

"Where is she?" I said, letting my eyes pan across the atrium and back out over the rotunda.

Jujubee said, "In the judge's chambers, I expect, trying to get him to drop the contempt of court charge he hit her with."

I said, "*Contempt of court?* Last I saw him he was about to doze off."

"That's before the Fanny-spankin' went down, so to speak. Now I don't expect you know this, but let me tell you straight up, Dewey: It's hard to sleep through a Fanny-spankin'. Mr. Early used to say you could sooner sleep through *a pack of lips*. Whatever that means, it must be right bad."

"Apocalypse?" I said.

Jujubee said, "Don't ask me; that's just what Mr. Early called it."

I said, "What in the world happened—this contempt of court debacle?" I eased down onto a stubby bench and massaged my temples.

Jujubee said, "That lawyer annoyed her, mainly."

I said, "He's good at that."

Jujubee said, "Now I'm not even sure exactly what it was he said, or even if Fanny heard it clear with her own two ears but Worthy heard it. He got right up next to Fanny."

I said, "What did he say?"

"I tried my best not to hear it," Jujubee said. "The Lord was speaking to me at that moment, and I tuned my ear to him and what he was saying about the trip down to the Altar Isles, or what have you here. I was trying to stay all up in there in the Spirit, and whatever it was he said would only have got me down in the flesh something terrible and I'd of probably ended up in the lockup and Worthy wouldn't get his chair today and we wouldn't be able to roll out on the trip to the ocean like the Salvation Navy. And this is the week we're called to go."

He said, "Anywho, Judge Sparks said, 'That'll be enough, Miz Fuller,' and she said, 'I'm just getting started, or what have you here,' and anywho he said, 'Bring it to a quick close then,' and then she said, 'You're not going to ask him what he said, are you?' and he said, 'Don't distaste the dignity of my court,' or something or other and all like that ... ."

"I heard what he said, Mr. Dewey," came Worthy's little voice, surprisingly clear for all the tangled mess he was in his chair, with all his tics and tremors. Jujubee hadn't heard him roll up, and I hadn't seen him roll up behind Jujubee's great mass doubled over before me on the bench.

Jujubee didn't so much spin around as pivot. He said, "Worthy Waddell, you can't very well get your new motor chair if you go and give me a heart attack."

I stood up. "What did Drice Weaver say to you, Worthy?"

He said, "He didn't say it to my face, Mr. Dewey."

I said, "Of course he didn't."

Worthy Waddell said, "He just looked down at me and then turned to that other man that was sitting there in the sweater. Daddy says if a man in a sweater offers you sweets you better roll on off away from him as fast as you can. Anyway, that man in the sweater whispered it to that other man, but everything happened to get real quiet right when he was saying it. And Aunt Fanny turned to me and put her hands on her sides and she goes, 'Worthy Waddell, *what* did he say to you? It had better not be what I thought it was.' I didn't want to tell her, but she said if I didn't it'd be worse for everybody, so finally I did, and she blew it out then."

Worthy Waddell said, "What he said is, 'All we need is a bunch of retards muleing around campus.'"

If I hadn't cared for Drice Weaver before, I positively hated the man just then (and it had nothing to do with the fact that he had outswum me in every meet we ever attended nor that by the time the report of the starter's gun had fallen silent he had me by a length and a half ... and looked as though he still could). I really did not want to believe he would say such a thing. He was a Delt fraternity brother, for one thing, and thus presumed to be of superior character and to "possess those gentlemanly qualities that promote the highest type of associational brotherhood." And then we were, after all, both of us Wentworth men, gentleman in public if nowhere else. I didn't want to, but I *could* believe it—especially on the word of Worthy Waddell who had struck me as one who told everything and nothing less. And I had once seen Drice Weaver derive sadistic pleasure in a fraternity initiation—hazing ritual gone terribly wrong. What was hardest to believe was that Dean Mobley—whom I knew to be a Southern gentleman in the truest sense of the word—would stand for it.

Jujubee said, "Now I hadn't heard that part of it." He stood there in his chalk stripe suit without a half inch of slack anywhere to be found and ground his big hands together for all the world as if to hold back some great dark force that would kill us all if he didn't. "I guess we best get you on out to the car, Mr. Worthy, and wait for Miss Franny to finish her business. Dewey, if you'd stay here and look after Miss Franny."

# March to the Sea

WHEN THE PHONE RANG AT A FEW MINUTES PAST FOUR THAT AFTERNOON I was at home, sprawled out on a lounge chair on the back deck looking at that giant lawn gnome I had stationed in the corner as if he might at any moment, as Fanny's lawn boy Jorge Ruiz testified, open his mouth and start speaking with tongues of angels. Meantime, I thought about Worthy Waddell, wondered if he was putting his new Pride Jazzy 1103 motorized wheelchair through its paces, maybe doing wheelies and spitting gravel out in the parking lot in front of the Town & Country Auction House. By the time I fetched my lemonade glass and waited for Dog Maddox to stretch and yawn and sneeze before finally making it into the house, the phone had, of course, stopped ringing.

I mashed the play button and refilled my lemonade while listening to the animated message Mitchell Bramlett had left only moments before. I knew he was something of a character, the self-proclaimed village idiot, who thought nothing—or quite a bit—of wearing an orange-and-green checked cutaway suit with orange suspenders and that kelly green porkpie hat with an orange feather in the band to the Maxey County Courthouse. When I first saw him, I couldn't help but think of Marryin' Sam, the preacher in *Li'l Abner* who married all and sundry for two dollars. Now I remember him as the Keebler elf, in all that orange and green and with that shock of gray-white hair.

He said, "Mitchell Bramlett here, calling on Diogenes Hazelriggs, whose acquaintance I had the good fortune to make this afternoon, Tuesday, at the county records office. I have some very interesting news to share about the W four thousand block of Medlyn, on U.S. Highway seventy-six. I will try calling you at the office number you left with me, the four-two-seven exchange .... "

His voice trailed off—no, it was more abrupt than that, really. The wind-up toy quality that had called up funny page characters went out not so much as a dying battery as a pulled plug, yanked even. And in the time it took me to hear him say, "My wife's granddaughter is being married up in Raleigh and we're taking our leave in just a little bit," and close with the awkward, "so I will be out of the office for a while, so then, goodbye," I thought I knew why.

Wentworth College is no trifling affair in Maxey County. In fact it has its very own telephone exchange—427. I could picture Mitchell Bramlett sitting at his desk in a sepia-tone office—gray as an old-time movie, but for his pumpkin-pie-orange and shamrock-green clothing—running a hand through his hair and wondering if maybe he wasn't, after all, more the village idiot than the most celebrated real estate lawyer in the county and quite the town historian, as that exchange tolled 4-2-7 like a death knell and he realized that I was not some disinterested town history buff but a Wentworth College official—for all he knew a lawyer representing Wentworth College sent there to the county records office to extract information from some bumbling idiot.

I tried calling him back at his office, but his secretary told me that he had left the office for the balance of the week. I told her that he had called me not ten minutes ago; she said he had left the office not five minutes ago. It was urgent, she said. I said, the wedding? She said, yes, the wedding, that *urgent* step-granddaughter's wedding. I said, I see, uh ... .

Thinking quick is not something we philosophy professors are either good at or fond of. Remember, it took hundreds of years of accumulating thought for us to come up with the concept of questioning as a means of getting at the truth.

Thinking *deep* is the goal. But I did the best I could under the circumstances to come up with and deliver a message that would neutralize the effect that seeing that 427 exchange had on Mitchell Bramlett. I said, "My dear lady, please tell Mr. Bramlett that discretion is of the utmost importance in this matter. Therefore, I would ask that he contact me only—*only*—at the home number I left with him or the cell phone number I am about to give you. Avoid the number with the four-two-seven exchange. And tell him that I am acting on behalf of Mr. Jujubee Forthright, who might need a real estate attorney to represent him."

If it wasn't the whole truth, I thought, it wasn't exactly a lie either. I gave my cell phone number to the secretary and asked her to have him call me as soon as he could, then I pulled the cell phone out of the kitchen drawer in which I had put it after mother's death, plugged it into the charger, and made a mental note to take it with me when the Salvation Navy set sail.

Back out on the deck a few moments later, having drained a second tall glass of lemonade, I stood there in my shorts, shirtsleeves, and thong sandals looking out over the tiptops of the pine trees, sweetgums, and hardwoods in the sanctuary that was my backyard.

If it sounds as though, in the span of a week, my whole life had changed … well, it had. Not that there weren't forces at work, looking back in hindsight (which, the old saying be damned, is in my case every bit as forty/forty as my foresight), forces moving.

It was the loss of everything that I had never, in any real sense, had. It was the understanding that, in the gospel according to Mitchell Bramlett, everything in this life is but a little piece of land that we squat on only in the end to find that our tears, if nothing else, were our rent and the title belongs to God. For some—for those who believe in God— that is comforting. "It's all in God's hands," they say. And never make the mistake of thinking this is a simple-minded profession of faith. It is as profound a statement as ever you'll hear, or make—if you make it and mean it. For those who don't have God and are too proud to realize that God has them, such as I was then, it is the last mile on the road to Despair and already there is a crack in the road.

That plate had been shifting for some time. When my father died, it lurched one way; when my mother died it lurched another; when one gray Wednesday morning I woke up late and could not, for all my effort, manage to get myself out of bed and drag a comb through my hair, the very ground of my world rumbled. On the advice of a colleague in the psychology department, I drove to Atlanta for sessions with a psychiatrist; tried antidepressants; tried talking it out; spent a small fortune (because I paid for the whole of it, in cash, out of my own pocket so that the journey into my madness would leave no paper trail).

And in the end, the psychiatrist, a kind man named Rubin who didn't believe in God and for whom a cigar was never *just a cigar*, suggested that I consider consulting a spiritual director (I half think he meant not a cleric but a psychic) because he said there didn't seem to be any obvious medical or psychological basis for my depression. He thought there was some anger there down deep though he didn't seem, he admitted, to be able to plumb it.

Instead, I took a semester sabbatical from teaching, flushed the Prozac, and started journaling in earnest, continuing the "therapeutic journaling" Dr. Rubin had me doing between sessions. The result was my book *Honest to God*.

All this is to say that I was questioning my sanity as I stood out on the back deck that Tuesday afternoon late in August on the day before we, Jujubee Forthright and I, were going to push off to the Altar Isles—he as if to find a new life, I as if to leave my old one behind, in the deeps of the wide blue sea. If I was crazy just then, or maybe even a little hopped up on the sugar from my lemonade, I was not depressed.

*  *  *

The next morning, at 7:30 on the head, I tossed my brown leather Pullman and matching traveler tote into the Big Healy and took off down the mountain with the top off and the breeze warm on my cheeks. I dropped Dog Maddox off at the Indian Trail Veterinary Clinic & Boarding House and bade him farewell with a kiss. He gave me that look of his that I associate more with cats—that look that said he couldn't have cared less, come what may. He was a proud dog.

I was giddy with excitement and drunk on nostalgia. Now of all the words I associated with "childhood," "mother," and "father" (when Dr. Rubin would have me recline on the fainting couch in the corner of his dusky office and free-associate) "happy" and "fun" and all their synonyms were not in the bunch.

"Serious," "proper," "stilted," "lonesome" best captured the tone, if not the volume, of my formative years. The exceptions that proved the rule were the sixteen weeks in August out of the sixteen years from the time I was two till I turned eighteen that I spent with mother and father on Jekyll Island on the Georgia coast. Those weeks we were not the Hazelriggses of Medlyn; father was not the Reverend Hazelriggs, Pastor of the First Presbyterian Church; mother was not busy keeping the *form* in Reformed as mother superior of the town church ladies, spearheading some campaign on behalf of the other Medlyn; and if I was expected to be "on my best behavior" I was allowed, more or less, to "act my age"—which for a child with Hazelriggs blood in his veins was about two years older than my actual age. We were not, for all practical purposes, Presbyterians on Jekyll Island.

For fifty-one weeks of every year I looked forward to that one week when we were not the Hazelriggs family. So maybe as much as anything I was giddy this Wednesday morning because, for however long we spent there on the Altar Isles, Jujubee Forthright and I, I would not be a Hazelriggs, or a Diogenes, or a doctor of philosophy, or a professor at Wentworth. I would be Dewey.

Well, when I, as Dewey, pulled the Big Healey into the parking lot of the Town & Country Auction House, I knew right off that something big was in the works. It looked like the set of a Cecil B. DeMille epic. People were milling around all over the lot, and a specially commissioned crew was unloading hardshell musical instrument cases and boxes of various shapes and sizes and relaying them to people standing in the back of the box truck. Larger parcels were sent down on the liftgate. On the side of the truck there had appeared overnight a dayglo-colored mural and a message lettered in red ink:

Come One, Come All
The SonRise Auction / The Alter (Isles) Call
J.J.B. Forth right, Dealer
Going once ... going twice ... going 70 times 7
No sin too big, no life too wore, tore,
rusted or busted
Salvation to the lowest bidder

The mural itself was a sight to behold. It was an airbrushed beach scene replete with all the clichés: sea oats sticking out like whiskers from the muzzles of sand dunes, logs of driftwood, the sand dollar here by the horseshoe crab, the starfish there beside the pink conch, the whitecaps and sea foam, a checkmark seagull soaring in the cotton ball clouds, and, of course, the sun, always the sun, a floating fireball impossibly orange, bisected by the perfect line of the horizon. All that was cliché. The giant Jesus high and lifted up and looming above it all was not. A cross between Cary Grant and Mama Cass was my original impression, and it hasn't changed. The body was all Mama Cass in a big lacy blue pleated go-go dress. I had to look away.

Others were skittering around peeling tape off the side of the Ford Club Wagon van with similar lettering on the sides of it. Worthy Waddell was, as I had imagined him the previous afternoon, cruising around in his new Pride Jazzy 1103 motorized wheelchair for all the world as though he were having the time of his life. And, to top it off, there was Jujubee Forthright in his red-and-yellow checked shortsleeve shirt and blue bib overalls, the pant legs of which ended at mid-calf, and shod in a pair of black high-top Converse All Stars. He was standing on the top step of the auction house porch directing the whole business through a red-and-black Georgia Bulldogs megaphone, his head listing to and fro like the ball of a great pendulum, turning his eyes, one after the other, on and then off, on and then off.

Jujubee held the megaphone to his face with his right hand and motioned toward a parking slot with his left. He said, "Dewey, pull that Austin-Harley open-face roadster right back in there alongside of Miss Franny's nice navy blue Mercury Grand Mar-keys right off yonder, or what have you here."

I waved at him and did as I was told, thinking that, with a bullhorn voice like his, a megaphone was not much help—though it did tend to equalize the singsong baritone-to-bass just a little. He was in auction form for the extreme unction auction traveling show and I wondered who on *earth* came up with that.

He said, "Listen up everybody, word to tell. We're at T minus ten minutes and counting down till we get this rolling auction show on the road, such as it is. If you ain't got you a ham biscuit and grits yet, you've missed a blessing, so to speak. They're in the house on the table—Miss Franny's laid out quite a spread, God love her, now that she's busted out of the county lockup."

My eye lighted for the first time that morning on Fanny, who was handing a large party platter covered with cellophane wrap to someone standing in the box of the truck whose face I couldn't see. She put her hand on her hip and wagged her finger at Jujubee. She had not, of course, been forced to do time for her contempt charge. In fact, Judge Nunnelly Sparks told her as soon as they were alone in his chambers that he had nodded to the stenographer—nodded, that is, his stern chastisement of her in open court right off the record. According to Fanny, the judge had a laugh at Drice Weaver's expense—got a charge out of some hardy-har wisecrack about Wentworth to the effect that one needn't wonder where the worth *went* when you had to suffer fools the likes of those three boobs. Fanny told me straight up that she was too angry to find the humor in it. Bristling was the word she used, and rankled, for Worthy deserved better than that, she said, even if it was the way they really felt.

Jujubee addressed me through the megaphone: "Dewey Hazelriggs, don't be shy, I promise I won't call on you out of the wide blue yonder, or what have you here, to bathe this thing in prayer and set the joy bells of heaven to ringing in the halls of our heart." He was in a wisecracking good mood himself that morning, I thought, though there was still no trace of a smile on his face. He said, "Good morning and put your bags in the van and let's go in and get us a biscuit and talk things out, if need be. There's some big things fixin' to go down here and we got an evangelistic team put together all roarin' to go."

I was still standing there in suspended animation by the Big Healy with my Pullman in one hand and the little grip in the other, trying to take in the scene, make some sense of it. I nodded toward Jujubee and then headed up onto the porch.

Jujubee showed me in to a picnic table set off to the side of the auction house vestibule and fixed me a plate. Over a salted ham biscuit as big around as a fist, Jujubee laid it all out, made some sense of it all for me. "Dewey Hazelriggs," he said, "blessed art thou. Why, what you did in helping me out first at the Wentworth College and then over to the Mt. Sinai institution was real kind. It was, as I've heard it put, above and beyond the call a duty. You're a kind man, a real gentleman, and all like that. Now I prayed last night a long time about a great big lot of things, but one of them was on account of the good Lord bringing us two together through Miss Franny. There's work to do before my time draweth any nigher than it already has."

"What do you mean?" I asked, but he nodded it off, his head still bobbing like a buoy in a choppy sea.

He said, "Dewey Hazelriggs, all I know is that I can't do it alone, such as it is. This work the good Lord has called me to do and this time won't take no for an answer is beyond me doing it all alone. I may be the heart of this ministry; you're the brains. I got thinking last night, laying all up in there on my pallet, and took to praying right earnest. And then I shut up and listened, and the Lord starting laying it all out. I woke up at midnight—rose up in the bed like as if there was a winch was doing it. I rang up Burden Blue and said get down here with your airbrush; the Lord has need of it. Bring your dulcimer, too, in case he needs that. If you're not good to drive, I'll come over and tote you up. You can't never tell at that hour any day of the week what condition you'll find old Burden Blue in. But, behold, Dewey Hazelriggs he said, 'I'm good,' and didn't say another word till after he'd applied the first coat of whitewash to the truck."

Jujubee drew breath and kept right on going. "Let's face it. I've got no more business in Wentworth College than I do on Mt. Sinai and no more there than I do in a tutu and ballet slippers trying to dance a jig with the Nutcrackers and the Sugar Plum's Fairy with my bum leg, flat feet, and built like a refridgiator box. I had a dream, see, and Dr. J.C. Wiley was in it plain as day—only he was wearing a Nero jacket over a Hawaiian shirt with pineapples and coconuts on it and gray chesthairs like sea oats was sticking out the top of it and in one scene he had on a pair of patent leather earth shoes with big sand-dune-like rubber souls maybe three-inch thick … and in the next he came bounding in on some black high-top granny boots like the old woman who lived in the shoe and had a kinky red afro a foot long that looked like a carrot-color palm tree waving around in a mighty wind. But it was him all right. No doubt about it."

He paused for a moment, as if I might argue against the possibility. I said, "I see."

"Well picture this then," he said. "We was in somebody's backyard by a lean-to privy. And now I know full good and well they don't go in for any of what they call 'penny-coastal shenanigans' over 't the Fu-Fi church, but lo and behold, he was talking in tongues a mile a minute, and he hitched his arm around my shoulder and said, real country, 'Jim Jack, kemosabe-san-souci or what have you here, what you need do is take and start you a congregation of people's down on their luck and can come Sundays in cutoff Daisy Duke shorts up in their you-know-what and won't nobody blink twice.' Then he laughed like something from a fright night spooky movie, and I said, 'Thank you so very much, or what have you here.'"

Jujubee's eyes pierced through me as he continued, "See, that's just about exactly what I'm called to do. And here's the kicker: A few minutes later, Jesus showed up, only I don't think I was dreaming then. That ah-ah-ah spooky laugh of Dr. Wiley woke me up in a sweat. Anywho, Jesus said, 'You're a auctioneer and accordion player, Jimmy Jack B. Forthright, and you'll follow after me and be a fisher of men. Thy fishing rod is they auction-dealing, if you will, and your mother-of-pearl Hohner accordion with gold-gilded bellows is your staff, or what have you. And they shall comfort many. See, not all fisher of mens need use the same bait or hook. There's all kinds of men needs fishing out of the deep sea like a pot of ointment that foameth dark with sin.' Dewey, he said, 'Canst thou draw out leviathan with a hook? Or his tongue with accordion which thou lettest down?' Job forty-one and verse one."

I wiped a biscuit crumb from the corner of my mouth, took a sip of coffee. A horn honked outside in the day breaking cool blue and shimmering. Even if those weren't exactly Jesus's words, I thought—and it's not for me to say whether they were or not—the gist rang true. The only thing I could think to say was, "So what does all this mean?"

And Jujubee said, "What all this means is that we're going to auction off salvation to the lowest bidder."

I said, "Auction it off."

He said, "Is there any other way? Think about it a minute before you answer, if need be."

I took a sip of coffee, thought about it a minute. "I see what you mean."

Jujubee said, "A rolling evangelistic auction."

I said, "From here to the Altar Isles."

He said, "From here to China if the Lord leads."

He set it all out for me then—the vision, the dream, the plan. "You and I are going to get in that GMC model Forward box truck that Burden Blue painted so dayglo nice by the dawn's early light and the utility lamp I ran out into the lot for him. Burden Blue and Dough-tree and Merlin Monroe and Wylynda's going to pilot that big old Ford Club Wagon van. There's nothing brings in the people like good music—and if Burden and Dough-tree's the heart of the Teensie Weensie band, then Merlin and Wylynda Monroe's the soul of it. We're going to stop off up in Lapsley Heights and see if we can't round up Banana Fosters. He'll be able to help out a good bit with the services and needs to get his mind clear of things back here in Medlyn. I called Bishop Lester Watts at the Good Shepherd A.M.E. church parsonage as soon as Jesus had finished saying his piece about fishing bait and the deep and all like that last night. Woke him up. He said, 'Boy, what kind devil's got in you to call some Negro man as old as Methuselah about some other old Negro man gone to Gadara in the second watch of the night? Why I'm of a mind to get me out of this dressing gown, come down there and administer some discipline to your big old hindparts.'"

Jujubee chortled, "When the Bishop finally got himself calmed down, he said, 'Now how'm I s'posed know where in God's creation is Barney Fosters? Am I my Barney Fosters' keeper? At that point I pretty much just said I was sorry, and he said, 'Boy, what good is it if you can't call on a man of God anytime of the day or in the pitch dark of the night? Acting like you bothered me. Boy, *STOP* !' It was then I thought I heard Mother Watts holler out to shush him up. Then Bishop Lester toned it down, he says, 'Lord's got his hands on you, boy. Now git 'bout his business, hear?' Now I say unto you, Dewey Hazelriggs, that right there brought the house down on me."

Of all the things I could have said after all that, or asked about, I said, "Who's Barney Fosters?"

Jujubee said, "He's some old colored man we all call Banana Fosters—all of us but Bishop Lester Watts anywho—on account of that he was a preacher of the word way back in the day before his wife got killed and he went through a hard time, went bananas in fact and lost everything, not least of which was his faith, so to speak, and he's been in and out of the 'sylum a time or two and has been known to hit the bottle."

I said, "Oh my," and Jujubee said, "There's more than *oh my* does justice, but I'll leave off there. He's come back around, thanks be to Jesus and the grace of God almighty, here lately, and anywho, the Lord laid him on my heart real heavy like the burden if you'd lay down a fifty-pound bag of Redi-mix concrete and then started pouring water in it. In my dream Jesus said, 'Was never a banana split I couldn't make it whole.' And I got the picture of a banana split so clear in my mind right then, saw it with whip cream and sauce and on top of it all the hot fudge, dark brown and shiny the color of Banana Fosters' skin, and there was a cherry on top, but no nuts. 'Hold the nuts,' I heard Lord Jesus saying."

He said, "Anywho, Banana Fosters needs Jesus put him to work just like we do. He's got a calling, and this time, this time, I say unto you, Dewey Hazelriggs, well dear Lord Jesus is not fixing to take no for an answer. Besides, Banana Fosters once had his own church before one of the elders that smoked like a chimney threw out a butt and set it ablaze and it burnt to the ground that sad season after his sweet wife Miss Gracie Mae got bad killed and his nerves broke down—whose wouldn't?—and he tried hanging himself from the rafters of his living room but the roof gave way and came down on him. Dewey, you'll see for your very own self that he weighs no more than ninety pounds now, and what with all the weight he lost after Miss Gracie Mae got bad killed, he was a string of yarn. Anywho, the roof didn't hold him, knocked him out cold. It was a miracle."

I opened my mouth to say something, thought better of it, and let Jujubee go right on, "Termites. Tell me that wasn't a divine innovation. They found him laying all up in there, down on the floor flat of his face with the pink bed sheet still hitched around his neck tied off in a slip-knot noose so there was no doubt what he'd been up to."

Jujubee lowered his voice, said, "Sewer-side. Anywho, they carried him off to the 'sylum down in Atlanta—locked *him* up—and didn't let him out for a good long time. It *was* terrible, though, Dewey Hazelriggs, the whole sad thing was. Everybody loves Banana Fosters, and we all loved poor old Miss Gracie Mae, too."

I wanted to know what killed poor old Miss Gracie Mae, bad killed her, but by then Fanny was helping Worthy Waddell get his new Pride Jazzy chair through the door. He was still trying to get the hang of steering the vehicle, she explained, with the little control that looked like a video game joystick that he worked with his one good hand—his left hand. Jujubee stood up from his side of the picnic table and I braced myself against having the table tip over on me.

Jujubee saw me grip the bench, said, "It's balanced pretty well, such as it is."

Worthy Waddell said, "I thought it was gonna roll you over, too, Mr. Dewey, when Mr. Jujubee Fluoride got up off that thing like a teeter-totter seesaw. And if he was to set back down hard on his you-know-what—his big old booty—I bet it would shoot you up through the roof like a rocket ship."

Jujubee said, "Why now I'm fixin' to set *you* down there in place of Dewey Hazelriggs and roar up off my business and shoot you up through the roof like a rocket ship, Worthy Waddell."

I stood up and swung my leg over the bench of the picnic table and shook Worthy's hand, kissed Fanny's cheek.

Jujubee had my empty paper plate in one hand and my Styrofoam coffee cup in the other. He rocked over to one side, said, "Poke fun all you want, Mr. Worthy Waddell, but if you was forced to live as big as all get out like this all these years you'd learn how not to kill people just going about your daily business, so to speak."

Worthy's face contorted into a smile. He said, "I'm just funning with you, Mr. Jujubee Flouride."

Jujubee said, "Shining me on, are you. Lord help me. Just because you got that jazzy new hot rod I guess you're too good for us now, or what have you here. Let's be frank: How's that thing running?"

Worthy said, "It's like the Everest and Jennings on steroids. It's like somebody gone and pimped my ride."

Fanny said, "Worthy Ray Waddell, I'm about to go in and fetch a bar of soap and whip up a nice bubbly lather and wash that nasty talk out of your mouth."

Jujubee said, "It's just a way of saying, Miss Franny. It's not near as bad as it sounds."

Fanny said, "Well, I should hope not."

Jujubee said, "Can you pop us a wheelie in that hog, Worthy?"

Fanny's face softened then, she said, "I can tell you this. He's given that chair a pretty thorough test drive. He was trying to roll it down the back deck to the patio at midnight last night."

Worthy said, "Daddy said he might have to get old Virgil Gower out there with his two-ton as—"

He paused for Fanny's benefit, then, just long enough for her to get her hand to hip-level, then he said:

"—phalt rolling machine and blacktop Fanny's front lawn so I can turn laps like as if I was Uncle Early Fuller."

Fanny said, "Well, we'll have to see about that."

Worthy said, "Looky here. Bert'n Ernie Blue painted our number on it."

The number 3:16—the very number Early Fuller had driven into victory lane more than 100 times at the Medlyn Dirt Track—was airbrushed on the side panel of Worthy's Pride Jazzy chair in red, white, and blue, with two white stars, one on top of the other, forming the colon.

Jujubee didn't smile then, but he nodded his head and there was a dreamy look in his onyx black eyes. He said, "Thanks be to Jesus."

Worthy said, "Thanks be to Mr. Jujubee Fluoride, too."

Jujubee said, "Now don't forget what else that three-sixteen stands for, now Worthy, hear?"

Worthy said, "My Aunt Fanny's birthday?"

Jujubee said, "Of course, that, such as it is, and what else?"

Worthy said, "Round about what you weigh in at when your under drawers ain't on."

"I remember back when," Jujubee said. He stood there wistful, trussed up in his bib overalls, suspender straps taut as butcher's twine on a rump roast, and a big thumb curled through the hammer loop.

Then Worthy started laughing—guffawing and snorting, foaming at the mouth laughing, the works—and, Lord help me, I did, too.

Fanny said, "I don't know who's more childish. David, I've never seen you carry on so."

When we finally quit laughing, Jujubee said, "Now let's try this again, one time. What else does that three-sixteen stand for?"

Worthy said, "Something about God so loving the world?"

Fanny said, "Let's give thanks and credit where they're due, too. Jesus was never one to mind sharing the limelight, Jujubee."

Jujubee said, "Anywho, let's just thank Lord Jesus and leave it go there." Then he turned to me, said, "This is the official Jujubee Fluoride fan club. All two members."

I said, "Count me in and make it three. I'll pay my dues."

Jujubee said, "Oh brother. You have no idea how you will."

Then he said, "Miss Franny and Marion's gonna stay back here on the western front, bring up the rear and take their galloping orders, or what have you here, from General Worthy Waddell of the Georgia Mountain Calvary saddled up on his jazzy new mount."

Worthy Waddell made a clapping motion with his hands, maybe as if pulling on some invisible reins, and Jujubee said, "Virgil Gower and his crew's going to help transform this old auction house into something new. You can't hold a new auction in a old auction house, so to speak."

I looked around to take it all in, said, "You're going to have the place renovated?"

"Reckon it's high time," he said. "Fumigated, too, most likely."

Fanny said, "Jujubee here's on a mission. He's going to turn his place into a *multi-use facility* pending the zoning commission's issue of a new permit."

I said, "Multi-use? Auction slash—"

"Slash shelter," Fanny said, "slash—"

"Group home," Jujubee said.

"Slash warm family en'firement," Worthy Waddell added, as the final word on the matter. He rolled his head around to the right and sought Fanny's eyes. "That's what Aunt Fanny calls it."

She patted him on the shoulder and when I said, "I see," Fanny said, "Let not your heart be troubled; neither let it be afraid. Judge Sparks said Jujubee won't face the same sort of opposition I faced from Wentworth and that nasty little Drice Weaver and Fundamental First Church because his property is already zoned commercial and is in a commercial district. Jujubee has had this project on his heart for a long time. He's scraped and saved every dime he's got to make it happen."

Jujubee was combing Worthy's hair with a little black barber's comb, getting the part straight. He said, "We were hoping to get Fanny's place rezoned so as we could have a good-size grounds, you know, combine the two properties so that we might could raise some more money and add another dormertory, for modesty or what have you here. My plot's only a hundred and twenty foot wide and not all that deep either, truth to tell. Why, I can spit off the back porch of my house which, as you seen for your own self, is directly back of this auction house, and with a little nod I can hit the trunk of a certain dogwood tree in the backyard of Miss Franny's rent property at 3712 Sugar Maple Lane."

Fanny put her hand on her hip, said, "Just don't let me catch you at it or Dark Vader, either; he's the one chews that nasty stuff."

Jujubee said, "I'm just saying is all, Miss Franny. Anywho, we got a notion to take and combine our plots being that they stand back-to-back and do something nice and Jesus-like with it, but now we'll have to just wait and see how Judge Nunnelly Sparks rules on the matter."

Worthy said, "Specially now Aunt Fanny's got prostituted for contempting the court."

Fanny slapped the air. "Oh, go on, Worthy Ray Waddell." She shook her head. "Sometimes I know he does that on purpose. His daddy Marion's a bad one for teasing like that. Our daddy was, too."

Something clicked in me just then. I walked over to where Jujubee was standing behind the counter where they sold auction tickets and fountain drinks. I lowered my voice and started speaking ... .

Now I have never, in all my life, been able so much as to use a hanger to open a locked car door or tongs to fish a cherry tomato out of a salad bowl, but for some reason I have always been fascinated with the dark science of lock-picking and safe-cracking. Dr. Rubin, my erstwhile psychiatrist, concluded after several months of analysis that it was because my heart was a lockbox of sorts with a key lock I could not pick, a fire-safe full of buried treasure secured by a combination lock I could not crack.

All that for five bucks a minute. If nothing else, it was charming, in a way not unlike the way of a cracker with a safe. Turning the dial now a half turn right, now a quarter turn left, then ... ever so slowly around till there's that faint little telltale click of the tumblers. At that very moment—as I stood there in the vestibule of the Town & Country Auction House with Jujubee Forthright behind the counter not only sounding but looking more like Satchmo than ever before with that head doing its sweet papa dip and cheeks b-flat full and Fanny O Fanny, with those arresting brown Gene Tierney eyes so lithe in her sleeveless summer sundress with swaths of Hawaiian tapa and petroglyph ukuleles, turtles, and palm trees splashed in earth tones all over it, standing there so right with a purple Tommy Tippee tumbler of soda pop raised just so the straw met Worthy Waddell's smiling mouth—at that very moment, I felt a faint little telltale click inside me, inside the lockbox safe that was my heart.

Jujubee was humming when he said, "What's up, Dewey Hazelriggs?"

And I said, "What say Worthy Waddell and Fanny Fuller go with us to the beach?"

He said, "Blessed art thou, Dewey Hazelriggs: for flesh and blood hath not revealed it unto thee."

A moment later, Worthy Waddell clapped his hands and Fanny Fuller winked at me, a slow wink that was so much more than a wink that it very nearly slew me.

*  *  *

Jujubee left Peanut Butterbean, Dark Vader, and Marion Waddell (Fanny's brother and Worthy's father) in charge of the renovation effort, and thirty minutes later, the Son-Rise Auction / The Alter (Isles) Call caravan rolled out of Medlyn, Georgia, east on U.S. Highway 76. Jujubee and I were leading the way in the cab of the GMC box truck with the airbrush mural of Jesus the Son rising over the Altar Isles on the sides. Hitched to the back of it was a maroon Dodge 3500 15-passenger van, which, Jujubee told me, belonged to Merlin and Wylynda Monroe, who were bringing up the rear in the Ford Club Wagon, itself a 15-passenger van, along with Burden Blue, Charles C. Doherty (called Dough-tree), Fanny Fuller, and Worthy Waddell.

Another half turn, another tumbler in the combination lock on my vaulted heart shifted when we pulled up outside a little cedar shake-sided cottage not a half a mile from the Good Shepherd A.M.E. church in the northern—also known as the *colorful*—part of Medlyn. I wondered if the living room of that gray weathered shack was the very room in which Banana Fosters had tried to end it all at the working end of a tied-off pink cotton bed sheet, wondered if the termite damage had been repaired, wondered what it was had bad killed Gracie Mae.

Banana Fosters was standing, not sitting, out at the end of the red clay driveway when Jujubee rumbled us up the gravel road, stopped, and honked the horn once. Banana had in his hand an old U.S. Trunk Co. flat-top, ivory in color and trimmed in oxblood leather, with, I couldn't help but noticing, a Corbin Sesamee combination lock on it. He had on white sneakers, dark blue jeans, a black T-shirt with white raised lettering that read "Malcolm Y?," and a white felt tam on his head. With skin smooth as dark Swiss chocolate contrasted by the dazzling white of his eyes and teeth and the words "Malcolm Y?," he might have been the most profoundly black man I have ever seen. He nodded and, without a cue, I opened my door and stepped down from the truck.

"Barney Foster," he said, shaking my hand with both of his, in the pastorly manner. "They call me Bananas, Reverend Bananas, or Banana Fosters, most them do, and I'll leave it on you to decide if addressing a spindly little old color man like me "Barney" ... or "Bananas" ... is more to your liking. Call me whatever you like. My granddaughter Gracie Mae calls me 'nana, and I answer to her all the same."

"Dewey," I said. "Dewey Hazelriggs. Pleased to meet you, Bananas." If Jujubee hadn't referred to the man as Bananas, I wondered what I would have called him—Barney or Bananas?

Jujubee had climbed down from the truck and made his way around to us. He picked up the valise, said, "You're looking real good, Reverend Bananas."

Banana Fosters said, "Boy, don't lie."

We watched Jujubee walk back and load the suitcase into the back of the Club Wagon. Then we climbed up into the cab of the box truck. Bananas insisted on taking the middle, as he was the smallest of the three of us.

Banana Fosters slapped his chest, said, "Sorta figured it'd be you-all come down to get me. Knew it'd be somebody coming. Mm hmm, I did. Lord Jesus woke me up early this morning. Early this morning?" he asked himself. "Mm hmm, he did. Now, of itself that's not unusual. No, no really: it's not. See, Jeez', he look in on me of the night two, three times a week usually. Bad weeks it's more—might be fo'. I'll wake up and he'll be in there looking around, and I'll say, 'Word, Jesus,' and he say, 'Make sure and keep that sheet folded down now, hear. I don't want no more monkey business in here involving the bedsheets, you hear?' And I say, 'Let not your heart be troubled, Jesus. I'm not fixin' to fashion some old noose and lynch myself again.' And he say, 'No noose is good noose.' And we both crack up laughing at that, and he say, 'That more like it. Gracie Mae says tell you hey—she'll be seeing you 'round.'"

Jujubee said, "Does my heart good to hear of it." He shifted the truck into second gear and then crossed his hand over his heart. "You about scared all of us half to death."

Banana Fosters said, "Ooh, it scared me too when I come to and got thinking about it. But be that as it may: See, last night Jesus won't just making rounds to do a bedcheck and collect the sharps. No sir, last night he was coming to give out doctor's orders. He said, 'Go to the ant, thou sluggard; consider her ways, and be wise ... . How long, wilt thou sleep, O sluggard? When wilt thou arise out of thy sleep? Yet a little sleep, a little slumber, a little folding of the hands to sleep: So shall thy poverty come as one that traveleth, and thy want as an armed man. A naughty person, a wicked man, walketh with a froward mouth.'"

Jujubee said, "Proverbs chapter seven. That'll preach, Reverend Bananas. Amen."

I said, "You men know your Scriptures."

Banana Fosters said, "One of us do. That was Proverbs chapter *six*. Chapter seven goes off into something else altogether, Jujubee."

Jujubee nodded. He said, "We might as well gas up and get prayed up before we hit I-eight-five."

He slowed the truck down, signaled, and pulled into the Shop-N-Hop. No sooner had we pulled into the diesel pump bay than Jujubee said, "Hold on, boys, this here has *encounter* written all over it." His head was bobbing around in the way of that Bobo doll Dr. Rubin once pulled out for me to assault with batakas on the outside chance my depression was fermented anger that needed to be vented. (It wasn't, though somehow that doll ended up popped—I think it was my inkpen.) At any rate, Jujubee's head was bobbing and he was taking the measure of something in the rearview mirror.

Bananas said, "I'll pump gas den. You go on about the Lord's bidness. You fill up with the Holy Ghost, and I'll fill up this GMC truck with the diesel fuel."

I remember wondering if Margaret Mead had felt the same mix of wonder and puzzlement that I was feeling then when she first touched down in American Samoa or Papua New Guinea and *encountered* the culture of those noble and ignoble savages with their strange tongues and primitive customs. Compared to philosophy, anthropology was dirty work, and I rolled up my sleeves and immersed myself for the first time in the culture of (Fanny forgive me) the "other" Medlyn: *Coming of Age in Medlyn.* In the passenger sideview mirror all I could see was the light morning traffic rumbling by on U.S. Highway 76, so I craned my neck around to see who or what it was Jujubee was looking at that had *encounter* written all over it—whatever that meant.

Turns out Jujubee was eyeing a rather savage-looking man sitting behind the wheel of a beat-up old Isuzu PUP pickup truck with tread-bare tires and a blue finish sun-dulled to white in places and rusted out in others. Debris was strewn so high on the dashboard that I wondered how the poor man could see to drive. A magnetic sign on the tailgate said: *Caution: Paper Delivery This Vehicle Makes Frequent Stops.*

The man stepped out of the truck and—oh my, I thought—he was indeed a savage. He had thick brown hair, fixed (if that's the word) in a mullet, and a three-day beard thin and red on his goitrous neck and puffy face that made all his features look mashed in. His blue jeans were soiled and way too tight and his tank top had come untucked in back, which, any way you looked at it, had *bad news* written all over it.

Jujubee opened his door and said, as he climbed down, "Dewey, I'm going to need some assistance."

I didn't say a word. I opened my door and eased down onto the pavement and followed Jujubee at a little distance across the parking lot and into the Shop-N-Hop. Merlin was fueling the van, and Fanny had preceded us into the store, no doubt, I thought, to get Worthy some sort of refreshment. By the time I made it into the store the man from the blue Isuzu pickup had found what he was looking for—the pornographic magazine section, which was set in the left corner of the store in a little alcove formed by three five-foot-high racks of shrink-wrapped slicks against the front and left wall of the store, opposite the checkout counter. The man was bending down and, not to put too graphic a point on it, the cleavage of his bottom was visible even to me, halfway across the store.

It was a dreadful sight, really. I looked around and was happy to find that Fanny, who was in the snack aisle on the right side of the store, was for the moment anyway spared the obscenity of it.

Not so the children. A little tow-head boy and his red-haired sister caught sight—if not wind—of it as they were milling around looking for sweets. The boy giggled, the little girl grimaced, said, "Ooh gross," and it was then I did what I felt "called" at the moment to do: I stepped over and stood a few feet behind the man in front of the mouth of the alcove, so to speak, to shield innocent eyes from the rude spectacle. Jujubee had taken up his position on the aspirin side of the rack the man was browsing.

I was close enough then to hear him, saying in that fine sandpaper Satchmo rasp barely louder than a whisper, "You look mighty tired today, or what have you here. Ask me, you look plum wore out. Getting them papers out to people before they get up to take their coffee of a morning will get a man weary way deep down in his bones. It's the Lord's work. Fact is, I have a friend was in that line of work, friend name Lord Jesus who was a Newsboy delivering up Good News."

I was facing the front counter, having seen enough, but I turned my head to see how the man would respond to Jujubee's homily, if he responded to it at all. The man seemed to heave a sigh and sink just a little, less as if from a weight bearing down on him as from a weight being lifted off of him. He didn't say anything, but he did grunt a little.

Jujubee said, "And that's not the answer—them books you're looking at. I've been down that road, my friend, and it's a No Outlet dead-end, and we both know it. That's five bucks and some change you don't have to spend, for one thing, and for another if it's just *that* you was looking for you'd save the money from your paper route and just go into your closet and pull out one of them other books you got stashed away in there but once you've looked at it one time it's wore off, as it were."

The man grunted again—or maybe this time, I thought, it was more a sigh of relief.

Jujubee said, "Anywho, that's not going to bring her back, friend, and it's sure not going to bring *you* back. You know?"

Perhaps Margaret Mead's greatest contribution to the field of anthropology, in particular, and to the history of ideas, in general, was that she demolished the myth that people from so-called primitive cultures were the children in the great family of humanity. Jujubee Forthright was doing the same thing to my myths that the "other Medlyn" was *unevolved,* in the parlance of Wentworth College, and that a

Sunday School quarterly in the hands of an evangelical was as deadly as a six-shooter in the mitt of a black hat outlaw. Jujubee was speaking to this man—maybe in his own voice, maybe in the Lord's—in a tongue the man could understand.

The man let go the magazine he had in his hands and looked up then for the first time and saw Jujubee. He said, "Who are you?"

"I am a friend," Jujubee said, "a friend, that's all. A friend that's been as wore out as you are, or what have you here, and met another friend who said, 'Come unto me, all ye that labor and are heavy laden, and I will give you rest. Take my yoke upon you, and learn of me; for I am meek and lowly in heart: and ye shall find rest unto your souls. And anywho, my yoke is easy, and my burden is light.' Matthew eleven and twenty-eight through thirty."

I turned my eyes upon Fanny who was standing at the checkout counter paying for a little bag of popcorn and a frozen Coke Icee. She snapped her change purse shut and paused for just a half-step and winked at me before she walked out the door.

The man said, "You a preacher man?"

Jujubee said, "No-sir, I'm not. Not one that's duly ordinated, such as it is, anywho. I'm a auctioneer by trade and see, I could use me a good man might like to take a trip with us for a few days down to the seashore in Altar Isles, Georgia, and earn a decent wage with a new job starting as soon as we get back to Medlyn."

The man's name was Otis Winters, and he didn't have a thing, he told me and Jujubee, as we waited in the checkout line with two bags of corn chips and fountains drinks in hand. There was no one he needed to tell he was going away—no wife or child, no mother or father, no employer. He had lost his paper route delivering the Rister (Georgia) *Weekly Standard* the week before for reasons, he said, he had rather not divulge.

Despite all our differences, Otis Winters and I had something in common: There hadn't been a soul I needed to tell that I was heading out to the Altar Isles with Jujubee Forthright, either.

Jujubee told Otis Winters to go out and fill up his blue Isuzu pickup with gas, water, and oil. He said, "I am drafting it into the Lord's own service. I think that by the time it's all said and done on our mission down to the Altar Isles we're going to need a good pickup truck, such as it is."

Jujubee took a fifty-dollar bill out of his wallet and slipped it into Otis Winters's hand. He said, "Let me know if this don't cover it. Keep the change, if need be. We'll use it for eats later or get you a bite now if you're hungry."

When Otis Winters was out of earshot, I pointed out that the tires on his Isuzu were showing signs of wear, and Jujubee said, "I reckon we all of us are."

I said, "But we don't seem as apt to have a blow out," and he patted me on the back, and said, "Speak for yourself."

Then Jujubee gathered us all together by the van, had us open all the doors and windows, and bade us all join hands around the vehicle—in which Worthy Waddell sat strapped into his car seat with a bag of popcorn on his lap and a frozen Coke Icee in his cupholder—bow our heads, and close our eyes.

He then broke hands and raised his big black preaching Bible into the air above us and commenced to pray, "Dearest Lord God Almighty, Lover of our Souls, in the precious sweet name of Jesus Christ your only begotten and beloved son, the Friend of Sinners, we come before you this day, such as it is, and beseech thee to pour out your blessings on us pilgrims and strangers, or what have you here, as we surrender to your call and fare forth to a promised land that floweth with milk and honey. We're all wrong, but you're all right! We are weak, but you are strong! Your power is made perfect in weakness. Give us the eyes of Lord Jesus to see them the world can't see, the heart of Lord Jesus to love them the world hateth, the ears of Lord Jesus to hear those who cry in the darkness of the night, the hands of Lord Jesus to touch the one don't nobody else care to touch … ."

The prayer went on for a full ten minutes, and for a full ten minutes Banana Fosters jogged in place, saying, "Yes, Lord Jesus, come on now and do it … bed sheets is not the answer, praise Gawd. Testify, testify, tell it out, Joo Joo Bee Forthright. Hallelujah, praise Gawd. No noose be good noose, Lawd Jes'."

I was startled when, at one point near the end of the prayer, I let my eyelids part just a little and saw through squinted eyes Jujubee lying on the ground flat on his back in his big blue overalls, and those black high-top 6E Chucks were waving around up in the air for all the world like a giant pair of Silent Mora's Chinese sticks. It was as though he were having an epileptic fit or some other manner of seizure—and even though I now take it as a moving of the Spirit in him, I still suspect that something of a medical nature, too, was going on. Out of the corner of my eye I caught Fanny looking down at the spectacle, too, with eyes wide open and a purl stitch in her brow.

Jujubee prayed, "Psalm twenty-two and verse twenty-four through twenty-six: 'For he hath not despised nor abhorred the affliction of the afflicted; neither hath he hid his face from him; but when he cried unto him, he heard. My praise shall be of thee in the great congregation: I will pay my vows before them that fear him.' And all God's people said, Amen."

We all said, "Amen."

Then Jujubee asked Merlin to fetch his fiddle out of the back of the box truck and bade Burden Blue and Doughtree to join him on a number. He said, "Dewey Hazelriggs here likes that song 'The Voice,' which y'all played for us so nice at the auction Friday night past. Dewey's been humming it like Moody Blues all morning, and now he's got it stuck in my big old head, such as it is, and I imagine it'll make as good a opening hymn as any to get us all going."

Then, on the four-count, they went to town, and the people of that town—whatever small backwater town we were in—came to them and huddled around the van to listen to their quick-step bluegrass version of "The Voice." They stomped their feet and clapped their hands in that joyful hand-over-hand manner, and for a moment we were all Jujubee Forthright with our heads listing to and fro and our eyes blinking on and off like the beacon of a lighthouse. A few of us sang along on the chorus, if we knew the words, and hummed along on the verses. A gray-haired couple did a spirited barn dance and everybody laughed.

It might have been 1958 there for a moment.

When the impromptu hoedown was over, Jujubee said, "Dewey Hazelriggs, for ten cent I'd get my Hohner keys out of the case and pitch the tent and have a SonRise auction right here in the parking lot of this Hop N Shop, or what have you here. I believe we could pack the place out."

But we didn't. He said the big Voice was calling us to get back on the road. So we all went back to our respective vehicles, and Jujubee dispatched Banana Fosters to ride in the truck with Otis Winters on Operation Isuzu PUP with the words of Scripture: "'For to him that is joined to all the living there is hope: for a living dog is better than a dead lion.' Ecclesiastes nine and verse four."

The day had broken perfect—as perfect as the day-glo day Burden Blue had airbrushed on the side of the truck in gradient splashes of lavender and pink—and we rolled down the windows and Jujubee shifted us into fourth gear and we were all diesel-gurgling glory as we rolled east on U.S. Highway 76 in search of redemption on the Golden Coast of Georgia.

* * *

An hour passed before either of us spoke a word, not so much, I think, because there was nothing to say as because there was so much to say that neither of us would have known where to begin or end. So instead of words, we took turns, more or less, humming a verse, the bridge, the chorus of "The Voice."

We might have ridden on another hundred miles content in our silence if it hadn't been for that wine-colored late-model Cadillac Seville with North Carolina plates pulled off on the shoulder of I-26 East with its hazard lights flashing. We were just east of a place called Irmo, just north of Columbia, South Carolina.

Jujubee let off the throttle as soon as the Cadillac came into view. And as we gradually slowed down, I could see his head bobbing, eyes cycling through several rotations—left on, right off, right on, left off—picking up what must have been a distress signal that only those with ears to hear could hear. Then he said, "Thank you, Jesus," and signaled our stop for the benefit of Merlin Monroe and Otis Winters behind us.

I said, "Another *encounter*?"

"Written all over it," he said. "All over it. Just think, Dewey Hazelriggs, how many people we rub elbows with every day that's just sitting around in the old john fish boat, or what have you here, just mending their nets, mending their nets and just waiting, waiting for somebody, anybody to come along and say, 'Come, follow me, and I'll make of you something, something different than what just sitting here stuck on your laurel and hardies mending nets in a pond that the fish are all dead in is going to make of you.'"

He engaged the emergency brake, and said, "So many folks, Dewey Hazelriggs, folks like me, for one, and old Otis Winters, for another, with nothing better to do on some nice day such as it is than lay around all up in there in his little old blue pickup truck looking at booty books wreathed in a cloud of ganja, or what have you, and his heart's so broke it'll take half of eternity for Jesus to take and get it all picked up and put back together again. There's folk smothercating with cares and can't make it through a week without pulling their Squeegie Board out of the closet and dimming the lights and laying on hands. There's folk sits around yakking on the horn with Dionne Warwicks two, three hours a night for a psychic consolation. I've been there. I know. I've been standing out on the ledge of life on a dark night and thinking about throwing down and getting shut of the pain. And, listen, Dewey ... ."

He lowered his voice—*sotto voce*—at this point, as if to assure me that what he was about to say was strictly *entre nous*, that I needn't worry one whit if the spirit should so move me to bare my soul. He said:

" ... if all you can do is to pick up the phone and get a psychic friend on the horn, I say: Make that call. Because, see, it can make you feel some better—depends on the type questions you're putting to her and whether your credit card checks out okay. But for the BIG questions it won't avail ye much. And that's where a lot of folks are—dropping a dime for an answer that can't be bought. Encounter, you say. That's when somebody comes roarin' up in the midst of a stir-fry life from out of the wide blue yonder and says, 'I myself ain't much, but I got a friend who's something else, come, go with us,' and he drops everything on a moment's notice and he's suddenly wondering why it took you so long to get there."

I thought about that, let the truth of it settle in, which was this: That's pretty much how it had happened with me. That was the only explanation for why I was sitting in that GMC box truck answering an Alter Call with Jujubee Forthright that Wednesday afternoon. The plain truth, when you got right down to it, is that I had nothing more constructive to do than Otis Winters. He had his girlie books; I had my heresy book; and honest to God, I had dropped everything on a moment's notice and here we all were.

I said, "I guess I'm a lot like Otis Winters myself."

And Jujubee said, "We all of us are."

Then he picked up his big black Bible and climbed down from the truck, and this time without waiting to be drafted into service, I, too, climbed down from the truck to assist Jujubee in the Lord's work. As we approached this particular thing that had encounter written all over it I couldn't help but think that a great many Samaritans passing by Irma, South Carolina, on that lonesome stretch of I-26 might, as well, have seen encounter (though of a very different kind than Jujubee Forthright saw) written all over the petite blonde-haired young woman.

She was alone there, leaning against the passenger-side door of the Seville with her chin in her hands and her heart on her sleeve. If she were poor in spirit, she seemed poor in no other way. She had on lots of jewelry, fine not tacky, tasteful not costume, set off to its best advantage on a simple white sheath of fine raw silk.

Jujubee said, "Sister, your spirit is low this day. It's not so much your car that's broke as your heart. Your heart's broke down; that's how come you're standing out here crying."

The scene would have made a fine addition to my shrink Dr. Rubin's collection of TAT picture cards, which he would sometimes resort to when there was an awkward silence in our sessions. He would select one of cards out from the deck (never at random), pull his knees in close together, and place the card facedown on his lap, saying: "Diogenes, please study the picture I am about to show you and tell me what you see going on there." Then, very slowly, to let the dramatic tension rise, he would roll the card over and I would try to come up with something thrilling enough to keep us both awake for the balance of the session.

What would I make of the picture of this poor woman, in her mid-forties, as far as I could tell, standing beside her purring Cadillac on a highway outside of Irma? Had she come to the very place on the highway where the love of her life had tragically lost his own one rain-slick night? Was this the anniversary of that awful day? Had she just found her husband in the arms of another woman? Was she on her way to or from a doctor on whose diagnosis her life turned? Was she merely carried away on the tender emotion of an old sweet song on her stereo as she made her way home to North Carolina from a long summer in Florida visiting her aging parents?

When you look at anybody, doing anything that we humans do, you can guess your head off and not really know what's going on, what's the story, the scoop, until you lay down the big TAT card and do what Jujubee Forthright was doing just then—enter that space and see with your own eyes, hear with your own ears, feel with your own heart.

If the sight of a five foot four inch tall 300-pound man in bib overalls and a gray-haired accomplice in belted blue jeans and canvas shoes happening upon her scared her at all, the pretty blonde gave no indication. She just gave us a little glance of her emerald green eyes as we approached and seemed as unfazed as though, well, as though she had been expecting us and was wondering not why we were there but why it had taken us so long to get there.

She said, "It was one year ago today."

Jujubee said, "And it's been a hard year, sister, I know it has."

She turned and looked at him then, standing there with that hair to end all hair—thick and black and defying gravity and every other law of physics, standing up literally on end—and all trussed up like Robert Earl Hughes's little brother in his denim overalls, his thumbs hitched under the taut elastic suspender straps.

She said, "How do you know?"

He said, "Sister, my name is Jujubee Forthright, and Lord Jesus told me to stop here this day, at this very hour, such as it is, and tell you something."

It was only then that I noticed the little memorial cross with faced silk flowers and the name RICKY on it set back from the shoulder about three feet, just at the edge of the woods. The dates below the name told the rest of the story:

Ricky had died there on August 28, one year prior to the day. He was 18 years and a few months young when he died.

The woman said, "Puh," and pulled her chin in and pursed her pretty red lips. It was not so much skeptical, that *Puh*, as it was angry, and maybe not so much just angry as anger fueled with sadness. It had a little of the *how dare he* edge to it. And standing downwind of her, I caught a whiff of liquored breath carried on the wind of a passing minivan. Her tears were ninety proof and the seal was broken.

Jujubee said, "I know, dear. I know. Sometimes a good old 'Puh' is all the Lord wants to hear from us. It's not all blue skies and sunshine and wish you was here's. Anywho, sometimes it's just '*Puh.*' And I think sometimes he has those days, too, when it's just 'Puh' and all like that."

She crossed her arms, said, "Well, what is it, then, that the Lord Jesus sent you to tell me?"

Jujubee said, "Couple things. First thing is, he wants me to tell you, Sister, that he's awful sorry about what happened to Ricky."

"*He* is sorry? That's a good one. He's sorry." She ran her hands through her hair and let go a big growling "Ahhhh." There was wrath in her eyes and venom on her lips.

Jujubee said, "Sometimes a big old 'Ah' is the most eloquious prayer we can offer. It's sincere, or what have you here."

She said, "Well tell him that I'm awful sorry that he's awful sorry. But if I could have spared him from feeling so awful, so awful sorry, believe me: I would have. He could have done me the same favor," she said, and the ninety-proof tear rolling down her cheek was proof positive that the liquor hadn't delivered on its namesake promise—Southern Comfort. Softer now: "But he didn't, now did he?"

Jujubee said, "No he didn't; see, he could but he couldn't really."

She said, "But he can do anything, right?"

"You have a lot of faith, sister," Jujubee said, "but it's like this: See, he could have kept Ricky from getting in that awful wreck, but then I reckon if he was going to take to stacking the deck like that, he would have had to keep his self from getting nailed up on that old rugged cross of cavalry. And that would be cheating, and the good Lord don't go for cutting corners and cheating. He's not big on gerry-riggin and jury-fixin'. Think of it like this: If he had jumped down off that cross or called a legion of angels to his rescue and they was to have reached up and pulled him down off the cross then see, ma'am, we'd all be in a bigger mess than we are now. Anywho, Jesus didn't make that man get stinkin' drunk and he didn't make him barrel out of control and cross the center median and hit Ricky head-on anymore than he made those Roman soldiers nail him to the cross. He's pretty much set his mind to let things happen as they're going to happen. Good book says he sparedeth not his own dear son. He spareth not your own dearly beloved son, Ricky, either, sister."

The woman lost it then, doubled right over and lost it, her grief coming out in great heaves and sobs. "My Ricky, my Ricky," she said, over and over and over again.

Jujubee said, "He knows, dear. He's a man of sorrows, acquainted with griefs, and when God the Father sat up there and watched them nail his little boy to that tree, he broke up and down about like you're doing here right now today. Good Book says at that hour the great veil of the temple was rent in twain; the sky was dark as pitch in the night."

My argument in *Honest to God*, which as I said before was largely my attempt to give the world my own two cents on why bad things happen to good people, was that one could not, given the fact of suffering in the world, logically maintain that there is a *loving* God if there be a God at all. That's the argument I made in 250 pages and which, if you can find one in a used book store, could be yours for the discounted price of about $3. A hamburger lunch plate would probably be a better use of money.

At any rate, here stood Jujubee Forthright presenting his own argument on the issue of God and suffering to some poor mother bereft of her son, and there was something elegant about it. His God was not embarrassed by tragedy; in fact, he took part in the tragedy of the world in order to do away with it once and for all. It was the big capital T tragedy that made sense of all the other tragedies of history; it was the cross of Calvary that made sense of the flower cross with Ricky's name on it there on a lonesome stretch of I-26 in Irma, South Carolina.

Jujubee knelt there on the gravelly soft shoulder and prayed with her, a prayer I couldn't hear for the traffic and didn't strain to hear. When they got up together, I did hear the woman say, "It might be the only hope I have of ever seeing Ricky again. Thank you for delivering His message to me."

Then I drove her Cadillac back to the hotel in Columbia where she was passing the sad anniversary week of Ricky's death because, as Jujubee put it to her, "Another thing Jesus said is, 'You're not good to drive in this state to keep from having to put up another little flower cross on the highway out here in Irma, South Carolina."

When our caravan was back on the road, I asked Jujubee about the Encounter with Ricky's mother. A cynic always has questions. For one, I wanted to know how Jujubee knew that Jesus wanted him to stop and "encounter" the woman, who might have been standing there on the side of the road for any number of reasons and whom he didn't know from Eve; for another, I wanted to know how Jesus communicated the messages he wanted Jujubee to deliver to her.

He said, "It's not a psychic thing, Dewey Hazelriggs, if that's what you're thinking. And it's not extra sensuous perception, or what have you here. I saw a show on the A and E channel a short time back. They said that most of us use maybe ten percent of our brain cells—give or take a few here or there—if you will. And there's a whole great big bunchload of them: billions. Now take and get you a genius like Einstein or that man wears black-frame glasses and sits there in a nice Sunday suit all hunched up in his black motor chair and looks kind of like young Worthy Waddell might look ten years from now if his hair darkens up some—well, a genius such as that might use twelve percent of his brainpower. Whereas, a big old boob like me might use five percent if there's no math involved."

He said, "In the things of the Spirit, I think it's safe to say we use about the same percent of our heart—about ten percent unless you're Mother Teresa or Billy Graham or even Bishop Lester Watts—if you will. Then we're probably talking about somewheres in the neighborhood of twelve or thirteen percent. I think that's what Jesus was getting at when he told people, 'Let him that has ears to hear, let him hear.' Now how many people there in the multitudes do you expect didn't have any ears? So what did he mean? He was talking about hearing with spiritual ears. Anywho, an awful lot of it is just a matter of keeping both our real ears and eyes and our spiritual ears and eyes open."

I said, "Jujubee Forthright, that is *quite* profound."

He said, "Tell me. They have some good shows on there on the A and E, if you catch them before they get sexy later on in the night."

I said, "No. I mean what was deep was not the part about how we use ten percent of our brains but what you said, Jujubee, the part about how we use ten percent of our heart, our spiritual sense. That was the original part. It was an incredible insight."

He was not *shining me on,* as they say in Medlyn. He really had thought I was referring to the show on A&E. Something about it touched me, his not knowing. The idea that he could have a deep thought seemed an alien, if not impossible, thing to him—but I'm not sure it bothered him much, if at all. There are those in the other Medlyn (the *other Medlyn* having no geographical reference at all to me, though my grandfather, Leicester Coat Hazelriggs, would have argued otherwise: To him, there was the highland and the lowland and all good things, like cream, rose) who miss the point of Jujubee Forthright and all his spiritual kin. Pity them for me. The feeling was never mutual. I have never heard Jujubee Forthright put anyone down. Never. Never once.

Jujubee said, "That means a awful lot coming from you, Dewey Hazelriggs, you being a professor and all." His head, which had been doing its sweet papa dip number the whole time as he drove us down the highway, stopped for a moment—a good long moment. "You're a Wentworth man and I'm not. I'll be honest with you. I read that book you wrote last night—*Honest to God*."

I said, "I'm flattered," when what I was really thinking is, *I'm sorry, and I wish you hadn't*.

He said, "It took me all night, and I'm not saying I could pass a pop quiz on any one part of it. I felt kind of like Peter trying to read Paul when he said: 'As also in all his epistles, speaking in them of these things; in which are some things hard to be understood, which they that are unlearned and unstable wrest, as they do also the other Scriptures, unto their own destruction.' Two Peter three and verse sixteen."

I had forgotten that verse, but I liked it.

Jujubee said, "Anywho, Mama, bless her heart, she used to say I don't test well, which was true. Who on God's green earth tests well on things he don't understand? Now it's like with the Holy Bible. I've read it over and over again from Genesis to Revelations and all like that. I've lost track how many times. I've done memory verses till I'm blue in the face to hide the Lord's word in mine heart that I might not sin against him. Psalms one-nineteen and verse eleven. It seems I've hidden it so well I can't even find it sometimes. Ask me, the King James Bible's easier to memorize but harder to understand. Anywho, I might not agree with everything you wrote up in there, but you sure are a smart man, Dewey Hazelriggs, and honest, too. And I think God could handle more of us being more honest with him, if you know what I mean."

I said, "Bless your heart," and this time that is exactly what I meant. "I'm afraid my father wouldn't see it that way."

He said, "That was one part of the book I did understand. How you felt so disgusted with your father for believing that Jesus woke up from the dead after they took and crucified him on the Cross and laid him in that grave."

I said, "I was a bit of an insolent young man and, to be honest, deep down inside I wanted to hurt him even though he was a good and decent man."

Jujubee said, "One night I wanted to hurt Allis Blackwell, honest to God I did. I was thirteen year old at the time, and I took a twelve-gauge shotgun down the hall to their room one Friday night, loaded with buckshot. Mama was screaming bloody murder and I was shaking so bad, worse than I am right now, it's a wonder the house didn't come down. I just couldn't take it anymore. I kicked the door open and there stood Allis Blackwell with his shirt off and Mama there on the bed crying, and I raised the barrel of the gun and made to pull the trigger, but a voice, the Lord's own voice, clear as I'm talking to you right now, said, 'Don't do it, Jujubee. "Thou shalt not kill, or what have you here."' I worked the gun around and tried to turn it on myself, but my arms was too short, and before I knew it Allis Blackwell was all over me, and Mama was on his back beating on him with her little bony fists."

I said, "I'm so sorry, so very sorry," and he said, "Allis Blackwell was a tortured man."

He should have been, I thought.

He said, "We all have our demons, our cross to bear."

I thought, Some of us should hang from them.

He said, "Judge not that ye be not judged."

I thought, I'm nailed.

Jujubee said, "Anywho, before I went and got all morbid on us, or what have you here, I was going to say how I got thinking when I read about you getting all disgusted with your father that I never thought about Jesus waking up as much as I thought about his father waking him up. Sometimes I study on it and get so carried away it's like my head's gonna come popping right off my shoulders. See, some people focus on the power and the glory of the resurrection; I always get thinking about how tender it was. I mean, there he was, laid up in there dead in that tomb, beaten all up to a bloody pulp, and his father loved him and so he comes in and looks at him in there in the cold and the dark and all alone with rock hard cold stone all around him. And his heart is breaking, and he says, 'Rise and shine, my son, my dear son.' It's the tender touch of the loving father that gets me about the whole thing. I couldn't doubt it because it's what I imagine a loving father—not that I know what that's like—what he would do."

He said, "You said in your book that it's just a story you can't bring yourself to believe; I can't think of any other story that does for me what that story does."

I said, "Father, forgive me, I know not what I do."

He said, "I'm going to get that book back to you and get me my very own copy of it, and I'd like for you to sign it for me, if you will. I've never known a author before."

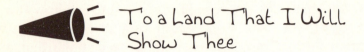

# To a Land That I Will Show Thee

SOME THREE HOURS AND AS MANY ENCOUNTERS LATER, with the smell of a storm in the air, at a Shoney's just north of Savannah, we stopped for dinner. It was time, and Jujubee said his head was swimming and he needed to get his sugar up so he could think straight with at least eight percent of his brain and twelve percent of his heart. The Lord, he said, was leading him, the way a patient father would lead his toddling son by the hand, taking little bitty baby steps, to something—something bold if not big, good if not great—but anywho, whatever it was, it was something he couldn't afford to miss.

Looking back, I guess I would have to say that it was in that ragged moment just after he backed the truck into a parking space behind the Shoney's and just before he stepped out of the truck to help them unload Worthy Waddell from Merlin Monroe's Club Wagon van that I noticed how shaky he was, not just his hands, but his whole body–jiggling. Then there was that strawberry-swirl blotchiness in his cheeks and the sweat beads clotted at his hairline.

It was enough to make me to lay my hand on his shoulder and say, "Are you feeling all right, Jujubee?"

He nodded, said, "Sugar's a little low is all."

I merely assumed he had diabetes, of the non-insulin dependent type, what with the excess weight he was carrying. I said, "Well, let's eat."

After dinner we spent a while out in the Shoney's parking lot resting our road-weary bones. Jujubee and Banana Fosters needed, they said, to have a little talk with Jesus and they staggered off into the woods for a little time apart to pray and listen. Fanny said what she needed was a little walk with Jesus, but since he was going to be tied up out in the woods with Jujubee and Banana Fosters for the next little bit, she would settle for me and Worthy Waddell. So off we went down the sidewalk that passed in front of a strip mall.

I lowered my voice. "Does Jujubee have diabetes?"

Fanny said, "Nope," and punctuated it with an elipsis. Dot. Dot. Dot.

And just as I was thinking she was doing it for Worthy Waddell's benefit and I was about to change the subject for the time being, Worthy said, "It's not the sugar he's got. Daddy says he got loufa-ed."

Fanny said, "Worthy Waddell, it's a good thing you got that new hot rod racing chair because you're going to need it to get away from me, if you keep carrying on like that."

She made a boxing gesture with her hands, said, "It's *lupus* and your Daddy's just talking. He doesn't know anymore than I do what's the matter with Jujubee Forthright. But I will level with you and tell you that it's got me a little worried. He told me he went to see Dr. Desai about it."

I stopped walking and turned to face her and the IGA behind her. I said, "And what did she say?"

Fanny said, "Jujubee said she drew several vials of blood, took some X-ray scans of his head and chest, told him to lose a hundred pounds to get him started, and sent him on his way telling him she would call when the results were in."

I said, "When was that?"

Fanny said, "About a month ago now, I imagine."

Worthy said, "Tell about that time Mr. Jujubee Fluoride bent over out in the backyard of your house pulling weeds and split the seat of his big old dungaree over-halls from here to yonder and stem to stern."

She said, "Worthy Waddell."

He said, "Lanny Dough-tree said he seen of it with his own eyes. Big old full moon cause he won't wearing any drawers." He was giggling then, and, despite myself, I was, too, picturing it.

Fanny said, "Boys, boys. Worthy Waddell, Lanny Doherty was not there that day, for one thing, and Jujubee was wearing underpants for another. He always does, and I never in my life expected I'd have to be out here on the street in Savannah, Georgia, talking about it."

Worthy said, "I love me some Jujubee Fluoride."

Fanny said, "Well don't we all now? And he sure does love you, Worthy Waddell, even if you do pick at him some." She turned to me. "My brother Marion talks a lot, says a lot of things—he always has—but probably not half as many as Worthy here says he says. I don't think it's lupus. I hope and *pray* it's not lupus. And I don't imagine Marion has any real idea about it either."

Worthy said, "Is Jujubee Fluoride gonna be all right, Aunt Fanny?"

She said, "Yes, but let's do remember him in our prayers all the same."

My cell phone with its *Fur Elise* ring tone was such an unfamiliar sound to me that it had rung three times before Worthy said, "Ain't you gonna get your phone, Mr. Dewey?" and I realized that it was my phone ringing. I had put it in my little blue fanny pack just in case Mitchell Bramlett saw his way clear to break away from the prenuptial rumpus long enough to return my call. My only chance had been that the opportunity to represent the rightful heir of Isaiah Longstreet Forthwright to the W4200 through W4400 properties would eclipse his fear that I might be representing Wentworth College. Suddenly, I was feeling very lucky.

I was also feeling very awkward, not merely because I was wearing a fanny pack but because I had been communicating with Mitchell Bramlett without the knowledge or consent of Jujubee himself. I hadn't even mentioned it to Fanny.

I said, "Excuse me, please," and sidestepped off the sidewalk into the grass a few paces. Fanny nodded in my direction; her hand on her hip. I fumbled around, finally figured out how to answer the phone. "Hello."

It was indeed Mitchell Bramlett, and he was so animated I could just picture him swaying on a glider on the shady front porch of a great Georgian colonial sipping a tall green mint julep, the kelly green porkpie hat with the orange feather in it resting on his lap.

He said, "Well, I'm hornswoggled. But best I can tell, yes, James Jackson Baldwin Forthright—Jimmy Jack B. Forthright, who runs the Town and Country Auction at W forty-three hundred U.S. Highway seventy-six, is the sole surviving heir of Isaiah Longfellow Forthwright."

I ambled a few paces farther away from Fanny and Worthy Waddell, who, at any rate, were peering through the bars of a pawn shop window at the merchandise displayed there. I lowered my voice. "So Jujubee *owns* the Wentworth College campus?"

"Well, God owns it, of course," he corrected, with a smile in his voice. "But, unless I have made some grievous error, James Jackson is the titleholder of the W forty-two, forty-three, and forty-four hundred plats of land in Medlyn, Georgia. That covers both Wentworth and the Fu-Fi Church there on the corner of Main and Whaley streets."

I said, "I see," and what I saw in my mind was the supercilious patronage of President Alisdair Knox, Dr. J.C. Wiley, and Drice Weaver, Esquire. "So he could evict them if he chose to do so?" If he could and he did, I thought, I wanted to be there to see it, to see those gray-haired old boys when he told them to get their stuff—all their stuff—and get the hell out. I closed my eyes and pictured Jujubee up on the terrace with Bette Davis as shotgun-wielding Charlotte Hollis and both of them pushing the urn off the rail and saying, in harmony, "Get off my property." And lo a Southern gothic voice, wistful and eerie, saying: *Hush ... hush, sweet Jujubee.*

Mitchell Bramlett said, "Well, his great grandfather, on his mother's side, let the land to Wentworth and Fundamental First Church—you know, they're the ones that put the *fun* in fundamentalist; ask me, they put the *mental* in it. It's a land-lease with ten-year terms. So, to answer your question about eviction, he could pursue eviction as a lawful remedy to some breach of landlord-tenant contract, but that's not likely and it tends to be a messy situation. Property rights are next to sacred even if you're merely a tenant letting property that technically belongs to someone else. Hearth and home, bed and board, all that. It's not just another right. If, however, it so happened that Mr. Forthright were considering making some sort of a change, even if it were merely to renegotiate the terms ... "

... *then, I, Mitchell Bramlett, would be proud to take his case.* He didn't say this, of course. Not in as many words anyway. But it was an unspoken subtext in italics and boldface and punctuated with an exclamation bang.

He continued, "Well, if that were his intention, he could do so a few weeks from now with considerably less fuss. You see, that is when the current ten-year term of lease expires."

I said, "Expiry September thirty."

He said, "Yes. That is correct."

I said, "I am curious. What are the terms of the lease?"

"Favorable," he said, "from the *tenants'* standpoint. Isaiah Longfellow Forthwright was in the liquor trade during Prohibition."

I said, "He was a moonshiner?"

"In the vernacular, yes—and a bootlegger to boot. He spent five years in the Federal Pen in Atlanta for it, and therein the good Lord found him and he got religion and upon his release put his land to the Lord's work—he let it out to the Wentworth College, a Christian institution, and the Fundamental First Church, a Christian institution. Words don't mean what they used to, I guess. Let each parcel out for one dollar a year renewable on October one of every tenth year. If you do the math, that's a bargain, shall we say."

I said, "I'll say. That spread is what, a hundred acres?"

He said, "Two hundred twelve acres combined for W forty-two hundred and W forty-four hundred, excluding the graveyard, of course." He sighed. I heard the rustle of papers. "One dollar per year each for their land. Wentworth College has made several attempts over the years to acquire title to the property. The last such attempt I can find a record of was in the middle nineteen-eighties. Jimmy Jack's mother Celia was advised against making any move on it because she was common-law married at the time to a scoundrel named—"

"Allis."

"—Blackwell."

I said, "Yes."

"Yes," he said. "And, later, a land developer who had done a title search on the property inquired about purchasing it, but Celia's lawyer, a drunken old coot named Ruskell, convinced her not to sell but to renew the lease. I'd bet the back forty he was on the take and got a handsome commission, most likely payable in Jack Daniels mash, for his trouble."

I said, "After all this time, couldn't they invoke squatter's rights?"

"Hardly," he said. "They would try that song and dance, of course, but squatters don't have too many rights, and it would never play to a judge or jury here in Maxey County. There's no adverse possession, for one thing, and as the fare-thee-well, they were leasing the land. You can only squat, so to speak, on public land; a tenant under lease is a horse of a different stripe. If it were otherwise, see, every renter in the state could simply claim the property he rents as his very own."

"Well," I said, "that all goes to show you how much I *don't* know about real estate law."

He said, "Well, I suppose it's not for all of us to give our hearts to such a wild woman as real estate law. The end of the matter is this: The land belongs to Jimmy Jack B. Forthright and, what's more, so do the all of the facilities that the trustees of the college and the church have built on their respective plats. That much is specified very clearly in the original lease in the Improvements clause; the force and effect of such survives down to this very day."

After I hung up with Mitchell Bramlett and zipped the cell phone up in the fanny pack it happened—another faint little telltale click of the tumblers on the great combination lock of my life. Jujubee's mother Celia's lawyer, who Mitchell Bramlett would have laid odds was on the take, was a drunken old coot named Ruskell. Theodore Cleary Ruskell. I knew a little about him. He was a lawyer, for one, and he was a drunk, for another, and he was the brother of none other than Sarah Beth Ruskell, who was the wife of none other than Drice Olin Weaver, *Esquire*, founding partner of the prestigious Atlanta law firm Blair-Polson-Weaver, which was the counsel of record for none other than Wentworth College, which was situated on none other than plat W4400.

\* \* \*

It was a little over an hour later when I finally mustered the nerve to tell Jujubee about my conversation with Mitchell Bramlett. Maybe it wasn't all about nerves. The little talk with Jesus that Jujubee and Banana Fosters had in the woods behind the Shoney's had done him wonders. He was not shaking—though maybe that was because he had gotten his sugar up—but truth is, he only had a small salad with Italian dressing and a little cup of vegetable soup.

He said, "Dewey Hazelriggs, I say unto you: The Lord Jesus told me something—me and the Banana Fosters both—when we was seeking his will back yonder behind the Shoney's. He said, 'You boys are all the time getting all up in there in folk business—*My* business, that is—and you couldn't find a shorter cut to misery.' Said, 'There you was, Jimmy Jack, sights set on getting you a college degree at the Wentworth or Mt. Sinai when I already told you to get a move on. Tell me something. When I told Father Abraham to 'get thee out of thy country, and from thy kindred, and from thy father's house, unto a land that I will show thee,' what'd he do? 'Did he take and get him a college degree? Come on, tell me.' Banana Fosters says, 'No, Lord, no.' And the Lord said, 'So get out of my business; let me in yours; and I'll take it from there.' Lord said, Look, he wasn't one to map out the whole journey before you took off because then you could just flip on the automatic pilot switch and where's the faith in that? He said he's not big on automatic pilot. He wants you to turn when you come to a fork in the road."

I said, "Yes."

Jujujbee said, "Yes. Anywho, Jesus said, 'Y'all get your big old business, on the one hand, and your old colored self, on the other, back on the road, if you will.' He said, 'I've got big news for you. There's something I need to tell you.'"

Then Jujubee fell silent, and I waited through the silence for a full minute until I couldn't take it any longer. I said, "And what was the something he needed to tell you, if you don't mind my asking?"

He said, "He left it at that."

I said, "He did?"

Jujubee said, "He does that sometimes—just lets it be. That's part of the faith-thing and all like that. Anywho, I think what he meant was for us to just get this show back on the road and he'd tell us whatever he wanted us to know, taking the road one fork at a time."

I said, "There's something I need to tell you."

Then, for some eighty miles traveling south of Savannah, Georgia, as we climbed up the great arc of the John Wesley Causeway that connects mainland Georgia to the Altar Isle known as Little Chancel Island, I told him the whole story—from my curiosity about why first Alisdair Knox then Dr. J.C. Wiley then Drice Weaver had made faces at the mention of his name to the full accounting Mitchell Bramlett gave me from his research into the matter of who held the deed to plats W4200–W4400 in Medlyn, Georgia.

Jujubee let his heavy right foot rise up off of the gas pedal and the truck slowed. He said, "Lo and behold what great work the Lord hath wrought." Then he said, "But now I do know this: They the county turned out old Wintson Peeler and took away all forty-some-odd acres of his land for a Super Wal-Mark. They said it was a easement. Old Winston Peeler, God love him, he raised Cain and Abel both, so to speak; he got the papers out there and the TV crew from Atlanta and was trying to get on Oprah Winfreys, but anywho in the end they did what they wanted and claimed they had the right to do it all under," here he lowered both the key and volume of his voice: "under *enema domain*."

I said, "Good heavens."

He said, "Tell me. What Jesus and me couldn't do with all that land."

Jujubee brought the truck, which had been decelerating this whole time, to a very easy stop on the lookout shoulder at the crest of the filigreed trestle of the John Wesley Causeway. Merlin Monroe and Otis Winters pulled alongside and we all got out, except Worthy Waddell, who stayed in his seat in the van. We formed a semi-circle around the double side door of the van and Jujubee led us in prayer. Every head bowed, every eye closed, he cried out there in the coastal Georgia twilight, when all that was left of the brilliant day were a few salmon pink strokes in the gray western sky.

He said, "Lord Jesus, yes, you have delivered your message to us through the mouth of your prophet Dewey Hazelriggs. Oh, Lord, you have prepared a place for me in the presence of mine enemies even as I walk through the valley of the shadow of death your light is shining all about me. Shine through me."

If I flinched a little to hear him speak of me—me, of all people—as a prophet, I shuddered to hear him speak of himself as walking through the valley of the shadow of death. But when he spoke of the Lord's light shining about him, well, I can tell you this: I was not the only one of the nine of us standing there who noticed what Fanny later said looked like a golden aura, not unlike the aura we had both of us seen on the lawn gnome by the lake in Fanny's backyard the previous Thursday evening, glowing around Jujubee from the top of his head down and around to the tips of his toes.

He raised both hands. "Lord Jesus, I love you. And all God's people said—"

"Amen," we chorused.

He said, "Now you all know that I left the others, Peanut Butterbean and Dark Vader and Marion Waddell, back there with a mission—to begin renegading the Teensie Auction House—to make a place suitable for them the Lord Jesus called the least of these my brethren. Miss Franny's sold me her place up the hill on Sugar Maple Lane for one dollar and a half—"

Fanny said, "A dollar is what we shook on, Jujubee. That fifty cents was a loan so you could get yourself a bottle of Coca-cola out of your own machine at the Teensie to get your sugar up."

He said, "That is true. I didn't have my change purse with me last evening when we cut that deal, or what have you here. Anywho, the point of it is we wanted to give folks a good-size yard with some woods on it and a little access to the Lake Sorghum stocked with a little brim."

Burden Blue had pulled that Lynyrd Skynyrd memorial cap off his head and his gray hair, pulled into a ponytail reminiscent of Willie Nelson, shone silver in the utility lights on the trestle of the bridge. He said, "What type people you got in mind, Jujubee?"

"Like I said, the least of these my brethren, and all like that." Jujubee was still glowing—though by then our eyes had pretty much adjusted to it. He had his hands in the pockets of his overalls. He said, "We don't want to start running people through the mill to get in. We're not going to make them meet a bunchload of what they call 'vigorous epidemic standards' and all like that. Believe me: I know what that's like: not fun. We're going to cast a wide net.

Now, see, after we rent out as many rooms as they got to let here on the Little Chancel Island and get us a hour or two of shut-eye here in the next little bit we're going to head back out on the road again, such as it is, bright and early of the morning. We're going to do a sweep from Jacksonville back up to Savannah then back here to the Altar Isles to hold a auction—we're gonna auction salvation to the lowest bidder."

Burden Blue said, "That's awful nice of you, Jujubee, turning your place up home into a shelter for people that needs it."

Jujubee said, "Awful nice of Lord Jesus is more like it. I'd have take and made it a brothel or a house of ill-repuke if it'd been my doing. The only cost of admission, if you will, is that people need a place to live in grace, and it's Lord Jesus works the door detail. Anywho, Lord Jesus has come through with Granddaddy's land in Medlyn, and all like that, and it's the cattle on a thousand hills and maybe he wants to auction off a head or two of moo or a acre or two, I don't know. It's his, not mine, such as it is. So I'm going to wait on the Lord and see what he wants to do about it, but it's going to be big and good, and it's going to be all for the least of these my brethren and sistren, too. And Otis Winters here is going to be our chief groundskeeper."

Worthy Waddell's voice came from the van: "Jujubee Fluoride, he's the man, if he can't do it no one can." He clapped his hands and had something of a little fit, and Fanny tended to him.

We all echoed his sentiment, and Jujubee said, "Let's get all up in there and rent out some rooms so we'll have someplace to put up all those that answers the Lord Jesus's Alter Call to join our auction on Friday night."

With holy hands lifted high into the brackish evening air heavy with creosote and saltwater, Banana Fosters led us in a closing word of prayer and benediction in the name of the Friend of Sinners. Before we broke company, Jujubee peeled off thick stacks of twenty-dollar bills and gave them, by turns, to Wylynda Monroe, the treasurer of the mission, and Otis Winters, who was its first official convert. All room tabs were to be paid in cash money, he said. Then off we went to divide and conquer the inns and outs of Little Chancel Island.

Jujubee consulted the little caricature map they had given us at the toll booth at the mainland end of the John Wesley Causeway. He was decisive: He and I would take the eastern part of the island where most of the larger hotels were clustered together because, as he put it, there were only two of us and between us we only had three real normal legs—in number if not in size, he noted, because his one real leg made three or four of Banana Fosters' toothpicks.

Worthy said, "That's three more'n I got," and Jujubee said, "I do say some stupid things, now don't I?"

Jujubee dispatched Merlin Monroe, captain of Team Club Wagon, and his troops to the northern end where the smaller establishments were—motels, rental beach bungalows, and condos. The PUP Team of Otis Winters and Banana Fosters were to hightail it down to the south end in Otis Winters' Isuzu PUP pickup where there were a few high-rises and a garage where they could have a set of tires put on to get the vehicle road-ready for the mission trip round-up to Savannah the next day. For their part, he charged Miss Franny and Worthy Waddell with the most important duty of all: They were to stay behind and commit themselves to prayer for the apostles and the Alter Call Auction (and between prayers they could take a dip in the hot tub and maybe order a pizza to refresh their spirits).

Jujubee charged the apostles thus: When—and only when—each team was satisfied that it had done its part in leaving no *No Vacancy* sign unlit on the whole island was it to call it a night and meet back here on Ocean Boulevard on the north end of Little Chancel Island at the Club Croquet (which he pronounced American style—"croquette"—and said he chose it because back in the day when he was on the road in his Kenworth eighteen-wheel transfer truck he used to stop at HoJo's and order two chicken croquette dinners and two large sweet teas, one for him and the other for him, too). Each member of the party would have a private room pre-paid in full and waiting for them.

As it turned out, the Club Croquet Seaside Resort where we would be staying was situated on the tract of beach between the Periwinkle-by-the-Sea complex, which was hosting the Fundamentalists, on the west and the Claymore Castle, which was hosting the Presbyterians, on the east. Their respective marquees welcomed their patrons. Which meant, I realized, that we were wedged smack dab in the middle of Dr. Alisdair Knox on our left and Dr. J.C. Wiley on our right.

Jujubee looked up at the marquees, his head swinging from one to the other. He raised his hands and prayed: "Clowns to the left of me, jokers to the right, here I am stuck in the middle with you. Here we are, Lord Jesus, stuck in the middle with you. The meat in a Medlyn sandwich."

I couldn't help but wonder how this could have happened. What were the chances that the two Medlyns would merge there several hundred miles from the north Georgia mountains? Coincidence? Were we stuck in the middle with Jesus?

Jujubee closed his charge with, "Now some of them rooms has got a big old jacozy hot tub in them that's as big as a fish pond, so take you a dip, but anywho don't party too late into the night in it because the Mission Alter Call caravan will roll out pronto at seventy-thirty in the morning."

Then we dispersed—each team to do its duty. Jujubee and I worked the eastern part of the island and, by the time we staggered into the Club Croquet Seaside Resort at midnight on our three real legs, we—Team Jujubee & Deweybee (Worthy Waddell named us)—had reserved a grand total of thirty-two rooms, which Jujubee paid for in cash from a seemingly endless roll of twenty- and fifty-dollar bills. I offered up my American Express for the work but Jujubee politely refused, saying the Lord doesn't pay in plastic.

He said, "Dewey Hazelriggs, fear not. I've sold off the few things I have that's worth more than two cents, such as it is. All but the Hohner squeezebox Mama gave me when I was eight year old. Lord Jesus drew the line at that; though if he hadn't, I might have … Dots used to say I was senti*mentally* ill."

He said, "I've been putting back all the receipts from the Teensie Auction for right on three year now—all except for the tenth part which was set aside as a tithe to the Good Shepherd A.M.E. Church and a little more that goes to keep Miss Lillian Bagwell in lights—for just such a time as this. Lord Jesus calls us *from* before he calls us *to*. Right?"

I nodded, thinking through what that really meant, and Jujubee said, "Angels unawares."

I said, "What's that, Jujubee?"

We were standing at the end of the great archway of the Club Croquet, which was opposite the registration desk at the foot of the grand winding staircase. I turned to see what Jujubee was looking at.

He said, "Hebrews thirteen and verse two: 'Be not forgetful to entertain strangers: for thereby, some have entertained angels unawares.'"

He was looking at a comely teenage couple standing in the shadows by the French doors that led out to the Grecian bath and swim-up bar on the beach side of the resort. When the doors swung open to let a patron in or out I could hear the mellow rhythm of reggae on steel drums and, in the glow of the Tiki torches, I could see that the couple was a boy and a girl, both with angel faces, both with silken hair. They were holding hands, and there was something of the itchy and urgent about it, as though it were stolen and needed to be held—held tight. They looked familiar, and I had the dreamy sense of déjà vu.

I said, "Angels unawares. Do you know them?"

Jujubee said, "From Adam and Eve? Yes. And you might, too, Dewey Hazelriggs, if you was to give it a little thought."

When I repaired to my room a little later, I stood out on the balcony and gave the young couple a little thought and came up only with more déjà vu as I watched the sparkling lights of barges passing out in the deep waters of the Atlantic. The waves sizzled and hissed on the hardpack sand of the north beach of Little Chancel Island and I craned my ear to eavesdrop on the great and terrible message in its ancient whisper. Next door, Jujubee was crooning a medley of hymns of old-time religion vintage on that black mother of pearl Hohner accordion his mother gave him when he was eight years old. "Old Rugged Cross," "Trust and Obey," "Holy, Holy, Holy," "Jesus, Lover of My Soul."

I sank into the deck chair and let the weight of my soul bear down on me with the blunt force of eternity. I was an old man now, and my best years, such as they were, were all behind me, but those waves breaking below in crash and whisper were breaking just the same as they had during those lost weeks we passed on Jekyll Island so many lifetimes ago, those weeks when we were not the Hazelriggses—Mother, Father, and I—not the Reverend David Umberton Hazelriggs II and family of 8400 Langley Lane, Medlyn, Georgia. If in my youth I had suspected, had *hoped*, that on Jekyll Island we were who we *really* were, the years proved only this: The memories were so vivid, so treasured, precisely because all those weeks on Jekyll Island we were who we were *not*, as the exception proves the rule.

Jujubee was on "Beulah Land"—I hear you calling—and I wondered if the ancient whisper of the breaking sea and the muffled crooning from the next room were not, in the big strange scheme of events as they were unfolding, unfolding so unlikely, one and the same thing.

 The Alter Call

At a little after eight the next morning, Jujubee was behind the wheel of the Dodge 3500 van pushing it hard up I-95 North toward Brunswick, Georgia. I was riding shotgun, Worthy was on the second row, and Fanny was on the third. Team PUP was off to Savannah; Team Country Club Wagon was headed down to Jacksonville. Jujubee the Heavy Foot, as Fanny styled him, from her white-knuckling place on third seat back, had us barreling full-bore. We were on a mission.

Fanny said, "And I thought Early Fuller could scare the dickens out of me with that lead foot of *his*."

Worthy Waddell said, "Jujubee Fluoride has a lead foot, literary a lead foot, Daddy says."

Fanny said, "The word is 'literally,' Worthy, and it's good to hear your Daddy hasn't lost his gift of gab."

Jujubee said, "It's not lead, it's stainless steel, or what have you here, and it *is* right heavy."

Fanny said, "I told Pastor Crowe he might could hire you out a couple Sundays a month for the invitation."

Jujubee said, "I have no idea what you're talking about." He was all business, as usual, with that head waving out like a maestro's wand to the meter of "Beulah Land."

The windows were down and the van was filled with the sound as of a rushing mighty wind. Fanny leaned forward a little. "I told him, said, 'You could get you a few more hearts for Jesus if you got Jujubee to come out and assist with the invitation.' I told him a spin around the block with you at the wheel would mash a profession of faith out of just about anybody. If he was to say, 'Every head bowed, every eye closed—Jujubee if you would, please pull the van up to the front steps,' and then the ushers could show all those who raised their hands with unspoken prayer requests out and get them seated in the van and off they'd go with you for a spin around the block. Give new meaning to the term 'conversion van.'"

Jujubee said, "Well, now I reckon a lot of folks needs to have the devil scared out of them. We all of us do from time to time. Anywho, I'm all for it—a new type church van ministry—a perversion van, you say?"

Fanny said, "*Con*version van, Jujubee. My heavens."

Jujubee said, "I'm not arguing with you, Miss Franny. Count me in."

Worthy Waddell said, "You ought to pimp this here perversion van with a set of mag wheels and a low-rider kit and some of them neon blinker lights makes the ground light up like a flying saucer at night. Now, put the hammer down in this here perversion van, Jujubee Fluoride, like Uncle Early used to do, go about a hunnert and ten."

Jujubee said, "Anywho, I better leave top-fuel speeds like that to the trained professionals like the great Early Fuller."

Fanny said, "Yes you had."

Worthy said, "You won't scare the devil out of me."

Jujubee said, "That's because there's no devil in you, so to speak."

A few minutes later, Jujubee said, "Dewey Hazelriggs, think about it for a minute. When was the last time you ever saw a church that actually *welcomed* sinners?"

I thought about it. It certainly hadn't been the First Presbyterian Church of Medlyn, where my father and his father before him had served for the better part of the twentieth century. In fact, for all our good intentions and well meaning ministries, we seemed to do just about everything we could to keep sinners out, lest they soil our sanitized Christian sanctuary. Or maybe it just disturbed our dream of self-righteousness. We were, after all, the living proof of sanctification—as if our good deeds proved we were of the Elect.

I said, "It's been a good long while."

He said, "The Lord's work is dirty work. Leave your three-piece suit and tie in your drawers and put on your overalls, or what have you here."

I took note of the triple-stitched Dickies denim bib overalls he had on over an orange T-shirt.

He said, "It's a dirty nasty job, but somebody's got to do it, if you will. And Jesus has told me I'm one of the somebodies that needs to let him have his own way. Lord, have thine own way, and do it through me—if it's the very last thing I ever do. It's like bathroom detail on the men's ward. Miss Franny, Worthy, I'm sorry if I've gone and offended you-all with all this nasty talk."

She said, "Honey, I've not heard anything that's shocked me so far."

Worthy said, "Aunt Fanny told me one time she made Jujubee Fluoride eat a cake of lye soap for making bathroom talk."

Jujubee said, "Lye soap wouldn't have been half as bad as what it really was. It was Earl Olay or Camay soap, I think. Some pink stuff the color of strawberry milk."

"Camay," Fanny said.

Jujubee said, "Whatever it was, it was some pink something reeking high heaven of perfume. I swear, to this day I can taste it in my mouth whenever I eat something with Italian dressing on it."

Worthy said, "What was it you said then, Jujubee, to make you have to eat that soap? Aunt Fanny ain't listening."

Jujubee said, "Don't kid yourself, Worthy. I learned a long time ago it's a mistake to ever think this Miss Franny's not listening."

Fanny said, "And I keep a bar or two of Camay in my pocketbook, Worthy Waddell, in case you didn't get enough to eat for breakfast."

Jujubee got back to his story. "Anywho, it's dirty work, all right, and when you go out to do it you'd better pack your pocketbook full with a couple three cakes of Earl Olay, or Cameo or whatever suits you best. Stop and think about it a minute: I reckon the Friend of Sinners might get bored with all them whitewashed folk that does good—but not *much* good—week in week out sitting all up in there in the Pine-Sol'ed meeting place in their pressed Sunday outfits smellin' of Airwick and Earl Olay. And putting on church bazaars when it's not so much a rummage sale they need as a rummage soul, if you catch my drift."

*Bizarre* is the word I think he meant—not bazaar—and again I was given to wonder just what moved him. I listened and listened as he went on, picturing Jujubee's Jesus against the backdrop of Club Med Christianity, the kingdom of heaven having given way to so many little "thiefdoms" lorded by free-enterprise preachers with bronzed cheeks and big wavy hair preaching their pick-and-pay, sow-and-reap gospel of name-it claim-it, which sounded, I had to admit, a lot like the sermon the devil had preached in the desert with a certain Nazarene who had just come off a forty-day fast. Yes, against all that worldly grubbing that no respectable Cynic or Christian could smile on, there he was someone so unfamiliar, so out of place, so dingy standing by in borrowed sandals and a dirty tunic.

Worthy, for one, caught Jujubee's drift. He said, "Daddy says them TV preachers is 'the bling leading the blind' and all of 'em got a lot of junk in the trunk, if you know what he means."

Fanny said, "I think that daddy of yours has a lot of gas in the tank, if you know what *I* mean."

Jujubee said, "A lot of wood under the hood, if you know what *I* mean. Anywho, ours is not to judge. Back to the story: I seen a vision of him sitting on the hobo row, the back pew, such as it is, in his white terrycloth robe with a big blue sash, and saying: 'Where's all my friends at? What came I out for to see? I came out for to see my friends, and there's not a single one of them in the whole stinkin' place—stinkin' of

Early Olay and Channel Number Five—not one sick dirty poor little old leper in the whole bunchload, the kind I used to have no trouble picking up way back when on the streets a Galilee? And all I see up in here is well people that gets three squares and has a Belk charge card and don't need a doctor.'"

I sat there in the silence that followed and let Jujubee's Jesus have his way with me. This was not my father's Jesus, not my grandfather's old-time religion—high church or low. And I'm not saying it was better or worse—though I think, really, that in his better (dirtier) moments, my father would have said it was better. He fantasized about getting his hands dirty in the Lord's work. Many times he had corresponded with our denomination's mission board about finding a suitable sabbatical assignment. Once he told Mother and me about an opportunity in Congo, but, bless her heart, neither mother's spirit nor her flesh was willing—she just couldn't picture herself holding the weekly coffee klatch with a group of Pygmy women deep in the African bush.

So we stayed put on the higher of the two Medlyns, and father resigned himself to vicarious mission work: He allocated a larger share of the church budget to mission giving and hosted missionary families three times each quarter and relinquished the pulpit and let them give their slideshows on life among the natives of the lowland plains of the Amazon Basin in Bolivia and harvesting bamboo on the banks of the Talo River in Irian Jaya. I think Father was the only one in the whole church who didn't nod off at least once during those services. I know I did.

I think my father would have donned the blue stretch coveralls he wore that time he tried changing the oil in the family Buick and we all found a week later that 10W-40 motor oil is hard on an automatic transmission. He would have suited up, I think, and answered Jujubee's call to ministry.

Worthy Waddell was the one who finally broke the silence. He said, "So that's what we're going to Brunswick for? To round up a bunch of sick dirty poor little old leopards?"

Jujubee said, "If we can find 'em and they need Jesus or a cold sip to drink or a place to lay their spotted heads, such as it is, yes, that's what we're going to do."

Worthy said, "Aunt Fanny says a leopard can't change its spots."

Jujubee said, "But a leper can."

"A leprechaun?"

Jujubee said, "They can, too, under the touch of Lord Jesus."

I had the map open on my lap and navigated us from I-95 through the low Georgia marshland to U.S. 17 North toward Brunswick, and though Jujubee had never been to Brunswick, as soon as we hit 17, he seemed to know exactly where we were going and how to get us there. We turned onto a deserted lane lined with Spanish moss-draped live oaks and Biloxi crape myrtles with their big pink flowers in full bloom.

Jujubee pulled the van into the gravel parking lot of a roadside peach stand with signage all over the place hand-painted with such memorable phrases as: *An apple is an excellent thing, until you have tried a peach—George du Maurier (1834–1896).* Then there were the side-splitting ones: *If you can eat this [picture of a peach], thank a peacher* and: *Take away the peach, and all that's left is the pits,* and: *A rose by any other name don't taste near as good* (a reference to the little known fact that peaches are in the rose family of flora).

The one I liked best was the faux Georgia license plate lettered with: *Lookout Mammy, I'm wilder'n a hog in a peach orchard.*

Jujubee approached the stand proper, a plywood-and-two-by-four affair with a trellis contraption on either side and pressboard checkout counter and weigh station attended by an oily little man in a tank top T-shirt soiled with peach juice, et cetera. He had the unlit stub of a fat cigar in his mouth and on his head he wore a pith helmet covered in fuzzy, golden-pink fabric obviously intended to make it look like a peach.

There wasn't another car around for miles and, for all I knew, might not have been since 1964, but the peach man said, "Was you-all with that peach blonde-hair broad with two big boobs looks like Wynonna Juggs?"

Jujubee said, "The only two big boobs I've seen this morning are the two you're looking at right now and nary one of us has blonde hair or could pass for the Juggs in a police line-up."

The man shook his head, grunted. "Well that's too bad for you all, I reckon."

"It might be," Jujubee told him. "I've always had a thing for blondes."

The man scissored the cigar stub out of his mouth, said, "I wouldn't sweat it too much if I was you, big feller. I'd lay a week's wage her real hair is black as your summer socks."

Jujubee said, "That part never bothered me none. Back in the day, before the Lord set the record straight for old Jimmy Jack B. Forthright, what things really was didn't mean near as much to me as the way they looked, and all like that."

Jujubee offered his hand and his head was doing its sweet papa dip like a great pendulum. "I'm Jimmy Jack B. Forthright, and this gentle man here with me is Dr. Dewey Hazelriggs, so to speak, from Medlyn, Georgia, way up yonder in the mountains."

The peach man said, "Billy Bob King's the name. They call me Peachy King."

We all shook hands and nodded at each other.

He said, "Six bushels, three each of freestone and clingstone. Some's the size of coconuts. Find so much as a single fuzz on one of 'em I got a five-spot says it come from your drawers. There's a carton of Minerva's chunky chutney and pickled peaches and a triple-decker tray of pies. They're on the trailer, so back it on in."

Next thing I knew Fanny was standing beside me and Jujubee was behind the wheel of the van backing it up to the side of the lean-to.

I said, "What on earth is going on?"

Fanny said, "Search me, David. It's just one of those *Jujubee Things*. Ever since he was a little boy he's been something of a lightning rod. I quit trying to figure out what he's attracting a long time ago."

I said, "Does he know this man, this Peachy King?"

She said, "Not that I know of. My guess is they have a mutual friend."

"The blonde-hair broad with big—?"

"Bazooms."

"Thank you," I said.

"I don't think *she's* their mutual friend," Fanny told me. "I think she was a friend of the mutual friend."

I said, "And they say philosophers are an obtuse bunch. I've never been so confused in all my life."

Fanny took hold of my hand, and I heard Worthy Waddell, who was still in the van, let out a snorting laugh. Fanny said, "That's because you try so hard to make sense of everything."

"*Too* hard?" I asked.

Fanny said, "Maybe you do and maybe you don't." She squeezed my hand.

Peachy King said, "Ho, such an one! Any more and I'll be mashed as flat as your feet, big feller," and Jujubee shut off the motor and came around to the back of the van and helped Peachy King hitch up the six-by-twelve refrigerated trailer full of peach goods of every kind.

I did what I could, which wasn't much. I knew very little about such things. I got behind the wheel of the van and they told me to mash the brake pedal then work the turn signals as they were wiring up the lights.

I relinquished the wheel to Jujubee and, a trailer full of peach products to the good, we were back on the road and wending our way through the streets of Brunswick, Georgia.

* * *

Our next stop was at the Cypress Shade nursing home, and whatever homing device or onboard navigational system had led Jujubee directly to Peachy King's out-of-the-way roadside peach stand for that *Jujubee Thing* must have shorted out for a moment because the route we took to Cypress Shade was anything but direct. We turned left on Glynn Street and proceeded on for a half mile only to discover it was a dead end. We turned around in somebody's driveway with a half-dozen black children in the front yard skipping rope and dogs ranging around with their teeth bared like dingos.

Jujubee honked the horn and waved, then we backed out and circled the same block three times. Finally Worthy Waddell said, "I'm getting dizzy, Jujubee Fluoride, with all this spinning around making circles."

Jujubee said, "Your Jujubee Florentine, or what have you here, is gonna turn some donuts'll make Krispy Kremes look twice and burn out and smoke the tires here in the middle of the road in a minute, if need be, and you'll *think* dizzy."

A few minutes more of this meandering from one false move to another inspired Worthy Waddell to break into song: "Yes and how many roads must Jujubee go down before he admits that we're lost?" It was such a fine impression of Bob Dylan that I found myself clapping my hands when he was finished.

Fanny said, "My my, Worthy, that was a pretty good Bob Dylan. We need to get you started on the harmonica."

Jujubee said, "I've got a Hohner and a nice little red kazoo in the rucksack back at the lodge, and you can blow you a little harp tonight for us. Anymore, I don't have the wind for it; seems like most of my fainting spells here lately have been when I get to playing the 'cordion and the harp at the same time. I fell out last week and, tell it right, a man could pop his bellows doing that, so to speak."

Fanny said, "Jujubee, we need to see about marching you up to see the doctor as soon as we get back home."

He said, "We'll see about all that," and on the rightward bob of his head he eyed Worthy in the rearview mirror. "That sure *was* a good Bob Dylan, Worthy Waddell. I'd like to hear you do a few bars of "All Along the Watchtower," such as it is."

Fanny said, "Your Daddy's always had a thing for Bob Dylan, Worthy, especially before he went electric. I was always partial to Simon and Garfunkel and the Mamas and the Papas back in that era."

Jujubee said, "Now I do like Mumma Cass."

Somehow in the midst of all this talk about the music of the late 1960s I noticed that our route became less circuitous, if not exactly more linear, and we turned right onto a two-lane road lined with dogwoods until we reached the third intersection, where we turned left onto a wide driveway with a camelback median dotted with patches of red and yellow wildflowers. A quarter of a mile back, set down in a swallow, there was a building which, from the looks of it, had once been an elementary school. Now worse for the wear, it showed its age, with crank-turn awning windows and chipped bricks the color of anemic blood.

Jujubee pulled into the parking lot with maybe a dozen old cars—old more in the sense that they were the kind of four-door sedans with whitewall tires that old people like to drive than in the sense that they had many years or miles on them. As we came to a stop between a Delta 88 and a Ford LTD, I noticed that Worthy Waddell, who had been singing the Mamas and the Papas' "California Dreaming" with Fanny, let down his end of the harmony until Fanny was going solo on "all the leaves are brown."

I pivoted around to my left and looked at him and he let go a wail so shrill and startling that Fanny yelled, "Ah," and Jujubee jerked his head, which at the moment was on a downward bob, around and bumped it on the steering wheel. I slapped my hand across my heart, wondering what on earth... .

Worthy went on, screaming: "Noooooo!"

Jujubee said, "Worthy Waddell, what's got into you?"

Worthy's face was burning red, and he was in the throes of apoplexy, his small trunk gyrating, arms flailing. He slapped his trembling hands over his ears. "I won't never tease you again, Mr. Jujubee. I promise I won't."

Fanny was on her feet, hunched over by his chair with his head against her breast. She said, "It's all right, Worthy. Shhhh now, baby. It's all right. There now, angel."

He cried, "Mama, mama, mama."

Jujubee had opened the sliding side door of the van and he looked in. "Worthy, Lord Jesus knows this life ain't fair, such as it is. And he also knows that I would never in a million years leave you off at a place the likes of this."

Then it hit me—only then, that Worthy Waddell's mortal fear was that we were at the Cypress Shade Nursing Home to check him in and be done with him here in this godforsaken south Georgia wasteland. Now, I had no idea what we were doing there, either, but I was sure it wasn't to institutionalize poor Worthy Waddell. But my heart broke for him.

He said, "Cody Grayson said they was going to put me in a home with one of them shirts with long sleeves that they wrap around you and fasten up in the back just like they did his cousin Leroy who was bad retarded and got run over by a forklift and had to get put in a rollin' chair just like me."

Fanny said, "I'm of a good mind to take a hickory switch to Mr. Cody's little old fanny myself for this, but I'll probably just take it up with his mama and let her see to Mr. Cody. For one thing, it's a lie. Leroy Vance, mind you, is not retarded. Leroy has *epilepsy*, and he has more smarts in his little toe than Cody Grayson has in that big head of his ... that was uncalled for, I'm sorry ... but Leroy Vance lives over in Blairsville with his mother and daddy and hasn't spent so much as a day of his sweet life in any home but his own."

Jujubee was sitting on the side-step of the van. He was looking down at his black chucks and his cheeks were damp, part sweat and part tears. He said, "Lord have mercy, Worthy, they're all back up in there right now turning the Teensie into a special place to live, such as it is. And anywho, you and your daddy are going to live right there in Miss Franny and Early's house right out by that Sour Gum Lake with that sloping backyard and birdbath with St. Franny in it—"

"St. Francis," Fanny said, and Jujubee said, "And all like that."

Worthy's sobs had subsided to a sniffle and a twitch. He said, "Am I retarded, Miss Franny?"

"Oh honey." Fanny stroked his hair. "I guess Cody Grayson told you you were .... He'll be retarded by the time I'm done with him."

If the exterior of the Cypress Shade Nursing Home promised a turn for the worse, the inside delivered on it, and we hadn't made it as far as the front desk before my mood was three shades darker. The place smelled of stale people and old urine; there were once-proud young men and women not much older (and a few even younger) than I in frumpy sleepwear hanging out of wheelchairs parked on both sides of the main corridor. Even the air in the place was somehow gray and washed out, and Jujubee's blue jean overalls and orange T-shirt cast a fluorescent glow against the backdrop of the drab nurses' station.

His head was bobbing the whole while he was making time with the nurse behind the counter. She had stringy gray hair and could have passed without a blink as Whistler's aunt. A few minutes later, she pointed down the hall and said, "She'll be glad you come."

I whispered to Fanny, "I think we must be in for another 'Jujubee Thing.'"

She said, "You might as well get used to them."

As we made our way down the hall, Jujubee sang a line from some Mamas and Papas' ditty I recalled from my graduate school days, a John Phillips song that, if memory serves, was probably composed under the influence of more drugs than were then available in all of Durham, North Carolina.

Jujubee led the way, singing, "And no one's gettin' fat except Mumma Cass." I had never cared for the song before I heard the Satchmo version of it as sung by Jujubee Forthright that day. I found myself humming along as we followed Jujubee through the rest home. He turned right onto a short hall and slowed to a stop in front of the third room on the left. He ran his hands over the sides of his head and fingered his hair as if to make himself presentable. He raised his right finger in the air and tilted his head with his ear to the wooden door, which was about halfway open. "You decent all up in there, Miz Greavin'? Because we're not looking to catch sight of nothing you'd rather keep to yourself, such as it is."

The old woman's voice, full and throaty, said, "Step one foot on my property and I'll kill you dead and tell the law the Lord done it on account of your making advantage of a old woman saint."

Worthy Waddell clapped his hands, Fanny said, "Shhh," and I took a little step back out of the line of fire in case Miss Greevy took a notion to make good on her threat and fired a shotgun blast through the window of her room.

Jujubee told her, "Now there's no need to let any blood over this, Miz Greavin'."

Unimpressed, Miss Greevy said, "First off, Mister, mister whatever your face is, my name is Greevy, not Greavin'."

Jujubee said, "My bad, my bad. I'm awful sorry. I must've misheard our Lord when he come to call on me about coming to call on you. I thought he said, 'Go forth and see

Miz Greavin'.' Even quoted a verse. He's big into that, you know. He said: 'And tell her to "*grieve* not the Holy Spirit of God, whereby ye are sealed unto the day of redemption." Ephesians four and verse twenty.' *Italian ice* added."

She said, "'They'll take and gnarl up word of the Lord to their own damnation, saith the Gourd,'" and added: "Jedediah thirty-five and verse two. Popsicles, twenty-five cent."

Jujubee said, "What Scripture ye quote I know not of." On the leftward list of his head, he drew back a little and tried to steal a glimpse into the room through a part in the curtain-drawn window. He said, "But fear not, for Jesus loves me this I know, for the Bible tells me so, and that very Jesus told me to come and pass a few minutes with you this afternoon."

"He could have come himself, if it was important as all that to him," she said, "instead of sending some big old form such as yourself."

Jujubee said, "But he said every single time he's come roarin' up in here to pay his respects you've turned him away with all that talk about shotguns and such."

Miss Greevy said, "Well then. And furthermore, you best move on now. Don't make me call the law on you."

Jujubee said, "'For sittest thou to judge me after the law,' Miz Greavin', 'and commandest me to be smitten contrary to the law?' Acts twenty-three and verse three, b."

Worthy let go a snorting laugh, and Fanny, again, told him to hush up.

Miss Greevy said, "'Shoot if you must this old gray head, but they'll carry you'n out in a bag.' Mace twelve and verse thirty-ought-six, a."

Jujubee was crossing the threshold into her room now, and when the curtain blew open a little in his wake, I caught sight of Miss Greevy for the first time. I had expected to see a Granny Goodheart, maybe with velvet-smooth cheeks glowing just a little from the burnt-orange coils of the warm oven from which she had just removed a full sheet of homemade ginger cookies—with both hands—a soft sweet face that smiled on the little cookie-men she was about to ice, or some such, like my own grandmother, who better matched the wisp-raspy voice than the murderous threats they carried. What I saw instead was—to speak plainly—a face not even (Lord forgive my honesty) a mother could love, I thought, and I turned away at the sight. It was the most hideous face I have ever seen. Hideous not merely by the cultural standards of beauty in America, but hideous by any standard, by the standard of a subterranean culture of trolls, hideous for all time. There was so much wrong with her face that I couldn't tell what was right, whether a genetic defect or an accident had caused all the mess.

I looked away and recalled Bierce Ambrose's quip that a "cynic is a blackguard whose faulty vision sees things as they are, and not as they ought to be," which I had always taken as a tribute rather than the aspersion Ambrose intended it to be. No rose-colored glasses and pie in the sky for me, thank you very much. I wanted (or so I said) to take life straight—straight out of the bottle, not watered down—to see things as they are unrefracted by wishful thinking. But things were changing, they were, on this surreal missionary journey I was on with Jujubee Forthright. Even though I could not see Miss Greevy *as she ought to be*—and for once in my life I was really trying to—I knew, knew, that Jujubee Forthright was seeing her as God, who is surely no Cynic, saw her reflecting his image in which she was created despite herself.

Jujubee approached the bed. He said, "So this is all it is, or what have you here?"

"All it is," she said. "*All* it is?"

"All it is," he said. He had his hands in the pockets of his overalls and his head was bobbing around.

"The demons," she said.

Jujubee said, "Jesus wanted me to tell you something—and, yes, he could have come by himself, but he said every time he's tried, you pretty well blessed him out and turned him out on his ear, which he understands, he said, and don't hold it against you. It's just that he got thinking that maybe some big old common form such as myself, such as it is, might could get through to you better."

Miss Greevy said, "You're shining me up, shining me on, Big'n." There was a raspy little laugh.

"Son's shine the only shine I got," Jujubee Forthright told her. I eased toward the door and poked my head in just so my right eye could see in the room, saw Jujubee take a step closer to her and pull his right hand out of his pocket and place his palm on her forehead. She was in the bed near the window, but the heavy curtain was pulled to, and a passing cloud cast her in a dark shadow. I couldn't help but notice that there were no flowers on her table, no greeting cards on the wall to remind her that she was thought of, if not loved, wishing her a happy birthday or Mother's Day or something. Though, if I had something in common with Otis Winters, I had to admit that I also had something in common with Miss Greevy. Who would send me a card if I were to find myself laid up for the duration in such a place?

Jujubee said, "Jesus told me to come here and tell you to your very face, Miz Evangelina Greevy, that you are beautiful to him, so beautiful, in fact, that he wants you to come live with him forever, if you will."

All was silent for a moment, and in that moment, I tell you, I knew that I was in the presence of one doing the Lord's work, that I was hearing the echo of the calling of Jujubee Forthright. There's simply no power on earth that would—even if it *could*—on its own initiative do what was being done in that long silent moment in Room 112 at the Cypress Shade Nursing Home when Miss Evangelina Greevy heard for the first time in her long life that *someone*—Jesus, no less—thought she was beautiful.

It was no random act of kindness I was witnessing, no senseless beauty that makes for a nice bumper sticker; it was better, higher by virtue of the fact that it was deliberate and sensible. Grace by its very nature, I decided, could never be random, never senseless.

A few minutes later, we were on the men's dormitory wing of the home, in the room of a crusty old geezer whose furrowed brow and bulldog jowls put me in mind of Winston Churchill. His name was Curtis P.R. Higginbotham. The Reverend Clarence P.R. Higginbotham, according to the block-lettered index card on the nameplate Scotch-taped to the door of room 224. And he seemed none too happy to see us, though for the record he did not threaten either to shoot us dead or call the law on us. Instead, from his little armchair where he sat eating Hershey's kisses from the bag and watching an episode of "Mr. Ed," he said, "What's this here kooky parade a near humanoids all about?"

Jujubee said, "Preacher Heiniebottom, or what have you here—"

The old man grimaced. "Why, what—?"

"Just hear me out," Jujubee said. He had his big hand up in a "halt" gesture.

Worthy Waddell was laughing, his head lolling around, and to my shame I admit that I joined him at it; and when Fanny elbowed me I ended up trying to fake-cough my way out of it, thinking that the Reverend William Archibald Spooner himself could never have transposed syllables to worse effect.

Fanny said, "*Higginbotham*, Jujubee."

Jujubee said, "Yes, Miss Franny, I know you're with me on this. Hay-looyah. A-man? Reverend Heiniebottom, incline your ear, if you will and if you have the ears to hear, the word of the Lord: 'O Lord, thy tender mercies and thy lovingkindnesses; for they have been ever of old. Remember not the sins of my youth, nor my transgressions: according to thy mercy remember thou me for thy goodness' sake,

O Lord. Good and upright is the Lord: therefore, will he teach sinners in the way.' Psalm twenty-five and verse six through eight."

Reverend Clarence P.R. Higginbotham pointed the remote control at the TV as though it were a searchlight, muted Mr. Ed. He said, "What all do you know, if all it told. And being colored or half-colored at least yourself, for all I know you're kin to Erastus Plummer?"

"We're all kin," Jujubee said. "You know how it is; cousins, or what have you."

Reverend Higginbotham nodded, said, "Figures." He folded his big hands in his lap.

Jujubee said, "Time to let it all come out. The Lord's got work to do through you, and he can't very well get to it till you come clean."

Reverend Higginbotham said, "Look here: I'm eighty and two years old."

Jujubee said, "That's young yet. Why I bet old Methuselah didn't even have a beard at that age. I had a uncle lived to see one o' six. But in your own case I imagine time's is of the incense, so you'd better hop to, fellow. Time's wasting. And you've been a-settin' all up in here how many years in your stri-ped terry cloth puh-jammas playing bingo on Friday nights and looking at TV when the whole place could've been saved for Jesus long ago? You can walk and you can talk every whit as good as you did when your were half this ancient, and the fire is shut up in your bones to where it's go'n sizzle you like a egg in a greasy iron skillet. 'Lift up your eyes, and look on the fields; for they are white already to harvest.' John four and verse thirty-five, b. The field here at the Cypress Shade Nurses Home is white unto harvest. And here you set."

The old man said, "I lost my calling many a year ago."

Jujubee said, "We all of us did. But Lord Jesus sent me here to help you find it. Lord's got a A-P-B out on you and we're the bounty hunting posse come to bring you to mercy. You'll get it dead or alive. Take your pick."

Reverend Higginbotham set that jaw, said, "Boy, I told you I don't have the calling anymore."

Jujubee said, "You have the calling, all right. It's not the calling you've lost. No sir, if you've lost anything, it's not the calling." He lowered his voice, said, "It's the *gonabs*."

The old man flinched as if a bee had stung him on the rump. He said, "The *what?*"

Jujubee said, "You heard what I said. I'm not fixin' to stand here and cowtail around the bush with you. So don't pull that old 'I can't hear you' number on me, Preacher. Nothing's wrong with your ears. When we first walked in your door you were able enough to hear what Mr. Ed was whispering to Wilbur Post, so as Miz Post wouldn't catch a word of it, and you heard Ed like as if he was in the room with you, heard it well enough to make you giggle and shiver and all like that with the sound on the TV set turned way down so you wouldn't wake up your bunkmate Mason Brubaker who's taking him a little shut-eye nap on bed number one yonder at this very hour. No sir, you heard full good and well what I said about 'nabs, just like you hear the Lord a-calling. You might try pulling that old 'I'm death' number on the Lord, but he's not buyin' it, and it's not gonna work with me, either. I think you heard it, all right, what I said about"—he lowered his voice to a whisper—"'*nabs*, co-*jo-nahs*, whatever you want to call them."

Reverend Higginbotham cocked his head, the moist pink tip of his tongue poking just through his red lips.

Jujubee said, "And don't you ask me again because I won't repeat it on account of Miss Franny not needing to hear such foul talk and this boy Worthy Waddell within earshot, and all like that."

This was the first time I had seen the side of Jujubee Forthright that was meant not so much to comfort as to exhort, to admonish. I wondered then if that "Freudian slip" of the tongue—calling him Reverend Heiniebottom—were really not, after all, just Jujubee's subconscious breaking through and telling it like it was, what he really thought of Reverend Higginbotham in this insolent state of discouragement.

Jujubee said, "The volume is fine, and your ears is fine … . So, let's get it all out and get you suited up with the whole armor of God, or what have you here, or maybe at least that brown Sears-sucker suit hanging up there in the chifforobe from your preaching days before you had that thing come up with colored Erastus Plummer."

That Churchillian jaw was set. Reverend Higginbotham said, "I can't be forgive' that and all the evil went down with Erastus Plummer."

Jujubee's head was arcing hither and yon now like the caged black bear I once saw in a bear zoo in western Carolina, pacing in place, wagging his head, wearing the claws off his feet and fur off his rump where he'd brush against the wall on each pass—as Jujubee might put it—roarin' to go. He said, "You're fixin' to be."

Jujubee said, "Miss Franny, as soon as we get the reverend out of the way a bit, would you be so kind as to fetch that suit in question, and we'll stand this man of God's very own cloth back up on to his feet shod with the 'preparation of the gospel of peace.' Ephesians six and verse fifteen."

I have no doubt that Reverend Higginbotham knew exactly what Jujubee meant—even though I didn't, even though I wouldn't have known colored Erastus Plummer if he had walked in in a red hat and coattails at that very moment, even though the term *gonabs* was one neither of us was quite familiar with, but for the context. Jujubee helped the old man to his feet and called us to gather around the foot of the preacher's bed.

"You, too, Worthy Waddell." he said. "Shift that Pride Jazzy eleven o'three motorized chair up into overdrive and hightail it on over here. Dewey, please wake up Mason Brubaker who's laid up there in bed number one, such as it is. A calling is a right serious thing, and we're gonna lay on hands and pray for the Reverend Clarence P.R. Heiniebottom here in a little bit."

Jujubee turned to Reverend Higginbotham. "You'll need your Bible. A preacher of your stock needs a brown Searssucker suit and a big old black preacher's Bible. If you held fast your suit but threw out your Bible in all your long season of nonsense after Erastus Plummer, the Gideons'll help us out."

Reverend Higginbotham said, "It's in the drawer of my nightstand—the bottom drawer." He grasped the top button of his flannel pajama top and cinched it together under his chin, lowered his voice to a tone suited to confession and said: "I can't recall really, and I hate to admit it, but there might—*might*—be a book, a *stag* book, in there with nudies in it and such. My nephew brought it in one time to lift my spirits. I did kind of lose my way."

Jujubee said, "We all have."

Fanny pulled Reverend Higginbotham's brown seersucker suit out of the open-front chifforobe, removed it from the hanger, and smoothed the slacks and arms of the coat. A pair of oxblood wingtips were set toes-out on the floor of the chifforobe, and I wondered how they would fit in with shoeing Reverend Higginbotham's feet with the "preparation of the gospel of peace," according to Ephesians 6:15, in the ceremony about to commence.

Jujubee said, "You can step into your little boys' room there, Preacher, and put your suit on, get gussied up, or what have you here."

The room smelled strong of mothballs and peppermint, and I couldn't help but think of my own father—the Reverend *David* Umberton Hazelriggs II—as I approached the sleeping form of Mason Brubaker, lying as still as dead on bed number one. And though for the life of me I couldn't imagine my father's dignified life devolving into a dusky room in the Cypress Shade Nursing Home, and though I wouldn't have wished it on him, I couldn't help but think it might have been good … in some way … good for both of us if it had.

I think Jujubee Forthright would agree with that statement, and I wouldn't even have to explain to him *why*.

At any rate, it was good for Mason Brubaker, I think, because when I gently jiggled his bony shoulder and said, "Sir, would you like to wake up?" he came awake with a smile, said, "Might as well, can't dance."

I said, "How's that?"

Mason Brubaker looked me dead in the eye and said, "I thought you'd never get here."

"Neither did I," I said, taking a note from Jujubee Forthright's notebook. I recalled Jujubee's words about Otis Winters when he said, "his heart's so broke it'll take half of eternity for Jesus to put it all back together. And you come along and say, 'I myself ain't much, but I got a friend who's something else; come, go with us,' and he drops everything on a moment's notice and he's suddenly wondering why it took you so long to get there."

I took old Mason Brubaker by the hand and helped him sit up in his bed. And again I said, "Neither did I, Mr. Brubaker. But I'm sure glad I did."

I meant it and *it* meant something to Mason Brubaker because his eyes were red-rimmed and damp, and when he closed them gently he said, "Thank you, Jesus."

And I, too, said, "Thank you, Jesus," and I meant that, too.

I guess it was in that moment that Jesus saved me. You see (bear with me for a moment), Cynicism with a capital C is what we students (or maybe only we teachers) of philosophy call a "philosophy of consolation," which is a pedantic way of saying that its purpose is to console people when all is lost, when their world has fallen apart—say, when the Greek City States are in ruin from striving within and warring without, when the streets of Athens flow knee deep with blood and guts and the Golden Age of Alexander the Great has bubbled green with corrosion. It is then, presumably, that the Cynic shows up bearing the good news, the

Gospel of Diogenes: *Grieve not, nothing matters—and you're grieving only because you thought it did.*

For the first time since I left Duke as Diogenes Umberton Hazelriggs, Ph.D. thirty-some odd years before, not only did I find no consolation whatsoever in that gospel—which was no good news at all—but I actually saw it for the pathetic counterfeit of the Gospel I had absorbed Sunday by Sunday, even if it was rather stilted, from my father's own pulpit. Though at first blush they were different, my father's gospel with its intellectual Jesus and Jujubee Forthright's gospel with its Jesus who was ... what? Surprising. Disturbing. Real. Well, they were saying the same thing, in different ways.

Against the faux consolation that nothing matters Jesus seemed to be saying that everything—absolutely *everything*, no matter how trivial—matters, and not only matters, but matters eternally. Take Ricky's mother—commemorating the anniversary of her dear young son's death with a fifth of Southern Comfort and an everflow of bitter tears. Take Otis Winters—a man in his mid-forties who had lost both his wife and his paper route in the course of a sad week and had nothing more edifying to do on a sunny afternoon than drop his lunch money on a stag book and a malt liquor tallboy. Take Miss Evangelina Greevy—poor old woman laid up for the duration in a dusky room in a Georgia backwater who had made it well into her seventies without ever once hearing that she was loved, that anyone on earth thought she was beautiful. Take Clarence P.R. Higginbotham—an octogenarian preacher who feared he had sinned his way out of reach of the very Lord who had called him to ministry three score and ten years ago over some incident involving a colored man named Erastus Plummer. Take old Mason Brubaker—take *me*: just waiting for somebody to come wake us up.

To come wake us up. I thought back to that long-ago Easter morning of my sixteenth year when I broke my father's heart. I was disappointed, I said, that a man of his intelligence could be so, so naïve as to believe that dead Jesus woke back up. The evidence I saw, as the Apostle John might put it, with my own eyes and heard with my own ears in the calling of Jujubee Forthright was proof enough for me—count me among the naïve, if you will—that Jesus had, indeed, been woken back up. It was a tender moment, and I remember Jujubee's take on the resurrection, which he shared as we rolled down I–26 out of Irma, South Carolina, after tending to Ricky's mother. He said, "See, some people focus on the power and the glory of the resurrection; I always get thinking about how tender it was. I mean, there he was, laid up in there dead in that tomb, and his father loved him and so he comes in and looks at him in there in the cold and the dark and all alone with rock hard cold stone all around him. And his heart is breaking, and he says, 'Rise and shine, my son, my dear son.'"

Fanny was fond of quoting Oscar Wilde's definition of a cynic to me: one who knows the cost of everything and the value of nothing. How different was this Jesus I was coming to know as he worked wonders—not random but deliberate—through Jujubee Forthright; this Jesus for whom *everything* mattered. This Jesus who knew both the cost and the value of everything.

Pardon me that digression, please. It's just that this was a really big moment for me, as it was for Reverend Clarence P.R. Higginbotham and the Cypress Shade Nursing Home on the low-country outskirts of Brunswick, Georgia.

Jujubee was riffling through the bottom drawer of Reverend Higginbotham's nightstand so as to excavate the big black preacher's Bible from whatever other less sacred literature might be in there with it. He was on his knees and had his head back so his eyes were on the ceiling and, from the back, the way his head was bobbing and his hands were weaving he might have been a jumbo Ray Charles with a big afro jamming on the last verse of "Ain't Misbehavin'." The voice, though, when he got back on his feet and held the Bible out in front of him, was all Satchmo.

He called us all into a circle at the foot of Reverend Higginbotham's unmade bed, and we waited for the preacher to emerge from the bathroom in his brown seersucker suit.

Jujubee said, "We'll need for you to get down on your knees here in the mist of us, if you will, so we can nip this in the butt before it goes any further than it already has."

Reverend Higginbotham said, "It might be the death of me if I do. My knees is all eat up with arthritis."

Jujubee placed his palm on the preacher's shoulder and pressed down gently, said, "Might be you're just a little out of practice hitting those knees of your'n and they're not so much eat up with arthur-itis as with a little bit of rust, or what have you here. Anywho, we'll stand you back up onto your feet when we're through if it takes a crowbar and a warn winch to do it. Dewey Hazelriggs here is a doctor and he'll see to you if need be." And then, as if any of the rest of the proceedings since we had walked in on Reverend Higginbotham in the middle of Mr. Ed were, Jujubee added: "This part's not a option in this case. See, this right here is all about gettin' a man back down on his knees so as we can set him right back up on his feet."

When the preacher, after making a rather big to-do of it, complete with a lot of moaning and groaning, managed finally to get down on all fours (and I couldn't help but think that Worthy Waddell would have had an easier time of it), Jujubee bade us all hearken unto his voice, let not our hearts be troubled, and gather round to lay hands on Reverend Higginbotham. Fanny and I helped old Mason Brubaker, who was wearing a long-john sleep suit, down from the edge of his bed and around Worthy Waddell's wheelchair. We eased him down onto the floor and propped him up against the TV stand. Worthy had backed his chair up in the space between the beds. He mashed a few buttons and lowered his seat so the preacher was in reach. Fanny and I knelt down, I on one knee, she on two, and laid our right hands on the preacher's meaty shoulders. It was a tight fit there, with the five of us huddled into a space that was perhaps just big enough to accommodate Jujubee Forthright.

And in that small space a big moment got bigger. Maybe it was the sacredness of the moment, or a moving of the Spirit, maybe; or maybe it was the way my sweet Fanny looked with the sunrays gilding her hair like a halo and the lingering scent of Peachy King's freestone peaches on all of us; or maybe it was something altogether less spiritual. Whatever it was, I made up my mind just then that I would do what I had wanted to do for the better part of forty-five years: I would ask Francine Mae "Fanny" Fuller to marry me, to come:

> "Grow old along with me!
> The best is yet to be,
> The last of life, for which the first was made:
> Our times are in His hand
> Who saith 'A whole I planned,
> Youth shows but half; trust God:
> see all, nor be afraid!'"

I would do it, I would, before the week was out. And in that state my head was already bowed and my eyes already closed when Jujubee, who had himself gone down on one knee, said: "Every head bowed, every eye closed. Dear Lord Jesus, we come before you this day, or what have you here, in the name of the Father and of the Son and of the Holy Ghost, to pray for our dear brother who's lost his way, such as it is."

Mason Brubaker was clapping his hands. He said, "Amen, praise be, glory to Jesus."

"Yes," Jujubee said. "We'll get to you in a minute, dear brother. Lord Jesus, though Reverend Heiniebottom might have got it in his head he was done with you, come to find out you weren't quite done with him. Sittin' all up in here, Lord, eating chocolate candies and passing time looking at Mr. Ed on the TV set all the livelong day is not what you've called him to do. There's a hundred old folk all up in here in the highways and byways of this here Cypress Shade conva-licentious home, or whatever they call it. We trust you know, Lord, for thy holy word teacheth: 'He heweth him down cedars, and taketh the cypress and the oak, which he strengtheneth for himself among the trees of the forest: he planteth an ash, and the rain doth nourish it.' Isaiah forty-four and verse fourteen.'"

"My knees is about shot," Reverend Higginbotham groaned. "Tarry not."

Immediately upon which Jujubee gave chapter and verse, "'For unto you it is given in the behalf of Christ, not only to believe on him, but also to *suffer* for his sake.' Philippians chapter one and verse number twenty-nine."

"Praise be," Mason Brubaker said. "Amen."

"Now, Lord, who knoweth Erastus Plummer, another dear child of your'n, whether he be quick or dead we knoweth not, but thou knoweth all things. Bless him here or there, or what have you here. Now is the time, dear Jesus, for repentance and restoration ... . "

Jujubee went on and on in that vein for a good long time. In fact, I could feel for old Reverend Higginbotham because I had to do some slow-motion *kazatskis* as they do in Russian kick dances to keep both my own legs from falling asleep. And when at last Jujubee brought the ceremony to a close by sounding the final Amen, Mason Brubaker was fast asleep with his hoary head slack as one lowered from the gallows. As Jujubee, Fanny, and I helped Reverend Clarence P.R. Higginbotham up onto his feet, I saw that the old preacher's face was wet with sweat and with tears, whether on account of repentance or the pain in his knees I would be hard-pressed to say. Probably both, I think.

But the really amazing thing is this: It worked! Now I must tell you the plain truth. I did not know much about the Day of Pentecost at that time. It was not one of my father's favorite sermon topics, for if you were to search the ranks of

Christendom for *the Anti-Pentecostal* (or, perhaps, the Anti-Charismatic) you would have to look no further than David Umberton Hazelriggs II, my father. It's not that the Spirit didn't move my father nor give him utterance, it's just that the cadence was measured, restrained. Squelched.

But that afternoon in Room 217 of the Cypress Shade Nursing Home somewhere on the coastal plains of Georgia the Day of Pentecost fully came. You see, after a few more stops along our way, as we were making our way back up the hall toward the nurses' station, Reverend Clarence P.R. Higginbotham, clad in his brown seersucker suit, feet shod in those shiny brown wingtips, was pushing Jesus's beloved Ms. Evangelina Greevy toward the dining room. On his way he stopped and spoke to an old man with the face of Geronimo who was hunched deep down in a wheelchair swaddled in a zigzag rainbow-striped serape.

Reverend Higginbotham offered him a few Hershey's kisses from the bag held under his left arm, and over the sweet hum of Worthy Waddell's Pride Jazzy 1103, I heard him say, "*Mi amigo, Jesús Cristo murió en la cruz para ahorrarle de sus pecados. Romans diez, verso nueve, dice 'si confiesas con tu boca que Jesús es el Señor, y crees en tu corazón que Dios lo levantó de entre los muertos, serás salvo.*"

I found it hard to believe that Reverend Higginbotham had ever studied Spanish. I hadn't, though I had enough Latin to know he was saying something about Jesus's dying on the cross for us. And truth to tell, I would have taken the old man who looked like Geronimo to be a native American, perhaps a Creek or a Cherokee, though maybe he was a Mesoamerican of Aztec descent, which would explain why he was fluent in Spanish (if in fact he knew a word of it), though I didn't doubt for a moment that the Spirit was seeing to it that the Gospel Reverend Higginbotham was sharing was not lost on him. I looked at Jujubee and when his head bobbed left on its paces, he winked at me. And, borrowing a line from Mason Brubaker, I said, "Praise be."

 The Rising Tide

As if Reverend Clarence P.R. Higginbotham's speaking in tongues to the old man in the poncho was not evidence enough of the Spirit's moving in our midst that afternoon, there came a rushing mighty Pentecostal wind that nearly blew all of us save Jujubee away as we made our way across the Cypress Shade parking lot to the van. Worthy Waddell's chair even did a 360 and would have toppled headlong off the curb if Fanny and I hadn't gotten there in time to get it turned toward the grass.

"Ilana," I said, as I bent down and picked up my eight-quarters cap, which a swirling gust had blown off my head.

"Holy Ghost," Jujubee said.

I was speaking of the tropical storm, Ilana, which for all I knew had been upgraded to a hurricane by then. A news buff for all time, I confess I had been so preoccupied in the calling of Jujubee Forthright since my lakeside encounter with the gnome in Fanny's backyard just one week before that I hadn't paid much attention to the news. When last I had heard of Ilana as I was on my way to Jujubee's place the previous morning, the eye of the storm was projected to make landfall somewhere between Jacksonville and Daytona Beach, or 100 miles or so south of the Altar Isles and Little Chancel Island.

Once we had gotten Worthy's chair up into the van and got him situated, Jujubee pulled around to the rear of the Cypress Shade and expertly backed the peach trailer up to the service entrance. I helped him unhitch the trailer and roll it onto the rusted blue scissor lift all the way back. Jujubee mashed a few buttons, then pulled a lever, and the lift raised up till it was level with the floor of the loading bay.

The door beside the loading bay opened, and a heavy-set black woman in a hairnet with a cigarette in one hand and a lighter in the other emerged from the darkness.

Jujubee said, "Sister, I say unto you, the Lord hath sent these peaches to you, in order that you might take and prepare a peach festival all up in there in honor of Miz Evangelina Gravy. I know it's late in the season for a peach festival, but her time draweth nigh."

The woman squinted and fixed her eyes on the side of the old trailer. "These be from Billy Bob Greevy. Gone called himself Billy Bob King. Peachy King."

Jujubee said, "Sister, yes. She's gone and wrote him off like a bad debt, but he wanted her to have these for the real nice peach festival Lord's called you to put on here … ."

The woman had the unlit cigarette between her lips, and it waved around as she said, "Just like when they was kids."

Jujubee said, "Bless your heart."

Then we left. A few miles down the road Fanny had me turn on the radio, and we heard that Ilana had indeed become a hurricane, a category four, and the ninth named storm system of the season, and she was bearing down on Ponte Vedra Beach just south of Jacksonville, Florida. Within the hour the leading edge of the eye wall would hit land, with sustained winds approaching 140 miles an hour. It was just after four p.m., and we were heading south on U.S. 17 toward the John Wesley Causeway that would take us back out to Little Chancel Island. The sunny day had taken a hard turn for the dark. Across the median from us, countless cars, their headbeams dim in the gray mist, crept slowly up the two northbound lanes, the evacuation route out of Florida.

Fanny said, "Ilana is driving them out by the droves, looks like."

Jujubee said, "Ask me, the Holy Ghost is calling them out."

Worthy Waddell said, "What do you reckon is the Holy Ghost calling them out to, pray tell, Jujubee Fluoride?"

Jujubee said, "Only thing he ever calls 'em out to, Worthy Waddell. glancing in the rearview mirror at the boy as he did. Calls 'em to the Lord Jesus, to the comfort of the Lord, if you will. Anywho, he's the one called *Comforter*."

Worthy Waddell said, "Aunt Fanny and drunken Davy Dyson's wife that ran off with the lunchlady that time give me a comforter for Christmas one time saying it was from Santa Claus when I seen the very one down at the Big Lots and was with drunken Davy Dyson's wife when she bought to keep my legs warm and it had on it these big—you want to know what it had on it, Jujubee Fluoride and Mister Dewey Häagen-Dazs? Guess."

"A flock of dinosaur?" Jujubee guessed.

Worthy Waddell laughed, and Fanny said, "Who ever heard of a *flock* of dinosaurs, Jujubee?"

"I know I haven't," Jujubee said. "Maybe they went about in droves, or what have you here, as you called all these motor vehicles called out from Florida by none other than the Holy Ghost."

"More like it," Fanny said. "Or try herds on for size." I felt her hand on my shoulder, her left hand, the very hand on which I would slip mother's fine diamond ring if Francine Mae Fuller would be so inclined to say to me, a cynic of a thousand No's, yes—yes, she would marry me for all time, or at least for the last of life for which the first was made.

I might have slipped out of my bucket seat and dipped to one knee right then and there on the floorboard of the rumbling V-8 van cruising down U.S. 17, but when I turned to look at her, she said, "Well, what say you, Mister Dewey Häagen-Dazs? What do you think was on the comforter that Judy Dyson gave Mister Worthy here last Christmas? And, for the record, Davy—not Judy—was the one who went off to Reno, Nevada, with Betty Sharpe, the lunch lady at Medlyn Middle School. And anyway, that's gossip, and Davy's back with Judy, and he's been off liquor for three-and-a-half months now, and Betty Sharpe is back with her husband, Subs, and they're all attending Sunday School, Sunday service, and Wednesday prayer meeting at Mount Moriah Baptist. And if the Lord has forgiven and forgotten, I suppose it's the least we can do."

Jujubee said, "People sin; forgive them. That's what the good book says anywho. But it sure is good to hear about Davy swearing off drink, Miss Franny, and boy I sure am proud Subs didn't kill the both of them with that sawed-off double-barrel rimfire Deringer he keeps under the seat of his truck. He would have been within his rights, according the flesh, such as it is. Preacher Carroll handled it all just right. Graceful as a butterfly that remembers when he was but a caterpillar his self."

Worthy Waddell said, "Daddy says Mount Moron Baptist Church is where all the literate folk in town goes to."

"Go to," Fanny corrected. "If you insist on ending a sentence with a preposition, Jujubee. And they most certainly do not, either. *Illiterate* is what he meant. If your Daddy had the sense he was whelped with he'd join the rest of us morons for Sunday service every once in a while. You'll not find nicer people or better music anywhere in Medlyn. Well, except for Jujubee and the Town and Country Band."

Jujubee said, "'Mount Moron'? I hadn't heard that one. Apostle Paul said, 'But God hath chosen the foolish things of the world to confound the wise.' One Corinthians Chapter one and verse twenty-seven. And I guess you can't find much more foolish things than morons."

Changing the subject, I said, "Race cars."

Worthy Waddell clapped his arms in big flailing strokes. "You're the man!"

No, I thought: Uncle Early Fuller was really the man; the real man.

All was quiet for a while, then Fanny said, "I hope Merlin and Wylynda take it easy in this stormy weather."

I remembered then that Jujubee had deployed them—and the Ford Country Club Wagon Team—to round up such as they could in Jacksonville. To the south and east the sky was a dangerous mass of gray clots and, as I let my head fall back against the headrest and gripped the armrests, I thought that, whatever else it was—an act of nature or an act of God in the moving of the Holy Spirit—it was dangerous.

The wind was gusting in great blasts that made the palm trees list and the van pull hard right, so Jujubee, who was struggling with the wheel, at last slowed us down a bit and pulled into the right-hand lane.

Worthy Waddell said, "Look at that." He was speaking of the traffic signal lights, which were swaying wildly, nearly doing a loop-the-loop and pulling the slack power lines taut.

Jujubee said, "Let not your heart be troubled, neither let it be afraid. Now let's see if we can't help this poor fellow out."

Jujubee signaled, though there was not a car behind us as far as I could see in my sideview mirror, and pulled the van off onto the shoulder behind an old Ford pickup truck with a Tennessee license plate and its hazard lights blinking. He shifted the van into Park and said, "You don't see too many nineteen hundred and sixty-four Econoline pickup trucks, or what have you here, on the road much anymore. No sir you don't."

He leaned forward and reached under the seat and pulled out a little bag, and as he opened the door, Jujubee said, "Miss Franny, you and Mister Worthy Waddell just stay put here in the van while Dewey Hazelriggs and I render to these folk such aid as we're able."

I was happy to have what little shield the van afforded against the sustained gust of wind pressing in on us from the Atlantic. Jujubee was not moved, or so it seemed to me, by the wind in the least. Only the legs of his overalls fluttered a little just above his black high-tops.

As we approached, I saw that the bed of the truck was filled with building materials—a thick stack of plywood and pressboard sheets, bundles of two-by-fours and two-by-eights in eight-foot lengths, and various and sundry tools—all battened down with a tarp that had blown loose of its moorings on the driver side and was waving around in the air like a mad magician's kerchief. A tall, dark-haired man in his early forties was standing at the cab end of the truck bed. He was in only his shirtsleeves and was paring the end of a frayed rope with a pocket knife. The undulating muscles in his forearms betrayed his power. Here, I thought, was a man who worked with his hands, but when he turned to see us approaching from the van, his dark eyes and the hard set of his brow told me that wasn't the whole story. Here was a wise man, I thought, a gentle man.

Over the whir of the wind Jujubee said, "Friend, do you think that a length of bungee cord might help some against all this wind, or what have you here?" He held the bag, which presumably contained a length of bungee cord, out toward the man.

I was standing directly behind the truck, between the white raised letters O and R on the tailgate. Out of the corner of my right eye I saw some movement and realized that the tall dark man with well muscled forearms and wise gentle eyes had a traveling companion. The movement in question was on this wise: In one sweeping motion the door of the truck flew open and a short, rather heavyset woman with black curly hair—which was a little stringy—and horn-rimmed glasses had turned herself about so that she was facing the highway and had set down what I took to be the barrel of a shotgun concealed in a baby blue sweater on the side of the truck. She was aiming directly at Jujubee Forthright's chest.

"Freeze," she said, in an unmistakable Tennessee mountain twang, "or I'll be forced to have to shoot the life out of you. Benton Oliver O'Casey, I told you we were bound to get looted out here in a monsoon. That's when they come out."

Now, to be honest, from where I stood it did look like there might be a gun in the brown paper sack Jujubee was holding out toward the man. First Miss Greevy, now this woman with a sawed-off shotgun. I half wondered if it was a double-barrel rimfire Deringer like the one Jujubee said Subs kept stashed under the seat of his truck. It was Jujubee Forthright's day to be in the crosshairs, and I wondered if he had ever been threatened with a gun twice in one day by two different women. For some reason, I was not the least bit scared, though I'm sure I would have been if the woman with the gun trained on Jujubee had been traveling with any other man on earth than the one with those kind wise eyes.

The man said, "Calm yourself now, Es'. No use you goin' and gettin' yourself all worked up. This man stopped to help us out. Stand down. Lay down your arms and put that thing, uh, your *gun* away."

Jujubee spoke up to be heard over the wall of wind. "Yes, dear sister, there's no need for taking up arms, or what have you here, right? I come in the name of the Lord Jesus. So let's us see about beating our shotguns into plowshares and make hay or a little peace whil'st it is still the day."

"I don't know about all that," the woman said. "Good book says many will come in the last times claiming to be Jesus."

Jujubee said, "Well, now I'm no Jesus. But anywho the Scripture does say, 'For many shall come in my name, saying, I am Christ; and shall deceive many.' Matthew twenty-four and verse number five. Anywho, I'd say you're wise to be wary as a serpent but harmless as a dove."

The man, Benton Oliver O'Casey, took the bag from Jujubee and pulled the bungee cord out of it. He held it up for the woman to see. He turned to Jujubee, said, "I'll be happy to pay you a fair price for this."

Jujubee said, "Just not getting my big ol' business shot off will probably be payment enough—and we'll call ourselves all square."

The man shrugged a little, and a little smile came over not just his mouth but his whole face—but was a little smile nonetheless.

The woman said, "Oh, for crying out loud." She yanked the blue sweater off of the shotgun, which turned out to be a tire tool, and draped the sweater over her shoulders, buttoning it against the wind. She tossed the tire tool back into the cab, and walked back toward me. "Must be the change," she said. "I get worked up over anything these days, or over nothing at all."

Jujubee said, "Some say change is good."

"I'm the living proof it's not," she said, and she smiled. She was wearing a faded yellow sundress with big orange blossoms, perhaps zinnias, on it. A gold oval photo miniature photo frame hung on a chain around her neck. In the gloaming I could just make out a picture of a little boy with the face of an angel on it, a face that put me in mind of Worthy Waddell, and I glanced back toward the van and saw Worthy sitting there only in silhouette.

Then my eye fixed on the face of the boy on the locket, and I wondered if perhaps he was there in the cab of the truck, maybe fast asleep on the front seat like Jesus in the hull of the boat tossed about on the stormy sea. It felt as though he were, though I saw no evidence of it.

Jujubee said, "I am Jimmy Jack B. Forthright, but most folk calls me Jujubee for short, so feel free, if you will."

The man said, "Benton O'Casey. Everybody calls me Olie, but I'll answer to about anything. This lovely woman here is my wife, Annie Oakley. We call her Esther."

Jujubee said, "Miz O'Casey, ma'am. I'm pleased."

I tipped my head, said, "I am Dewey. Dewey Hazelriggs."

Jujubee said, "Dewey is a fine man."

We made a little small talk there on the windswept shoulder of Highway 17. I looked back toward the van to check on Fanny and she, ever graceful dear, made a calming gesture and, if my lip-reading served, said, "Take your time. We're fine." Or something to that effect. She really believed in Jujubee Forthright, and I could only hope that she would believe in me, too.

Esther was telling us that the Lord had been good to the O'Caseys that year, so good that, more or less on a whim, Olie had gone to the lumberyard in Sevierville and bought some materials and they headed out to help the poor folks in Florida board up their houses ahead of the storm, but then, she said, Olie, bless his heart, took a left when he should have taken a right somewhere in Georgia and she said there were three signs that told her they were headed in the wrong direction: The first was a big orange-and-yellow sign that said "You're a TOP Banana with Pedro" advertising a place called the South of the Border Motel, the second said "You're only 50 Miles from South of the Border," and the third, which finally convinced Olie that she was right and he needed to turn the truck around, said: *Welcome to North Carolina.*

She said, "Now I imagine we'll just have to be here to help them to build back their houses and such after Ivana's blowed them all to bits."

Then Jujubee's right eye did its sweet papa dip and he looked Olie O'Casey in the eye and said, "*O'Casey*, you say? What part of Tennessee are you good folk from?"

Olie O'Casey said, "Town called Tynbee. Little bitty place way up in the mountains, in Avery County, not too far from Pigeon Forge."

Jujubee said, "You wouldn't by any chance be kin to a fellow by the name of Hey*weird* O'Casey, would you?"

"Why, yes," Olie said. "Heyward O'Casey is my brother."

Esther O'Casey didn't so much clap her hands as slap them together. "Well, I declare. Mother was right—it really is a small world after all. How on God's green earth is it that you are knowin' Hey' O'Ca'y?"

"Oh, well," Jujubee said. He cleared his throat. "Let's just say we shared a truck route way back in the day. Years and years ago now."

I recalled the autobiographical account Jujubee rendered to Dr. J.C. Wiley, pastor of the Fundamental First Church, as we sat in his office—in the *laigh cellar* of the church, as Alisdair Knox put it—at the Mount Sinai Fundamental Bible College & Institute of Theology. That admissions interview, too, seemed like it had occurred *years and years ago*, though in fact it had been less than three days before. Jujubee had mentioned a certain incident from his truck-driving days that went down just outside Lenoir City, Tennessee, and involved five state troopers and some blonde-haired doll named Edna Mae Shilgroth ... with the face of Barbie and the body of Kewpie. I couldn't help but wonder, seeing how vague Jujubee suddenly was, whether old Heyward O'Casey had been riding shotgun in the cab of the Jujubee's eighteen-wheeler on that fateful day and maybe he thought he'd just let that bygone be gone.

All was silent for a long moment then Jujubee said, "Anywho. Well ... how is old Heyward getting along these days?"

Esther O'Casey said, "God be praised, he's been dry now going on, what is it, Olie? Thirteen months."

Jujubee said, "Jesus, we thank you. Yes, Lord. You tell old Heyweird that Jesus has been good to Jujubee Forthright, too, and if he ever needs a job, ever needs anything, to just get on the horn and give me a call. I'm not too far off from Tiny-bee, down in Medlyn, Georgia, or what have you, and the good Lord and me are going to need some good men like him to help us out in our work."

No sooner had he said it than Esther O'Casey was heading back to the cab of the truck to fetch some paper. She was back a moment later with a pencil and notebook. She took down Jujubee's name and phone number to give to

Heyward, and when Jujubee handed it to her his blinking eyes fixed, one after the other, on the photo of the little angel on her necklace.

"Suffer not the little children," he said. His breath caught. "What a beautiful little angel that is."

"He's with Jesus," Esther O'Casey announced.

"Kind of makes you homesick, sister," he said. "But it looks like that's about the only place he'd be at home—with Jesus." Then he rolled his head back and raised his hands slowly, palms up. "Lord Jesus says to tell you that ... to tell you that your little *Rind* is doing just fine, dancing with a great many playmates in the deep green grass in the Father's backyard."

All I can say is that, in that moment, the glory of the Lord shone all about that lonesome stretch of U.S. 17. The gray firmament opened just over us and the rays of the sun sprayed down like liquid gold and—for a moment, just a moment—the wind died down and Jujubee's blue denim Dickies overalls, orange T-shirt, and black high-top Chucks became, as John on Patmos might have put it, white as snow. I didn't know then and I don't know now whether there was a perfectly plausible meteorological explanation for the sunburst or whatever it was (and even if there is it wouldn't detract from what it meant to me and the others there in the least), but what I do know is this: I have never in my three-score-and-some odd years seen, heard, or felt anything at all to which I can liken this Miracle on Highway 17.

As we walked back to the car, I said, "Who is Rind, Jujubee?" and his bobbing head twitched as though he were a pitcher looking off a slider when he said, "Lord knows."

Fanny Fuller and Worthy Waddell saw it all right—the roadside transfiguration. When we got back into the van, Jujubee and I, after bidding godspeed and farewell to Olie and Esther O'Casey (she was sobbing, the dear woman, saying "Thank you, dear sweet Jesus" over and over and over),

Fanny said, "For a minute there I think Heaven—not just the heavens with a small h—opened up on us. What in the world was going on out there?"

I said, "Lord knows," and Jujubee said: "It is as you said."

And we left it at that and rode the rest of the twelve miles back to the Club Croquet on the north end of Little Chancel Island in silence not even broken by the AM radio weather report.

* * *

As Jujubee pulled the van into the parking lot of the Club Croquet and wedged us in a tight spot between a VW Beetle and the GMC Box Truck with the dayglo mural, he prayed, "'Many, O Lord my God, are thy wonderful works which thou hast done, and thy thoughts which are to usward: they cannot be reckoned up in order unto thee: if I would declare and speak of them, they are more than can be numbered.' Psalm forty and verse number five."

"Amen," I said, as I surveyed what I can only describe as the sequel to the Cecil B. DeMille production I had come across when I showed up at Jujubee's place the day before. The large roadside marquee of the Club Croquet was dazzling white against the stormy gray day, and up in lights there it was: Merlin Monroe had arranged to have the hotel announce our assembly with the very words Jujubee had painted on the side of the box truck:

Welcome

Come One, Come All<br>
The SonRise Auction / The Alter (Isles) Call<br>
J.J.B. Forth right, Dealer<br>
Going once ... going twice ... going 70 times 7<br>
No sin too big, no life too wore, tore,<br>
rusted or busted<br>
Salvation to the lowest bidder

Since we had, after all, rented every available room in the place, which was a lot of rooms considering the no-shows and cancellations occasioned by the storm, and paid for them all in cash, I'm sure it didn't take a lot of arm-twisting to get the marquee customized for us, but "wonderful works" did the scene justice, all the same, the Psalmist surely would have agreed. The wind was pummeling the coast now as the outer bands of Ilana delivered a big looping haymaker right to Little Chancel Island. But there was Otis Winters with a road flare burning in each hand directing traffic. His legs were wide-set against the wind as he guided a red AEC Routemaster double-decker bus around the cobblestone circular drive that led to the Club Croquet's grand entrance and into the drive-under terrace where it would be less likely to topple over.

Speaking of toppling over, Jujubee appeared to do just that. He had walked around to the passenger side of the van, waddling Sumo-style almost, and his knees buckled and he went down. With hands raised he said, "Praise be. Dewey Hazelriggs, I say unto you, fear not. You have not seen the likes of such, nay in all the land, such as it is."

"I most certainly haven't," I said, and before I was finished he was back on his feet and shambling toward Banana Fosters. I threw open the sliding side door of the van and helped Fanny out, then pulled a lever to lower Worthy Waddell's chair down to ground level.

Fanny's voice was strained. She said, "Did Jujubee slip or did he fall or did he go down in that way of his to praise and worship?"

I said, "I think he fell. Though it might have been all three."

Traffic was building and the wind was whistling and whirring, but above all the clamor, I could hear Jujubee proclaiming: "'Give unto the Lord the glory due unto his name: bring an offering, and come before him: worship the Lord in the beauty of holiness. First Chronicles … .'"

A horn honked, someone shouted "Yee haw," and we turned to see Merlin Monroe pulling into the parking lot with perhaps twenty-five people crammed into the fifteen-seat Ford Club Wagon. I waved at the van, at no one in particular, with a sort of presidential tambourine-like wave, and aptly strange, in a breathy voice reminiscent of Marilyn (not Merlin) Monroe, Worthy Waddell clapped his hands and rolled his head and said, "Happy birthday, Mr. President."

Fanny caught it, too, and said, "This is all getting a little strange even by Jujubee-Thing standards, but Worthy, that father of yours really ought to have his head examined." Then she waved at Merlin Monroe, too, and said, "Now they can't *all* be buckled in."

I tried to take in the scene—the whole surreal scene—to turn this great moving picture into a still so that I could—at some later time—return to it, not so much to make sense of it (the habit of the philosopher in me) as to see if in some way *it* could make sense of me. The irony was overwhelming. The Fundamentalists were at the Periwinkle just west of us, they with their Jesus who was so straightlaced, so well behaved, so whitewashed—a moralist above all. A turn of the head and I was looking at that Claymore Castle where the high-brow Reformed were, they with their Jesus so politically correct, with soft hands and weak knees and a spot of tea and a crumpet in place of the offensive Elements. The Two Medlyns. And here I was smack dab in the middle with Jujubee Forthright—rejected by both Medlyns and condemned as too bad and too uncouth by both of their Jesuses, with his Jesus so unlikely and inspired that—dare I say it?—he wasn't merely "Christian" if he was Christian at all, as we have come to understand the word.

I turned to Fanny and said, "Fanny, do you have any idea what this, this auction is going to be about?" Despite everything that I had been through with Jujubee since we first met after the Town & Country Auction a mere six days earlier I still wanted to find, for want of a better cliché, the method to his ministry—if not his madness. I knew by then well enough that they were one and the same. Things were happening, just happening, random things that seemed to lead us from one cul-de-sac to another only to open up into a road that couldn't have led anywhere else but where we were supposed to go.

When I asked her the question, half of me was hoping that Fanny would say it all made sense to her and the other half was hoping that she would say that she, too, was puzzled, as I puzzled as I. Either answer, any answer, would have satisfied me just then. Fanny didn't disappoint. I turned to face her and was a little surprised when she turned to face me. There we stood, eyes locked. Gene Tierney couldn't hold a candle for her to brush that bubble-cut Barbie brown hair by, I thought, as I lost myself in the deep of her dark eyes. She drew her right arm up and let her cheek come to rest on her palm, crossed her arms. She said, "David, I have no earthly idea."

"Hallelujah for that," I said.

She said, "If you thought I was fooling when I said you might as well throw away the map when you head out with Jujubee, well, I wasn't, see?"

I thought I saw her lip quiver as I stood there nodding my head, though it might have been a gale-force gust of wind, and I might have kissed her if Worthy Waddell hadn't popped a wheelie in his Pride Jazzy chair and I hadn't turned to look at him and seen the decal 3:16, Early Fuller's racing stripe. When I looked back at Fanny, she shrugged her shoulders a little, and I felt like Adam, suddenly exposed.

She said, "I guess we'll see, now won't we?" Then she curtsied and offered us her hands, which she flapped like graceful wings, and said, "Gentleman, the lady deserves a hand."

\* \* \*

The Club Croquet was a magnificent place overwrought with all the trappings of the Victorian Era. The promenade archway in which the registration desk was set was rather embarrassing with its exquisite scrollwork and high coffered ceilings. Nothing about it was understated. What a place, I thought, to host the Alter Call. And there stood Jujubee at the front desk in his overalls and orange T-shirt, chatting with a debonair young concierge in a white summer suit. To say it was a study in contrasts doesn't do it justice, but after all I'd seen that week it didn't seem as improbable as I would have predicted.

All those who had been called from points as far north as Beaufort, South Carolina, and as far south as Jacksonville, Florida, were milling about in that grand hall. And the hotel staff (and this *was* improbable) were treating them—*us*—as valued guests rather than as the ragtag mess of humanity we were. As you might imagine, those most likely to accept an invitation to attend an auction where salvation was sold to the lowest bidder (and where food and lodging were free) were down and out—though I for one was there, and some might say I was up and out. The guilty and ashamed, criminal, destitute, handicapped, mentally ill, spiritually poor. Needy all; proud none. I couldn't help but think how at home Jesus would have felt—did feel—there in the midst of such as he called his friends. I wondered how at home he would feel in the company of the Claymore Castle Presbyterians to the east and the Periwinkle Fundamentalists to the west.

I shared the insight with Jujubee, but he would have none of it. He shrugged and said, "Dewey Hazelriggs, I say unto you, 'Wherefore let him that thinketh he standeth take heed lest he fall.' One Corinthians ten and verse number twelve. It's blasphemious, or what have you, to carry on as if we knew the mind of Jesus. We say he's partial to the underdog. But who's to say who's the underdog? I know I can't. See, Lord Jesus has a whole 'nother perspective on us. Before it's over you'll see some suits among us. We always say Lord Jesus doesn't care if you're wearing a three-piece Sears-sucker suit, such as it is. But if that's the case then he doesn't care if you're wearing holey rags like that dear colored sister over there making time with Otis Winters."

"I see," I said. I didn't feel at all chastised, merely mentored. I said, "That's perfectly logical, Jujubee."

Jujubee said, "Logic alone will get us into a world of hurt. The Word says, 'But God hath chosen the foolish things of the world to confound the wise.' One Corinthians Chapter one and verse twenty-seven."

"How profound," I said, seeing wisdom rise like smoke from the ashes of all this nonsense.

He lowered his voice, said, "We need to see to it that poor sister gets some new duds."

"Indeed," I said.

Then Jujubee called the team together—the team being all the original members of the SonRise Caravan as it had crossed the Georgia line into South Carolina, including Otis Winters—in a reading nook of the promenade to lay out the Plan.

The SonRise Auction was going to take place at 7:00 p.m. in the best room in the house, the Croquet Club's Grand Ballroom. A great feast was going to be laid out for all to eat and drink as much as they pleased. The Teensie Weensie Band was going to make some music—gospel, bluegrass, country, whatever. Point, he said, was to have some entertainment. Then the auction proper was going to commence with Jujubee Forthright, dealer, presiding.

Merlin Monroe, who had been twisting the ends of his long gray moustache into French horns the whole time, said, "What's the merchandise we're going to put on the block, Juju'?"

Jujubee said, "Salvation."

No one said a word. We all waited, expecting Jujubee to elaborate. Because if anything at all, ever in the whole history of ideas, had demanded elaboration, I thought, it was this—this notion that salvation was going to be put on the auction block and sold to the lowest bidder. Jujubee just stood there. And we all tried avoiding eyelock with him as his head did its listing like a buoy.

Legend has it that Diogenes of Sinope, my namesake, the founder of Cynicism, would climb out of his tub and mill about the streets of Athens in broad daylight with a lantern in his hand in search of an honorable man—and never ever found one. How different this Jesus whom Jujubee Forthright proclaimed—this Jesus of Nazareth who went about looking not for the honorable man but for the dishonorable, the disgraceful, the sinner, the distraught, who needed a physician and knew it. The *honorable* Pharisees, the teachers of the law, did not "win" salvation *precisely* because they bid *too high*. They brought their best to him—their strict observance of the Law of Moses, their righteousness, such as it was.

I thought: *O Diogenes, my sometime hero—what has the Nazarene carpenter done to you? How he has made you seem a piffler and a trifler and cantankerous old fool. How dark a shadow his cross casts on your bathtub.*

"I think we understand," I said, as giddy as a schoolboy.

Fanny patted me on the shoulder, whispered, "Speak for yourself. I haven't the foggiest idea what this is all about."

Jujubee said, "Miss Franny, I say unto you: You do. You were the one—you and Mister Early Fuller—who got me thinking about all this way back when you took me in and put me up after Allis Blackwell went bad berserk."

Worthy Waddell said, "Daddy says one time Jujubee Fluoride took out after Allis Blackwell with a sling shot four-ten loaded with a silver bullet."

Jujubee said, "That was a bad thing that the good Lord kept from getting any worse. And it was a single-shot forty-five, but I reckon a sling shot four-ten would have served me well in that pinch." Then he looked at me and said, "Dewey Hazelriggs, you were going to tell us what it all meant."

For just a moment I wondered if Jujubee, no doubt led by the Spirit, was as "in the dark" as the rest of us and walking by faith and not by sight, and was asking me to explain what it meant not as Socrates might have asked—to lead me to the truth—but because he was himself really curious about what he and Jesus meant in all this.

I said, "Grace, boiled down to its very essence, is salvation to the lowest bidder."

"Dewey Hazelriggs, I say unto you: Yes."

Otis Winters said, "You're kidding?"

Fanny said, "Can't get it at Sotheby's or Christie's."

Jujubee raised his hands up high. "'But we are all as an unclean thing, and all our righteousnesses are as filthy rags; and we all do fade as a leaf; and our iniquities, like the wind, have taken us away.' Isaiah sixty-four and verse six."

Otis Winters was still after it. He said, "How do you auction off something like salvation?"

Jujubee said, "Only reason we're doing a auction instead of a regular old-fashion tent meeting is because it's the only thing I've ever even been sorta good at in my whole life, such as it is. I can't preach. Believe me, I've tried to, and I'm no Billy Graham or Billy Sunday or Billy Monday or Tuesday, either, for that matter. Anywho, I've put on my suit and stood all up in there in the empty auction house back yonder at home with all the doors locked up tight and tried to do it. I've got a message the Lord has laid on my heart and called me to deliver. But some messages can't be preached. They have to be delivered in some other way."

Wylynda Monroe said, "Then what?"

Jujubee said, "Well, first things first. The Grand Ballroom seats about five hundred and we'll be full up. There's going to be some real bad weather this evening that's going to give us a full house, so it'll be something."

How he knew this, I didn't know, because we had not heard a weather report since just after we left the Cypress Shade Nursing Home.

Fanny said, "Jujubee, how did you set all this up? This must be a five-star resort."

Jujubee said, "If I was the one set all this up we'd be in a big old mess right about now, Miss Franny. The Lord Jesus set it all up. That's his business, such as it is. And if he can hang a million stars in the filament I imagine it's no big deal for him to get us put up in a five-star joint. That young clerk with the fair face and fine white suit over yonder there at the counter told me that the man that owns this Croquette Club, or what have you here, was born again not but a week or two ago and he's all ablaze with the Spirit, saying he's going to sell all he has and give it to the poor."

# To the Lowest Bidder

THE TEENSIE WEENSIE BAND HIT THE STAGE in the Grand Ballroom at 7:30 p.m. sharp and opened up with that uptempo bluegrass version of "The Voice." Jujubee was seated stage left way up high on a makeshift riser madly pumping that vintage mother-of-pearl Hohner accordion with gold-gilded bellows. I was skipping in time to the song as I dutifully carried out my food-service detail, which entailed helping the waitstaff roll in and set up huge silver roll-top chafers full of beef pot roast, low country boil, broiled halibut, chicken croquettes, and breads and vegetables of every color and type.

A dozen young hosts, festooned in black Victorian sack coats complete with period cravats, were showing the swelling flow of guests to their places at large white linen-draped tables. I was in a white waiter smock with pockets for my order pad and a rag for bussing tables. They suited Fanny up—over her pedal pushers and crewneck—in a houndstooth chef's tunic with the CC monogram in charcoal stitching on the breast pocket and a matching twill flat-top toque. They even had Worthy Waddell outfitted in a double-breasted houndstooth chef jacket and a white toque that made him look like the Pillsbury Doughboy—and Fanny just had to get a picture of it; it was simply too cute, she said, not to. And I said, same to you, and got several shots of her and Worthy before the latter took off motoring around the room in his Pride Jazzy chair with a smile on his face and divulging heaven knew what to the guests.

What a grand room it was. *Yes, Jujubee,* I thought, *Jesus has done a fine job of setting it all up.* It was stately, royal, a "hymn to Victorian design," with eighteen-foot coffered ceilings, scalloped Victorian columns, exquisite chair rail, pilasters with ornate bases, and all those huge gaslight-style chandeliers dripping brass and crystal.

As Jujubee had prophesied, the bad weather got worse. Hurricane Ilana was producing a storm surge that assaulted the coast of Little Chancel Island with fifteen-foot waves and spawning tornadoes from Daytona to Charleston and a hundred miles inland. One of the caterers told me that the locals all knew that the Croquet Club's Grand Ballroom was the safest place on the whole island. The owner of the Croquet Club, T. Everett Winslow, had gone so far (I assume in the days before he was born again and ablaze with the Spirit) as to deem his resort's main building "hurricane proof," a claim that warranted a front-page feature in the *Altar Isles Gazette*.

Apparently the publicity stunt had worked. Of course, it helped that we had put up a big backlit road sign complete with flashing arrow lights advertising the "Feast for Free with all the Fixin's."

I was adjusting the heat on a big chafing dish of peach cobbler when the lights in the room flickered a few times, then went out. Jujubee and the Teensie Weensie Band, which was all acoustic, played on in the pitch black ballroom. A long moment later the lights came back on, and my young catering confidant told me that the Croquet Club was also one of two resorts on the island that had a power generator capable of supplying the whole facility.

Jujubee led the Teensie Weensie Band in a medley of songs that included "This Little Light of Mine," "Holy Spirit, Light Divine," and "I Saw the Light."

Jujubee said, "All together now," and led us *a capella* on the final chorus.

> *I saw the light,*
> *I saw the light,*
> *No more darkness,*
> *No more night,*
> *Now I'm so happy,*

*No sorrow in sight.*
*Praise the Lord,*
*I saw the light.*

After blessing the food, Jujubee urged everyone to dig in, which they did, with gusto. A little later, as the guests were washing down their peach cobbler *a la mode* and red velvet cake with strong Columbian coffee, Jujubee got the auction going in that baritone-to-bass-and-back auctioneer voice I had heard him use only that first night in the Teensie Auction House.

"Welcome to the SonRise Auction, oh," Jujubee bellowed, the microphone looking like a black lollipop in front of that wide face. "Eat up, all of you, all you want, if you will. Squeeze on in and cozy up so everybody can get a place to rest their laurel and hardies, or what have you. How 'bout say we get this here show on the road? We got a Dealer's all up in here roarin' to go—souls pouring in here like forty goin' north—and I'm a setting here roarin' to go, too. *Come* on!"

Fanny was helping those who couldn't help themselves—serving the old and infirm guests to dessert and coffee, and, with my polyethylene food handling gloves still on, I moved in close to her when she went to the service cart to fetch the pitcher of sweet tea and said (no, not "Will you marry me?" though the thought did cross my mind, but), "Does he always do that voice when he's playing the auctioneer?"

She said, "It's not 'playing'—especially not tonight. Not here. But, yes, I guess that's part of his auctioneer's rattle."

"It has a certain charm," I said.

The chatter of suppertime conversation among all us strangers faded to near silence in the great ballroom. Necks craned and backs turned, as all eyes searched out the source of that thunderous voice projecting through the house speakers. The chandeliers dimmed, and for a moment I thought we were about to break a circuit again, but they stayed low—for effect, I assumed. The effect on me at that moment of silence was to walk over and stand close to Fanny, who was standing with her back against the wall, as rapt as the rest of us by that voice and where it was going to take us. I took her hand in mine and she swung our arms out a little, which took me back to the carefree and careful days (such as they were) of my youth.

Jujubee said, "What we've got on the auction block tonight, here, all right, is something you won't find at any other old auction you're likely to 'tend, or what have you. Anywho, it's real relief. Redemption. Forgiveness of sins and cleansing from all unrighteousness. One John one and verse nine. It's salvation. Lord Jesus's salvation."

There was murmuring amongst the guests. One old man with peach cobbler dribbling down his bib said, "Come off it. Whoever heard of such a thing? A auction for Lord Jesus's salvation."

"Yes, *whoever* ... ?" I whispered.

Fanny elbowed me in the side, said, "You come off it, David. After all, you're the one who had it all figured out. Grace."

Jujubee said, "If you've already got it, fear not. What's on the block tonight is something that will do away with your past—such as it is. If you'd paid anything for it, it would come with a unconditional money back guarantee. Anywho, let's straighten up and get serious here a minute. Listen up, Lord Jesus could care less about your past. It's your present and your future he's interested in. If you're a thief, a adulteress, a fornicationer, a shiftless crooked low-down no-good something or other, full up with pride, Lord Jesus will give you a brand new start, new and fresh, right here, right now. Because it's not about you—what *you* can do for Him. As Jimmy Carter said one time: 'Ask not what you can do for the Lord, such as it is, but ask rather what Lord Jesus can do for you.' So, if you're so bone-weary tired carrying the weight of this mean world on your back, Jesus will crack you open like a egg and give you a new yolk."

I overheard one of the hosts say that a tornado warning had been issued for all of the Altar Isles and, scarier still, one had already touched down and ripped through St. Simon's Island, which, he noted, was 18 miles from where we stood in grand ballroom of the Croquet Club on Little Chancel Island. I wondered if old T. Everett Winslow would warrant his Grand Ballroom "tornado proof," too.

Jujubee said, "You're bidding on salvation all up in here on the auction block. If you'd like to try it before you buy, you can't, but you can come on up here—and if you can't walk, we'll tote you—and talk to some folks that knows all about the goods being auctioned off up in here tonight."

We watched as Merlin Monroe and his wife Wylynda climbed down from the stage and stood by the auction block, which was a little side table with nothing—well, nothing that you could see with your physical eyes—on it. Then Dough-tree and Banana Fosters, who had been up on the stage tap dancing to the music, followed suit.

Jujubee sucked in some wind and started the bidding with his trademark pitch: "Who'll give a start? Let's go. Tell me what you wanna give."

Nobody moved. No one raised his hand.

Jujubee said, "Now lookit, now we got this priceless thing up here for sale, just a setting there, and I'm waiting on the opening bid. Don't be fooled: Just because you can't see it doesn't mean nothing's there. Y'all come on. Anywho, who'll give a start, let's go. I'm looking for somebody with something worthy of salvation. Raise your hand." Then the scat: "Got nothing, give a start, need sin, give a sin, any sin, get it going, need a sin."

*What manner of catechism was this?*

A door closed behind me, and for a moment I thought I was hearing my dignified high church father roll over in his grave. People were still coming in.

Fanny said, "Leave it to Jujubee to come up with this type of Alter Call."

I said, "You've got to hand it to old Jujubee."

She said, "I think we both know that God's working in and through him."

I said, "Indeed."

She said, "And don't be surprised at how He moves in here."

I said, "I don't think anything could surprise me at this point."

She said, "Don't kid yourself."

Jujubee was gaining momentum, his voice that odd mix of Al Jarreau and Louis Armstrong, almost more a rap than a scat: "Salvation's on the block, on the block, on the block, and redemption is the deal, the real deal, what a deal, seal the deal …"

Finally, a middle-aged man seated at a table on the left half of the room stood up. He was one of the better dressed guests—chino slacks and a peach-colored golf shirt—and was well kempt. He raised both hands, cleared his throat as if to quiet the crowd, and spoke up. It was clear he wanted all to hear what he was saying. He said, "Okay, Mr. Auctioneer, I'll take this salvation."

Fanny said, "Uh-oh. He's a wise guy."

I said, "How do you know?"

She said, "He thinks he's going to toy with Jujubee."

Jujubee said, "Got a bid, now a bid, give your bid … . This handsome young fellow up in here in the peachy alligator-type shirt, or what have you, says he wants the salvation and the whole package deal. What do you bid?"

The man cleared his throat again, said, "Well, I'm an honest man, a family man, happily married ten years with three children—good children. Well educated. I have several degrees. I give blood. I give to charity. I was raised in the church and I don't smoke, drink, or run around."

If Jujubee had planted a shill in the audience, he couldn't have worked it to better advantage. He said it as though he were giving a poetry reading: "Got a bid, now a bid, says he's honest, that's his bid; family man, says he's good, doesn't smoke, real good, doesn't drink, doesn't wink, says he's never been a fink. Well now, folk, that's his bid."

Jujubee let a moment pass then said, "Sir, you'll have to bid lower than that to take this merchandise off the block. Why the floor bid is lower than that. Anywho, giving blood is good, having it give to you—and for you—is even better."

A collective murmur arose among the guests. *What manner of auction was this?* It was clear that some were starting to get it. A woman in a tattered old gray Mother Hubbard frock stood up and said, "I had a fling once with another's man's wife, and I know it was a sin, knew it at the time. I was reared to fear God. And I lay it down and confess it right here for that forgiveness you was talking about up yonder."

Jujubee in singsong again: "Got a bid, had a fling, awful thing, what a bid, bless your heart, hit your knees, close your eyes, bow your head."

Worthy Waddell was clapping his arms. He said, "Rap on, hip-hoppin Jujubee Fluoride, know'm sayin'?"

Then Jujubee spoke up in a deep but pastoral—African American pastoral—voice: "Give your bid to Jesus, sister. You've confessed of your sin, adultery. Now repent: In the name of Jesus the Friend of Sinners and by the Holy Ghost power invested in me I say unto you: Go and sin no more."

The man in the peach golf shirt who had bid his good name said, "What sort of nonsense is this?"

Jujubee said, "Just the kind that can save your soul."

Then I recognized him. "Wait a minute, I know him," I told Fanny. "Yes, yes, of course, he's from Wentworth. He's on the faculty. Maybe the Sociology department. No, that shirt screams Business. He's an elder at First Presbyterian. He tells everyone."

"Your father's church," Fanny said.

I said, "The very one."

Just then I heard a crash outside the door we were standing next to, and I turned and nudged it open with my knee

(I was still holding hands with my beloved Fanny) and asked my young catering confidant what was going on.

He said, "Tornadoes are ripping through the island. Cop told me one took out the Periwinkle. Said it was a force three. That's what they call an F three. Man oh man, can you believe that?"

"I don't know," I said. *Was it unbelievable?* Even though I was not familiar with tornado classifications, I figured that an F3 was worse than an F1 or an F2.

He said, "An F three can take down bearing walls like a game of Pickup Sticks. I hear that all the Periwinkle's outbuildings are pancake flat, windows busted out of the hotel. Power's out all over the island. Just watch. Before you know it, everybody'll wash up here at ye olde Club Croquet."

I turned to Fanny, said, "Fu-Fi Fo-Fum … ."

And she chimed in, "Devil's gonna get you if you drink that rum … ."

I sang the second verse of the little ditty that children in Medlyn in my and Fanny's era used to sing: "Fi-Fu Fum-Fo … ."

And ever the good sport, Fanny echoed: "Preacher's gonna get you if your ankles show."

A moment later the great raised-panel double door of the Grand Ballroom opened and in they rushed like the Children of Israel crossing the Red Sea dryshod.

Fanny said, "So *that* is why you were singing the Fu-Fi song. There's Dr. J.C. Wiley of the Fu-Fi Church. And there's his wife, Beulah. Bless her heart."

"Bless her heart is right," I said.

Fanny elbowed me in the side, said, "Now, now. Let's be sweet."

I said, "Yes, ma'am," then: "I thought old Jujubee was kidding when he said the approaching bands of Ilana were a moving of the Holy Ghost, but now I'm not so sure."

She said, "Pastor Clay always says everything—every single thing—has a spiritual aspect to it. I guess maybe Jujubee's just better at seeing it than most of us."

"Indeed he is," I said, and that giant gnome appeared center stage in my mind again, and again I considered how even though the glow may have been a reflection of the porch light off the metal on my shoes that didn't mean—at all—that it wasn't also something else, that there wasn't a spiritual aspect to it. I said, "I think my father would have smiled on the whole idea of the ubiquitous spiritual aspect."

She said, "And you, David? Do you smile on it? Does it make sense?"

"Not at all," I told her. "Not at all. And therein lies the charm." I said, "Speaking of my father, I used to tease him that despite all his theological certitude concerning divine providence and predestination and all that Reformed theology, he always looked twice before crossing the street."

Fanny said, "God willed him to use the sense he was given."

I said, "Yes indeed, and I'll lay you odds the Presbyterians attending the Pew 'n' Pulp will be along as soon as they can get their umbrellas up and their hairnets on."

Turns out not a minute later I started seeing some familiar Presbyterian faces from the north Georgia delegation. I wasn't at all surprised that the first to enter the room was none other than the illustrious Alisdair Knox, President of Wentworth College, with a look of horror on his pinched face and an inverted umbrella in his hand—first in line, I thought, not because he was playing follow the leader but that it was the better to save his own hide, the hide of the leader, of course, being the most precious hide of all. His eyes desperately searched the crowd—*for whom?* I wondered. It must have been someone important he sought; he grew more wild eyed by the moment. As interested as I was to discover the source of Alisdair's despair, I was drawn irresistibly back into the action of the auction.

Through it all, Jujubee and the auction went on as though the island weren't about to become just another knot in the

Atlantic seaboard. Guests were rising all over the ballroom and entering their bid for salvation. The hosts were attending to the bidders with wireless microphones, at Jujubee's urging, so that the bids could be heard above the din of murmurs and chatter in the room. Because, he said, private confession is good for yourself, but public confession is good for everybody. One by one, Jujubee was dealing with the bids like a Big Brother Confessor, charging the bidders to repent and believe on the name of Lord Jesus.

A very elderly black woman with spackled gray-black hair that looked like an uncrushed cigarette ash rolled her wheelchair down to the front edge of the stage. She spoke into the microphone they handed her: "Honey child, I'm here to say that by the time you live four-score-and-five years, or however old I happen to really be, you've done so many wretched things, and hurt so many people, and hurt the Savior so, that all you can do is pray for mercy."

Jujubee said, "Sister, I say unto you, bless your heart. Jesus said, 'Peace I leave with you, my peace I give unto you: not as the world giveth, give I unto you. Let not your heart be troubled, neither let it be afraid.' John fourteen and verse twenty-seven."

I scanned the room for Alisdair Knox. What must he be thinking of the *big lad what likes his meat* now? How foreign such a notion as the lowest bidder wins must be to a man of economics.

I looked over at Dr. J.C.Wiley, leaning against a shiny silver dumbwaiter, forking large bites of red velvet cake into his mouth. And he, what must be going through his mind, seeing this spectacle? I wondered if he was finding the salvation-auction to his liking. After all, I thought, Jujubee was not speaking in tongues and *was* quoting Scripture from the King James Version of 1611.

I didn't have to wait long for an answer.

When Jujubee told a bidder who confessed that, although he had been born again when he was but a boy—

"and, yes, it had took the first time, Lord Jesus don't leave a loaf half-baked,"—he had backslidden into the deep dark abyss of sin, Dr. J.C.Wiley set down his empty cake plate and marched up toward the stage. He commandeered a microphone from one of the hosts and said, "People, this is not the way it's supposed to be. This is cheap grace."

Jujubee said, "It's free, but it ain't cheap. Dr. Wiley, I'm proud to see you all in the mist of us this night up in here in the Croquette Club ballroom for the SonRise Auction. Now, anywho, would you care to enter a bid?"

Dr. Wiley said, "A bid? Me? Are you crazy? What balderdash!"

Jujubee said, "Seems I've heard that one already this evening."

Dr. J.C.Wiley said, "We are to be separated, as called-out ones."

Jujubee said, "I can quote you chapter and verse on that, from the very word of God, and you could me, too, I'm sure of it. We *are* called out, or what have you here. And I am doing the very thing that Jesus has called me out to do: an auction of salvation and forgiveness."

Dr. J.C.Wiley, red-faced, stood there quaking, wagging his head. "A sideshow is more like it. This is an outrage. Why, you've no right to say such things. *You*, you of all people, you who have been divorced and drunk fire water and done all those other shameful things."

Jujubee said, "Shameful is right. The things you mentioned right there was only a teenie-weenie part of my bid and probably not the lowest I ever bid, either, if we're telling the truth here. There was more to it than that. But the Lord was true to his word and forgave and forgot all that mess, so I don't want him to overhear me drudging it back up again. And there's womenfolk and young'ns up in here that don't need to hear such stuff. Anywho, the thing of it is, Jesus has restored me from those sins. And if there is therefore now no condamnition, as the good book says in Romans chapter eight, why is it I feel like I'm being condemned now? Could it be it's not *real* condemnation, but somebody's else's fear or something or other? Jesus has forgive' me. If you can't, maybe it's not the sins in *my* past that we ought to be talkin' about. A bid?"

Dr. Wiley clenched his fists and raised them in the air, and for a moment I thought he might rend his garments. He hollered, "I don't know what you're talking about."

"Could be that I don't either," Jujubee said. "But I know this: Lord Jesus loves you, Dr. Wiley, and he knows how many thousand Bibles you've printed and shipped all over the world and he wants you to know that they've made a difference, shined a light in some pitch dark places. And now Lord Jesus is saying it's high time you let go that burden you've been toting around for so long. So very, *very* long. It's high time you lay it down, such as it is. Because until you do, you won't be able to really love anybody in this whole hateful world."

Dr. Wiley's face was as red velvet as the cake he had just eaten. He muttered something, gibberish, look confused, as though he was a stranger in a strange land frantically riffling through a foreign phrasebook, then silent: There was no such phrase.

Jujubee said, "You may brand me a hairy tick, or what have you, but verily I say unto you, you won't be able to really love anybody in this *whole hateful world.* Not even Sister Brender Cheeley."

Dr. Wiley shrieked, and it merged with a tremendous cracking sound above us (which we found out later was the sound of the third floor of the Croquet Club's being relocated to another part of the island by an F5 tornado). We all cowered.

Jujubee was on his feet then. He said, "Preacher here was talking about being separated and called out. So ... " He paused and it was weird. The cryptic reference to Wiley's statement left Fanny and me looking at each other through squinted eyes.

"What's that about?" I said.

"Search me," Fanny said, "but apt as not it's about to be big."

Jujubee said, "Dr. J.C.Wiley, come with me. I'm calling ye out. President Alice Dare Knocks, you, too. Tarry not. *Now!*"

And just like that, Jujubee climbed down from the makeshift riser and bounded over and cupped a hand over Banana Fosters' ear and passed the microphone as if it were the passing of a torch. Banana Fosters stood there, cocked head nodding, and, apparently without pause or protest, Dr. Wiley and President Knox joined Jujubee on the stage.

Another great crack above, greater still, nearly drove me to my knees.

Fanny said, "Jujubee's got that look. Go with him, David. I'll look after Worthy. *Git.*"

Without a word, I was on my feet and rushing toward the bandstand. By the time I had spun my way through the crowd before the altar, Jujubee and the men were passing through the exit door stage right. Banana Fosters was saying, "Let us pray. Dear Jesus, sweet sweet Lord done gone pulled down the roof once before and saved Nana Fosters's life that be swinging up in there by a cotton bed sheet tied off in a slipknot, self-impose' capital punishment, strung up like some old Christmas bu'b that's blowed-out. And Lord we know they be good news, but ain't no good noose … ."

I passed an old man with no teeth, no legs, lying across a table lifting holy hands, shouting, "Hal E. Loo."

"Amen," I said as I mounted the stairs and bounded across the stage toward the exit door.

Jujubee and the men were already across the tropical atrium, with its Grecian bath in the center and sticky green plant leaves swirling all around. Then they were in the once-magnificent solarium, which was blown to bits, and heading out beyond what had once been the back, the seaside, wall of the Croquet Club. The bushy frond-headed palms lining the shore were drooping as if they had bowed their heads, knowing they were helpless to contain the storm's furious beachhead, and the air was all gray stinging grit. We were exposed now, as exposed as could be, to the act of God, and the wind was having its way with me—though Jujubee, who was leading the way and shielding his friends (who together made perhaps half his width) from the worst of it, was, as they say in Medlyn, "steady gettin' it." I hunkered down and surged ahead, arms cycling in great swiping butterfly strokes reminiscent of all those blasted times I used to try—always in vain—to chase down Drice Weaver on the final leg of a 400-meter freestyle heat.

I looked up and saw that the grand terrace, which was perhaps twenty feet above ground-level and made for ocean-view dining on top and sunshade below, was swaying on the remaining half of the dozen or so peristyle columns bearing it. Still swimming along I struggled after them, quicker if more careful now, for a false step would land me in the oblong pool that became a faux river farther out where Jujubee was, and it was a treacherous soup of debris. Down and around the fountain they went, through the swim-up bar that was now a wading pool, out onto the landing just above the storm surge crashing over the sandbank.

Suddenly Jujubee stopped and dropped to his knees, and at first I thought he had slipped, fallen. I closed quickly at that point, sloshing and huffing the final fifty yards with the awful angry howl of the wind in my ears and the crash-bang of havoc all around, propelled as much by concern for Jujubee now as anything else.

At last we were all there together beside a gray cement-block outbuilding of some sort—the pump house for the pool, I guessed. Jujubee was on the ground, on his rump, straining with all his might to pry open the double doors at the rear—the oceanfront side—of the pump house, which was jammed shut by a section of a steel utility pole thirty inches in diameter that had been sheared in two by a lightning bolt, a twister, some preternatural *force majeure*.

Jujubee had his shoulder on the pole, his teeth were clenched, his eyes narrowed to slits, and seen from my angle he might have been a giant winding up to snap off a length of the thing and hurl it like a metal boot in a wellie-wanging match. Then he put a hand on each of the double doors, grunted, growled: "Boys, help me get this thing off here—shed's near about full up with water."

Through the three- or four-inch space between the pried-open doors I could see that the building was indeed a pump and filter shed, where rainwater and pool run-off drained out into a water treatment facility for recycling—or at any rate not into the protected waters of the Atlantic.

"What in the world are we doing?" I said, but a strong wind spirited my voice away before it made it as far as my own ears. I was on my knees then, beside Jujubee and the others, none of us but Jujubee seeming to know what we should be doing.

Then I saw it: a bit of flesh—an arm? A leg? A swath of clothing? Blue. Light blue. Yes, the hem of a shirt. I heard a sound, echoing in the close watery shed, a child's whimper, plaintive: *Help*.

I pushed against the jammed utility pole then with all I had. So did Dr. Wiley. So did President Knox. The pumping machine itself was already covered, its domed top an inch beneath the surface, and water was within a foot of the ceiling of the windowless pump house. And behind the pump, thank God, heads, two of them, necks stiff, tilted back, and straining to keep the airways open.

Dr. Wiley's glasses had fallen off his face and the lenses lay shattered on the concrete walkway. He peered hard into the pump house, seeing the only thing that mattered to him at that moment, that shock of wet hair, wet but still unmistakably blond. He said, "Hold on there, Daniel, son. We'll get you. Hold on. Dear Jesus, please, save my boy."

In so close and straining in the deafening babel of the storm I could not so much hear as *feel* the panic in his voice.

He yanked his red striped necktie off and was trying to loop it around the pole. His legs were jammed up against it, and the veins over his temples were bulging blue and angry.

President Knox, the cantankerous man of economics, was in for a pound, too, his very last pound, if need be. "Althea," he said, "just hold oon tae the lad. Ye'll be fine. We hae aboot got ye." He looked up into the infinite gray above us, cried: "*Laird save us we perish!*"

Daniel. Althea. Daniel Wiley. Althea Knox. The cherub-face boy and the angel-hair girl. Alone. Together. Stealing forbidden time in a little spot out of the way … . Now it made sense. Now I understood President Knox's wild-eyed searching in the ballroom. Yes, Jujubee, I do know them. The Two Medlyns come together in a taboo romance—he with the call, she with the apple: falling from grace—and soon dead as dead could be if we could not somehow manage to jar that mammoth pole and loose that door and drag them out.

Dr. Wiley's son.

President Knox's daughter.

Jujubee Forthright's only concern.

The pole was beyond budging. Diminishing returns. I looked around, spotted a large slab of concrete, periwinkle blue, jarred loose from the Periwinkle Resort, a long slab cracked open and filled with tied steel rebar, sloped steel rebar.

*Might work*, I thought.

I shouted, "Jujubee, here. Let's try this."

He rolled over and up onto his feet, and the four of us pulled-kicked-lugged the great concrete slab over and positioned it adjacent to the pole. Now if we could only manage somehow—*Lord* help *us, amen*—to get that pole to budge one inch it would take off rolling off the pump door and down over the dune and, I hoped, into the very cold dark Leviathan-infested depths of the Atlantic Ocean.

Jujubee heaved and shook, said, "On three!"

And on three we four battered that steel pole with all we had and, for all I knew at the moment, with four dislocated shoulders.

Little shift.

And again.

This time it gave, and Jujubee jumped up on the pole and bore down, balancing on his left—his real—leg for all the world as if he were a one-legged river dance log roller. And that did it. The pole was spinning down toward a little dune. Jujubee bailed off of it just before it crested the beachhead and fell out of sight. Then we hit our knees, all of us, and dragged the children out of the water and hugged them for all time as we stagger-stumbled across the atrium and made our way back into the Grand Ballroom of the Croquet Club … .

And we gave them to eat and to drink and warmed them by the fire and swaddled them in snug clean clothes and hugged them close.

* * *

The auction was still going strong when we got back.

Jujubee was a soaking wet mess. We all were. But he was the auctioneer, and this was the auction that Jesus, the Great Auctioneer, through him was hosting.

He took to the stage again, said, "'As the whirlwind passeth, so is the wicked no more: but the righteous is an everlasting foundation.' Proverbs ten and verse twenty-five. Only way you'll be righteous is if you admit with Saint Paul that you have no righteousness of your own but 'that which is through the faith of Christ, the righteousness which is of God by faith: That I may know him, and the power of his resurrection, and the fellowship of his sufferings.' Philippians three and verse nine and ten."

Someone shouted "Amen," another shrieked a long-drawn-out "Hallelujah," and Jujubee stood up tall then, the straps of his wet overalls snug as stitches, lifted his hands up high, as if spreading great hefty wings, and said, "Lord

Jesus said I came not to con-damn the world but to save it. There's folk all up in here that's shackled by a heavy burden, 'neath a load of guilt and shame, and—"

Fanny was there, God love her, wringing water from the hem of my smock, swathing me with table linens warm from the dryer. When I quit shivering, she took my hand, and somehow we were moving toward the stage, very slowly. Nearly everyone else was, too. And when I looked up—I kid you not—Jujubee seemed to be glowing again, like a buttercup when you cup it in your hands on a July evening at dusk, like that giant lawn gnome in Fanny's backyard when she tossed her cape over our heads. Now maybe it was the forelight shining from the small lamp on the makeshift auctioneer booth they had fashioned for him. Maybe it was the light reflecting off the crystal chandelier closest to the stage. I prefer to think of it as a halo cast by the very Light of the World shining through him.

And a revival broke out in earnest just then as people answered the call and rolled slowly, seeping, like the backwash of a great wave toward the auction block where salvation was free, free to the lowest bidder by the grace of almighty God.

Jujubee mopped rainwater and sweat from his forehead with a linen napkin—as white as his rich voice was black—and said: "There's young girls and old up in here that's gotten in trouble and had a abortion, and now they're heartbroke', laboring under a load of guilt. There's a man in here that cheats on his income tax and knows it's wrong whole time he's filling out the papers and licking the stamp'll take it to Uncle Sam. There's folk that's run around on their husband or wife, having illustrious relations. There's folk turns head-on to voodoo, folk that pulls out the Squeegie Board every time they need a answer and get fondling that wooden thing looks like a big wood guitar pick on a air hockey table and picks up more channels than a cable TV set—even though it may be the evil one is all up in there, working. There's kinky folk in here that only the Lord can get straightened out. And nasty talk, ah: There's folk in here uses language. Folk that's got a friend sticketh closer than a brother—and his name's Jim Beam and he has a sister name Mary Jane. There's men that beats their wife and women that sits there and takes it. There's folk nerved-up such that they'll blow their big top every time you say so much as boo to them. There's folk pops a jug of pills just to roll out of the bed in the morning."

His arms were swimming now, making great treading arcs, like two stout oars. He said, "There's men can't stop looking at booty books to save their soul. There's women that strips off their raiments and does a seedy jig for filthy lucres—lookers that ogles them up one side and down the other—and all the while deep down they still feel cheap as a fifty-cent part and can't seem to buy theirselves enough stuff to cover the stark butt-nakedness of their soul. There's folk here that's grieved the Spirit of almighty God their whole life, believing any fool thing but the truth. Listen: There's folk having relations outside of marriage—before, during, and after—but always outside. There's folk up in here that's got the sticky fingers and practices the pretty larceny. There's folk sick and tired, and seven months into 'you got six months to live.' There's folk that's been baptized so many times and rededicated more ways than Waffle House griddles hash browns: they've been scattered-smothered-covered-chunked-topped-diced-and-peppered and they're about to conk out. Wore out from all their striving with that sense of emergency to be good and get it all right instead of letting the One who *is* good make them all right, be in them and live through them. It's not about coming and kneeling down at the altar but about letting the Lord of all alter you. Praise be! Let Lord Jesus have his way with you, friend. 'Have thine own way, Lord. Have thine own way.' There's folk pays more allegiance to the Donkey and the Elephant than they do to the Lamb of God slain from the foundation of the world. There's folk full up with spiritual pride, patting theirself on the back for being better than the rest of us. There's somebody in here thinks he has no sin and he makes God a liar and the word is not in him. One John one and verse ten .... "

On and on he went, calling sinners to repent. And when he was finished, he said, "And, to one and all, Lord Jesus says, 'Confess your sin. Turn around: Repent. Then you do this—but don't try this at home till you let me, Lord Jesus, set up housekeeping and housecleaning in the home sweet home of your heart: Go and sin no more. Then you just love one another and let me, Lord Jesus, take care of cleaning the house and keeping the homefires burning. And, when you do, I will never hold—that sin of your past against you. Never ever *ever*.' Folk, listen—You can't give him your best and expect to earn your way in; you just give him your worst and trust him with it. If you do, you'll never be sorry. You see, Lord doesn't care how you got into such trouble with all your sins. He just wants to make you a deal of a lifetime and lift that great weight off you and set you free from it once and for all."

A few in the room were sobbing, but most were merely sniveling, as I was, my cheeks damp again but not with rainwater, stinging. A few feet ahead of us stood Dr. J.C. Wiley, with his cherub-face prodigal son Daniel snuggled against his side. He was stroking his son's damp head, tenderly. He said, "Listen to him, people. Listen. He's speaking truth."

Fanny was in a daze of her own. She whispered, "Fo-Fum Fi-Fu .... "

And I rejoined: "The Lord's gonna get you if you don't be true."

All was pandemonium then in that magnificent hall as sinners and backsliders gave their worst to Jesus and received, in return, God's best. Many from the Fundamentalist party answered the Alter Call, and not a few from the Presbyterian party could be seen kneeling down with their heads bowed. The venerable Scotsman Alisdair Knox hugged his daughter Althea for dear life and was down on one knee—whether because he had strained himself in the rescue mission or because he, too, was answering an alter call of his own, I know not. But I am quite sure that the few drops I saw falling around him were not rain but tears—and perhaps just then that was enough.

Now you may very well question the timing of it, along with my sense of propriety, but it was in that dim hall with souls being saved and lives being delivered from bondage all around us that I did it. I knelt down on both knees and prayed and, as I made to stand back up, something resisted, a heavy phantom hand on my shoulder, and so I stayed down on one knee, took Fanny Fuller's warm hand in mine.

I said, "Fanny, I have always loved you."

She said, "I know you have."

I said, "I may be the lowest bidder of all, but … "

"Yes, David … "

I said, "Will *you* marry *me*?"

She swung our hands out a little bit, then removed the flat-top toque from her head, and let those eyes, all Fanny Fuller's eyes, slay me. She said, "I cannot believe my ears, David Umberton Hazelriggs. I must be hearing things. I could have sworn I just heard you propose marriage—marriage between *you* and *me*."

I heard the buzz-hum of a motor and a chortling laugh and turned to see none other than Worthy Waddell pulling alongside us in his chair with Early's number 3:16 painted on the sideboard. His white toque was tousled. He said, "Haagen-Dazs and Fanny sitting in the trees, K-I-S-S-I-N-G. First comes lust, then comes marriage, then comes Aunt Fanny with a baby carriage."

I let go Fanny's hand and she mine, and we stood there serenaded with Worthy Waddell's laughter and applause.

Fanny said, "Worthy Waddell, you little dickens. It is *not* polite to eavesdrop. And here we are, with people giving their heart to Jesus, and you're carrying on like we're at a circus."

Fearing the jig was up, and feeling the click of a tumbler on that safe that was my heart, I started to rise from my kneeling position, but Fanny placed her hand on my left shoulder, pressed and held me down.

She said, "Ask me again—that question you asked before."

I swallowed, said, "Fanny Mae Waddell Fuller, will you marry me?"

And she said, "David Umberton Hazelriggs, yes, I will."

*Joy to the world!*

*Praise be!*

*Jujubee Forthright, have I got some news for you!*

Worthy Waddell popped a wheelie then and turned doughnuts right there on the polished hardwood floor of the Grand Ballroom. And he wasn't alone in his merry-making, though the others dancing a jig with a do-si-do were celebrating their big win at the auction—forgiveness and salvation, deliverance from the past and hope for the future. It was a party then, and everyone there was the guest of honor.

A little while later, Jujubee said, "Listen up, folks, I want this party to go on now. But the time has come for me to quit preachin' and get on to Medlyn. Anywho, here it is. Jesus wants me to tell you this: If you don't have a home, you have one now. If you can't read, we'll learn you. If you need clothes, we'll get you suited up. If you're hungry, we'll feed you. If you need a job, we'll put you to work on the Lord's payroll in the mountains of north Georgia."

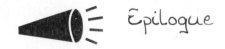

# Epilogue

THREE DAYS LATER THE SONRISE CONVOY, with cars of every make and model—and motorcycles, pickups, panel vans, and box trucks, school and motor coaches—carrying those who had answered the Alter Call rolled into Medlyn, Georgia, on a wave of good cheer. Jujubee said that the same penny-coastal moving of the Holy Ghost that blew folks onto Little Chancel Island in that great rushing mighty wind (aka Ilana) kept right on blowing unto the blue hills of Georgia. Hard now to see it any other way.

We were a boon for the local economy. We secured temporary lodging for the "ministry team"—all who had answered the call—in motels and hotels throughout north Georgia at negotiated rates for long-term stays, long-term because the radical transformation of the Town & Country Auction into a Christian community called A Place Worthy was a big undertaking. In fact, as of this writing, we are still several months from the official ribbon-cutting and dedication ceremony.

Jujubee retained the flamboyant barrister Mitchell Bramlett, Esquire, to put his property affairs in order. In late September, in the City Court of Medlyn, Bramlett entered a petition to reclaim fifty-five acres of the property on the W4200 block of U.S. Highway 76, Medlyn's Main Street, of which James Jackson Baldwin Forthright was the rightful owner. The acreage in question was annexed mainly from the eastern portion of the Wentworth College campus—a densely wooded tract that used to save me from the eyesore of Jujubee's ramshackle farmhouse and the auction house and its outbuildings; used to, that is, when I was a teacher of philosophy at Wentworth. (I resigned my post at Wentworth College immediately upon my return to Medlyn and lobbied hard for them to consider me a scapegoat for the good of the philosophy department, for without the discipline of philosophy it is hard for one to judge what is either liberal or art; the Board of Trustees agreed; I have no regrets.) Jujubee's petition was granted without ado and sealed by order of the City Court of Medlyn, the honorable Judge Nunnelly Sparks presiding.

Of the reclaimed acreage, Jujubee sold twenty-five acres with ample frontage on both Main and Sycamore Streets to a commercial developer in order to raise what he called "adventure capital" for A Place Worthy—the campus, chapel, dormitories, and workshops of which would occupy the remaining thirty acres adjacent to the property at 3712 Sugar Maple Lane, the house that Fanny and her dearly departed Early Edwin Fuller Jr. shared for nearly thirty years, and which was now up for sale.

Though he was not in any wise constrained to do so, Jujubee continued to lease the remaining land to both Wentworth College and the First Fundamental Church for a fair price—as each was able to pay—with a term of one year, renewable by consent of the parties.

Jujubee is hard at work in his role as Director of the Epic that is A Place Worthy, and the heart, hands, and soul of the ministry to which God called him, and through him, the rest of us.

Turns out, those physical symptoms that had us all so concerned about Jujubee's health betokened something a bit more serious than a mild case of anemia, as some originally thought. Fanny has done virtually everything short of breaking into Dr. Naresh Desai's office under cover of night and reading Jujubee's file, including working the phones: rumors all, with diagnoses ranging from acid reflux to angina to diabetes (juvenile, Type I, Type II, Type III, you name it) to lupus to Parkinson's. Jujubee keeps his own counsel about it, tells us not to worry about him, but of course we do … .

Speaking of Fanny. We are, my betrothed and I, going to be united in holy matrimony in A Place Worthy's chapel on June 12. My best man will be none other than Worthy Waddell, and my groomsmen will include, among a few others, my brothers in the Lord: Banana Fosters, Bennett "Merlin" Monroe, Charles C. "Dough-tree" Doherty, Jr., and Otis Winters. The Rev. James Jackson Baldwin Forthright will be officiating.

I guess to bring my account of Jujubee Forthright's calling to a close I should tell you how astounded I am at how it all happened that I, the Cynic, erstwhile disciple of Diogenes of Sinope, got out of my tub, put down my lantern, and took up my cross. How could I have known that my rather teasing encounter with a six-foot-tall lawn gnome on the shores of Lake Sorghum (in Fanny's backyard) would lead me to Jujubee, who led me (not by the hand but by the heart) to Jesus. You see, all those years I simply couldn't believe that he woke back up by the power of almighty God until I had seen him living in and through Jujubee Forthright. But oh how I did see him … and pray that others might see, a fraction so clearly, him living in and through me.

# About the Author

Scott Stewart lives in Atlanta with the great blessings of his life—his wife Lena and sons Scott, Chace, and Aidan. When not writing or drumming, Scott is busy with CarePoint Support Group Ministries, Inc., a grace-full, people-helping ministry that he founded in 2004. Scott is the author of *The Healing of Ryne O'Casey* (FaithWalk 2004). Read more about his work at www.scottphilipstewart.com.